D0149464

THE MAN FROM BOOT HILL

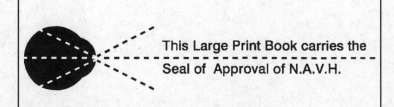

This Large Print Book carries the Seal of Approval of N.A.V.H.

THE MAN FROM BOOT HILL

MARCUS GALLOWAY

THORNDIKE PRESS
A part of Gale, Cengage Learning

GALE
CENGAGE Learning·

Farmington Hills, Mich • San Francisco • New York • Waterville, Maine
Meriden, Conn • Mason, Ohio • Chicago

GALE
CENGAGE Learning·

LIBRARY OF CONGRESS CATALOGING-IN-PUBLICATION DATA

Galloway, Marcus.
    The man from Boot Hill / by Marcus Galloway. — Large Print edition.
        pages cm. — (Thorndike Press Large Print Western)
    ISBN 978-1-4104-6488-0 (hardcover) — ISBN 1-4104-6488-1 (hardcover)
    1. Large type books. I. Title.
PS3607.A4196M36 2014
813'.6—dc23   2013042912

Published in 2014 by arrangement with Harper, an imprint of HarperCollins Publishers

Printed in the United States of America
1 2 3 4 5 6 7 18 17 16 15 14

*To Mom and Bob,
for helping me go on
when it felt like I was six feet under.
And to Megan,
for being the light at the end of the
tunnel.*

PROLOGUE

Boston Harbor
1849

No matter how much time had passed, the smell of revolution still hung in the air of Boston Harbor. Old folks wandered the streets recalling tales of their relatives and their supposed involvement in the War for Independence. Even though the Redcoats were nowhere to be seen, those old-timers still spat out those names like poisoned meat when they referred to their ancestral nemeses.

Visitors couldn't get enough of that kind of talk. In fact, many of them had traveled a long way to hear those stories from the lips of those who knew what they were talking about firsthand. Tales of Paul Revere and George Washington floated through the air like insects buzzing around their faces. Those visitors sat along the waterfront, buying drinks for the old-timers, fueling their fires while watching the ships drift toward the docks.

One of those ships was marked with a few words in a Baltic language that nobody could quite make out. Some of the letters were worn away by salty air, and the rest were simply beyond the comprehension of their audience. The visitors watched it sail in all the same, taking in the sight of vessels from exotic lands while listening to stories from a time that was already turning into legend.

That ship was actually Polish. On board, several rows of passengers lined the decks, staring out at a shoreline they'd been dreaming about since they first started saving up to pay for the voyage. Etched upon their faces was a mixture of hope, fear, nervousness, and joy. They were a group marked by sunken cheeks and pasty skin, and their numbers had been thinned throughout the rigors of oversea travel.

One of those faces belonged to a stout man in his late forties. He stood with his arm around a small boy who was just tall enough to peek over the ship's rail. "You see there, *sunus*?" the man said, keeping only the word for "son" in his native tongue. "That is your new home. Where do you want to live, Nicolai?"

The boy strained his legs and feet to try and make himself just a bit taller. He knew his father wasn't going to help. After all he'd learned before and during the voyage, he didn't expect any help. Clamping his strong, bony hands around the rail and tugging himself up, the child dug his toes into the rough wooden surface of the rail until he finally got the view he was looking for.

"There," the child said, nodding his head toward the shore. "But farther away."

The man grinned down at his boy the way he always did when the child climbed like a plant through the soil. Ever since the first time he'd seen his son scamper over a fence like it was hardly there, he'd called him his little *spurgas;* his sprout. "How much farther, *spurgas*?"

Smiling at the all-too-familiar nickname, the child pulled himself up a little higher. "Far away, Tevai," he answered, leaving only the word for father in his native tongue. "Far away. I don't want to see the water anymore."

The older man looked appalled to hear such a thing. "What? But the sea is glorious! She brought us all this way to our new life."

"It killed *motina.*" He scrunched his little face and corrected himself without being

9

told to do so. Ever since the decision had been made to come to America, he'd been encouraged to speak in that land's tongue. "It killed Mother. I don't want to see it anymore. I don't even want to smell it."

For the first time since he'd walked up to the rail and set his sights upon America, the older man let his eyes drop away from the shore and the rolling waves. "I understand, *spurgas.* You came with me this far . . . so the least I can do is let you pick our spot once we get our feet on solid ground. We wanted to travel some more anyway, right?"

"Yes, Tevai," the child said with a wide grin.

The ship wasn't primarily a passenger vessel. Instead, it's main purpose was to haul foodstuffs and dry goods to Massachusetts, while bringing farming supplies and tools back to its native port. It wasn't an exotic route in the least, and it left the ship's passengers smelling like the inside of a musty silo. For the most part, the man and his son reeked of potatoes and brine. Their skin was smudged with dirt and their hair was plastered to their heads.

If either one cared about any of that, they didn't show it. Instead, they both smiled as the ship came to a rough stop, bumping against the side of the dock before the gangplank was finally dropped to bridge the gap from ship to pier. The crew was first off. The passengers walked timidly onto shore a while later, hoping not to draw any attention from the rowdy sailors who'd barely been tolerating them for the last several weeks.

There were a few men in uniform waiting to talk to the people that came off the boat. They asked questions and checked names off a list before allowing them to pass. They spoke in English to the sailors, which brought a worried look to the child's face. His young mind had picked up the new language quickly, but Tevai couldn't quite make the transition so well when he got flustered. Of the passengers, he and his father were first in line to meet the uniformed men. Since his father seemed fairly brimming with confidence, the child followed that example and puffed out his chest while lifting his chin.

Fascinated and scared at the same time, the child watched everything he could, soaking it up with wide, sparkling eyes. Just as the first uniformed man allowed the last sailor off the dock and looked over toward the gathering passengers, a sudden commotion broke out directly behind him. The official still had his hand in mid-wave when one of the sailors was approached by a man who'd stormed out from one of the nearby buildings.

The sailor was one of the largest men on the ship, and had also been one of the most vocal when it came to putting the passengers in their "proper place"; that place being at the bottom of the pecking order, even behind the rats living in the darkest corners of the storage hold.

Smaller and leaner than the sailor, the other man wore dirty black pants and a heavy coat that reminded the child of clothing he'd seen on the soldiers boarding one of the military ships in his homeland. This smaller man spoke English in a voice so loud and harsh that the child didn't have to understand all the words for him to know their intent.

"You dumb son of a bitch!" the man in the black jacket snarled. "I told you last time to never show your face in this country again or I'd blow it off!"

The sailor looked around and noticed that his buddies were smiling and looking at him to see what he'd do next. "Settle, *drauge.* There is no reason for fighting," he said in a thick accent. Holding his hands out, he walked toward the smaller man. "Let me buy you drink and we can put this behind you."

But the other man would have none of it. Stepping back, he made sure to keep himself out of arm's reach. "Turn around right now . . . and get back on that boat," he said, pulling his jacket open to reveal the gun belt strapped around his waist. "Do it quick, and I might let you live."

If the sailor understood, he didn't seem to care. He stopped for a second, took another look at his friends, and plastered the same shit-eating smile that had become so familiar to all the passengers who'd tasted the back of his hand throughout the voyage. "Come now, *drauge* . . . there are so many people here that —"

In a flash of motion, the man in the black jacket dropped his hand to his side and drew his pistol from its holster. The only thing the child heard before the shot was a distinct *click* as the hammer was thumbed back. Next came the roar of gunfire and the slap of lead drilling through meaty flesh.

The sailor straightened up and reached out as if to grab hold of the man who'd shot him, but he was stopped dead in his tracks by another fiery round, which punched a messy hole through his skull.

Women nearby screamed, and the rest of

the onlookers simply stood rooted in place, unable to tear their eyes from the bloody spectacle. The child's attention was focused on the man in the jacket. He watched as the pistol was calmly dropped back into its holster by its owner, who turned and walked away.

Two other men in uniforms ran up and started shouting. They took out guns of their own and made the man in the jacket drop to his knees and fold his hands behind his head.

"Come now, Nicolai," the older man said as he pushed his son forward. They both walked the length of the pier and made it to the spot where the uniformed men were gathered around the dead man and his killer, who was being taken into custody. The child's father was the only passenger who still seemed anxious to leave the boat at that point. In fact, he walked straight up to the first uniformed man he saw and waited.

"Oh . . . uh . . . you're one of the new arrivals?" the uniformed man asked.

Nicolai's father nodded once.

"This is a bad time, but . . . well . . . it's just as good as any I guess."

Although his father knew enough English to get by, Nicolai could tell that the uni-

14

formed man's words were coming too quickly, which flustered his father even more. From there, much of what the official was saying went straight over the older man's head.

"What's your name?" the uniformed man asked.

"Stasys."

"Stah—seees?"

He nodded. The older man's eyes kept darting toward the body.

"Last name?"

Stasys pointed toward the body and spoke reflexively in his own language. "I can take care of that for you," he said in a flood of syllables that were so much nonsense to the man in uniform. "I can put him in the ground and take care of him. I dig graves. It's what I do for a living, and I need the money. I need a job to take care of myself and my son. I will work for cheap and —"

"Hold on there, mister," the uniformed man said impatiently. "Can you speak English? I mean . . . can . . . you . . . speak . . . English?"

Nicolai had seen his father push for work like this before. It was such persistence that allowed him and his family to survive back home. But now, with Stasys at such a disadvantage, even young Nicolai wondered how his father could get this uniformed man to understand.

Nodding, Stasys spoke in hesitant English. "Yes. I speak a little. I can —"

"Just tell me your last name and we can move this along. We need to get this mess cleaned up."

Stasys nodded vigorously. "Yes. I can . . ." Finally, he spat out the word, "Graves. I can . . . make graves."

"Graves?"

Smiling victoriously, Stasys nodded again. "Yes! Graves. I can —"

The uniformed man nodded as well, noting something on a small pad of paper. "Stasys Graves. And this is your son?"

"Yes. My son . . . is Nicolai."

"Any more with you?" Seeing the confusion on the other man's face, the official asked, "Just you two?"

"Yes, yes."

"All right then, Mr. Graves. Just head over there and someone will see about getting you a place for the night."

"But, my work," Stasys said, motioning toward the body. "Should I . . . ?"

"We'll take care of that, Mr. Graves. Just head over that way so we can process the rest of these folks. Welcome to America."

With that, the official handed Stasys and

16

Nicolai over to the next official. Once Stasys saw that he wasn't going to be let anywhere near the body, he took hold of Nicolai's hand and tugged him along behind the smiling man.

Nicolai looked up while trying to keep up with his rushing father. "Did you get a job, Tevai?" he asked without attempting English.

"No, *spurgas*. No job."

"But the man was —"

"I know. These people don't . . ." Pausing, Stafsys looked down before admitting to his inability to communicate with the official. "They already have a man to dig the grave."

"Oh."

"I think you're right, *spurgas*. We need to move away from this city. Away from the sea. That would be nice, wouldn't it?"

"Yes, Tevai! I can't wait to see the trees and the open fields."

Stasys nodded and did his best to keep from squelching his son's enthusiasm.

ONE

It was autumn. Not only that, but it was far enough into autumn that the wind carried the steely edge of winter upon its breath as it raced over the withered weeds and through the barren branches that stuck up from the Nebraska plains like uneven stubble on an old man's chin. The sky was wide and gray, streaked with clouds that hardly seemed to move no matter how long he stared at them. Instead, they hung like cobwebs from the rafters of his father's woodshed, only stirring occasionally when a big enough wind rolled through.

That wind tore through his body as well, chilling the blood in his veins and causing his muscles to tense. Gritting his teeth, he clenched the reins in his fists and gave them a little snap, causing the two mismatched horses to quicken their pace toward the distant town. Adjusting naturally to the bumps in the road, Nicolai shifted as the wagon jostled beneath and around him. The clattering of the wheels upon the rocky trail had combined with the rattle of his equipment in the back to form a constant flow of noise that he'd stopped hearing long ago.

Looking up, he saw the Nebraska plains stretching out in every direction like a drab-colored quilt that the good Lord had laid down in front of him. Nicolai grinned as his father's words drifted through his mind.

"There isn't much," Stasys had said when referring to the American prairie. "But at least there's no sea."

Nodding, Nicolai snapped the reins and thought about just how true that was. To someone who didn't like the sea or even the coast, Nebraska was something close to paradise. The land was flat and in some places barren, but it was as far from the seacoast as a man could get. The only thing to break up his view of the rolling prairie was the town that lay directly ahead of him.

That town would be Jessup, Nebraska. Either that, Nicolai thought, or he owed a good beating to the man who'd given him directions to the place before he'd left Iowa. Supposedly, Jessup was a nice enough place. Not that it mattered, of course. His visit there wasn't exactly for pleasure. He had some business to tend to in Jessup. Some of it was new, and some of it was so old that it had started to rot in the back of Nicolai's mind.

From the bits and pieces he'd put together, Nicolai knew a man he'd been after for some time was in Jessup. Of course, the town was more than just a hiding place. He had heard there was more than one saloon and enough restaurants to give him a wide variety of meals during his stay. One thing Nicolai couldn't stand was a town that served up bland food. He'd had enough of that when he was a boy. Stasys was a good man and a great provider, but there were only so many ways to boil potatoes.

Also, Jessup was one of the smaller stops on the local gambler's circuit. Playing cards was another one of Nicolai's requirements for a town, and he was already looking forward to sitting down to a good, solid game. As luck would have it, he was also fairly certain an acquaintance of his had already found his way to Jessup, and Nicolai was looking forward to possibly catching up on old times.

Jessup had also appealed to him because the place was in need of a man of his particular talents. According to the Iowan he'd spoken to, Jessup was starting to develop a rotten air to it. That was due to two things. First of all, there was a problem with some gunmen who'd also taken a liking to the town's food and card games. Like most men trying to make themselves look tougher than average, those men weren't shy about backing up their tempers with the occasional bit of lead.

Every so often even the drunkest shooter got lucky and those chunks of lead found their way into live targets. Unfortunately, one of those live targets had been Jessup's resident grave digger. From what Nicolai had heard, the poor fool was doing his job while some other local was visiting a fresh mound of dirt in the cemetery. Since that grieving man was still on someone else's shit list, a fight broke out and everyone in front of the killer wound up buried in that same cemetery . . . including the unfortunate grave digger.

Nicolai didn't know every last detail and he didn't much care. All he knew was that Jessup was in need of a strong worker, and he was looking to put his newly inherited wagon to good use. He figured he'd learn whatever else he needed once he got to Jessup and started asking around. Since bad news and dirty gossip traveled like a greased log through a plume, Nicolai had no doubts that he would become an expert on the grave digger's story before he even asked for the dead man's job.

It seemed to be a nice bit of luck that two such good opportunities had presented themselves within the space of one town. Then again, just how good that luck truly was depended on who you asked. There was bound to be someone who wouldn't find it anything close to good.

"Come on now, Rasa," Nicolai said as he snapped the rein that stretched over the first horse's back. "No time to get tired. We're almost there. You don't see Kazys acting lazy, do you?"

Both horses nodded their heads and quickened their pace a little. Nicolai passed the time by conversing with the two animals. Although the talk was one-sided, it occupied his thoughts enough to make the last leg of his trip speed away.

He reached Jessup as the sun was starting to dip in the sky. That was Nicolai's favorite time of day since the clouds took on the same colors as the leaves when they died on their branches. Dark reds and oranges smeared across the heavens like swipes from a careless yet brilliant painter. Also, it was the brightest time of day when he could look up at the sky without it hurting his eyes. His mother used to say that it was the grave digger's blood in his veins that made him like such times, a trait honestly inherited from his father.

Since it was useless to argue with his mother, Nicolai used to nod and accept her prognosis. Now, whenever someone commented on his tastes, Nicolai offered his mother's words as his only explanation. Not that many people asked him anyway. Most folks he saw regarded him in much the same way as the people he saw while driving into the town of Jessup.

The locals glanced in his direction and looked away as soon as they got a look at the dark, somewhat ominous figure huddled over the wagon's reins. After so much time on the trail, Nicolai was looking scruffy and rough. His hair was unkempt and his chin was full of thick stubble. Beyond that, however, his eyes carried a seething kind of presence that had been acquired during the years before he'd decided to pick up a shovel to make his living.

Before that, his primary working tool had been the gun. Those were the years that he wasn't so proud of. They were the years that had forged him into a man, from the boy who'd broken away from his family. They were the years that had caused his father to all but disown him until only recently. They were the years that had taken up permanent residence in his nightmares. And they were the years that Nicolai thought might have already won him a choice place in hell.

He still carried a gun, but it was as different from the one he used to wear as he was different from the kid who used to wear it.

Shaking away his morbid thoughts, Nicolai snapped the reins and nodded to one of the men who actually held his gaze for more than a second or two. So far, he'd ridden past a few rows of houses and a small livery. The main body of the town was a little ways off, but close enough for him to hear the sound of traffic rumbling down the larger streets.

"Good day to you," Nicolai said to the man who still looked up at him.

By now the other man was staring as though he'd discovered a new, sour taste in his mouth and couldn't decide if he'd rather spit it out or swallow it down. He reached out and grabbed hold of Kazys's reins. The horse protested and started to fight, but Nicolai brought the wagon to a stop before Kazys got too worked up.

Working the brake with his right foot,

Nicolai shifted in his seat so he could look down at the man head-on. "Something I can help you with, friend?" Nicolai's voice still carried a hint of his native accent, just enough to add a curl to every other word.

"I was just about to ask you the same thing."

"No help needed. I'm just on my way to a hotel and see about a job." Even though he knew better, Nicolai started to release the brake as if he meant to go merrily about his business.

Just as he'd expected, the other man slapped his foot away and stepped forward. His hand dropped to rest upon the handle of his own pistol as he let his jaw drop in a silent sneer. Nicolai looked around and noticed that almost everyone else who had been around was no longer to be seen. All that remained were a few slivers of faces peeking from behind half-closed shutters.

"What's in the wagon?" the other man asked.

"Just tools and such. Nothing of any value."

The other man was clean shaven and dressed just as well as any of the others who had been on the street. Something separated him from the rest, however. It was a roughness in his features that no amount of soap or smiling could cover up. He had a natural brutishness that made him seem more like a drawing from a book on natural history instead of something that should be up and walking around with modern men. Suddenly appearing more confident, this throwback said, "How about you let me decide that. Get off the wagon and step away before I toss you out of there. I bet I can at least get something for them two fine horses." He said the last part more to himself, grunting as though he figured Nicolai had already left.

But Nicolai hadn't left. Instead, he had yet to move so much as an inch from where he was sitting. His foot was still propped on the brake handle and his eyes were still fixed on the throwback's ugly, brutish face. The only thing that had moved at all was his hand, which was working its way toward the nub of gnarled wood protruding from his holster.

"This isn't a very private place for a robbery, is it?" Nicolai asked. "I mean, aren't these things usually done outside of town without so many witnesses?"

The throwback turned and looked around. When he faced Nicolai once again, he was wearing a smirk that was even uglier, since it was now tainted by arrogant smugness. "I don't see no witnesses. And you ain't even in town yet. So how about saving yourself some trouble and stepping off that wagon?"

Narrowing his eyes as he glared up at the wagon's driver, the throwback poured all his hate into his stare, as though the force of it alone would knock the other man to the ground. His breath started churning in his throat as the tension began to thicken between himself and Nicolai.

"Step away from there!"

The voice broke the relative silence that had fallen around the dirt path since most of the other locals had evacuated it. The words were spoken with volume and force, but anyone listening for more could easily have detected the nervousness running beneath the bluster.

Without even looking over his shoulder, the throwback replied, "Knock it off, Jed. This don't even concern you."

Nicolai's eyes only left the throwback for a fraction of a second, but that was more than enough time for him to catch a glimpse of the other man, who looked as though he meant to approach the wagon. He emerged from a nearby farmhouse and was dressed in thick cotton pants held up by worn suspenders. A tan shirt covered a muscular frame, and rolled-up sleeves revealed thick, brawny arms. Callused, dirty hands were wrapped around a battered Winchester rifle that looked more suited for hunting small game than anything on two legs.

The first impression Nicolai got of this newest arrival was that he was a farmer. Jed's dirty face, strong hands, and simple clothes spoke of a man more than accustomed to an honest day's work. Plus, the tentative way he held a gun made it obvious that he wasn't used to shooting at anything bigger than a squirrel.

"You'd best take a look at who you're talking to before you use that tone, Abe."

Abe turned to look, while shifting his feet so he could keep both Jed and Nicolai in his field of vision. His eyes shifted sluggishly beneath the protruding ridge of his brow. That was when he noticed the rifle held in both of Jed's hands like a steel snake that might awaken and bite the farmer at any second.

When he saw the rifle, Abe actually smiled. "What're you set to do with that?"

"Shoot you down if you don't leave that man alone."

"What's he to you?"

"I don't know who he is, but I do know he don't deserve to wind up like them others that you pulled this business with."

Nicolai shook his head and addressed the farmer. "Don't bother with me. I don't have much to steal anyway."

"I've seen it more times than I can stomach, mister," Jed replied. "This man'll kill you just to clean out your pockets. Me and the rest of us who live here have sat by and watched it too many times. It ends now." To Abe, he said, "You hear me? It ends now!"

"Does it?" Those were the only words Abe said before his hand flashed toward the gun at his side.

Nicolai was impressed with the throwback's speed, but not overly so.

A shot blasted through the air, shattering the tense quiet like a brick through a plateglass window. The single explosion echoed between the homes and outhouses and was quickly followed by the screams of those who'd been watching from their hiding places nearby.

Abe pulled in a breath and aimed his pistol at Jed, gritting his teeth as he set his sights upon the farmer.

His eyes wide with shock, Jed raised his shaking hands and bumped the rifle stock against his shoulder before pressing his cheek against the splintered wood and sighting down the barrel. The process took no more than a second, but to him it was an eternity that would be etched forever into his mind.

Even with the ferocious pounding in his chest and the cold beads of sweat that had pushed through his skin, Jed cocked back his hammer and tightened his finger around the trigger. At first he'd thought Abe shot him, but there wasn't even a hint of smoke coming from the throwback's barrel. Then the old rifle in his hands spat out a gout of sparks and smoke while bucking against his arm. Lead flew through the air and slammed into Abe's torso just below his ribs.

Abe squeezed off a shot that seemed more of a surprised reaction to Jed's rifle going off than anything else. The shot went wild and hissed through the air high over his target's head. As his body began falling backward, he instinctively prepared to take another shot. It wasn't until his rump hit the ground that he realized he was bleeding like a gutted deer.

With the last bit of foul distemper he could dredge up, Abe lifted his gun, about to pull the trigger. There was a rustle of movement behind him, and suddenly he couldn't raise his arm another inch. He looked down at his wrist to find it pinned to the earth by a single, scuffed boot.

Nicolai looked down at him and slowly

shook his head while twisting his heel in the same manner he would use to stamp out a cigarette.

The gun slipped from Abe's hand moments before the life drained from his body. Every muscle went slack, and he let out his final breath with a haggard wheeze.

Jed rushed forward, keeping his smoking rifle aimed at the corpse. The gun trembled in his hands. "Good lord, are you all right?" he asked.

"Yeah," Nicolai said. "Thanks to you."

"I . . . didn't know I had it in me. Tell you the truth . . . I didn't even know I hit him that bad."

Moving his hand to his side, Nicolai took advantage of the fact that everyone emerging from their hiding places was watching the farmer with the rifle and dropped his pistol back into its holster at his side. Its barrel was still warm to the touch. "You hit him well enough," he said.

Jed looked around, his eyes still nervous. "I thought I heard another shot. Right before this one missed me. Did you hear that?"

"In all the excitement, I couldn't rightly tell how many shots were fired. Just so long as we're both standing, I'd say we should consider ourselves lucky and be done with it."

Jed nodded. He took to that suggestion easily and without question . . . just like Nicolai thought he would.

Two

After dusting himself off and tipping his hat to Jed Arvey, Nicolai drove the rest of the way into town and put his horses up at the first livery he could find. Even though he was doing a good job of keeping himself calm after what had just happened, he still felt his insides rattling and the gunshots ringing through his mind.

It was all coming back to him. No matter how much he'd wanted to put it all behind him, the ways of his past were creeping back into his present. It had been all too easy to draw his gun and pull that trigger. The only thing that made it sit better with him was the fact that Jed seemed convinced that he'd been the one to put that throwback down. If Jed could be convinced, then perhaps he could as well.

It became easier the more he practiced; lying, that is. If it was to himself or to others, coming up with a truth that better suited his purposes was something Nicolai felt he would have to do if this new life of his had any chance of working. It wasn't a difficult sin for him to commit, especially when compared to the pile of sins he was trying to leave behind.

The kid at the livery took Nicolai's money as it was handed to him, his bright eyes darting away from his customer to the open door leading out to the street beyond. "You hear them shots?" he said in a quick, excited voice.

Nicolai shrugged. "Yeah, I did. That happen often around here?"

"No sir! I'll bet the sheriff's down there right now, with his gun drawn and everything."

Reaching out with his left hand, Nicolai took hold of the kid's shoulder before he could dart outside through the open door. "Hold on now, before you go." His right hand extended down to the kid's level, and when it opened, a half dollar was revealed. "Here's the rest of your payment. I intend on staying for a while."

At first the kid had looked up at Nicolai as though expecting to get into trouble. Then, seeing why he'd been detained, he grinned and lowered his eyes. "Thanks, mister." Straightening up and shaking Nicolai's hand the way he'd been taught, the kid pocketed the money and ran toward Nicolai's wagon.

The youthful body flew around the horses and cart like a swarm of bees, unfastening hitches and taking hold of reins. In no time at all the horses were shown to their stalls and the wagon was left in the middle of the barn. "My pa will see to your wagon, mister," the kid said as he took off running for the door. "Don't worry about nothing."

"I'll be staying at —" Nicolai started to say, but stopped himself when he realized he didn't know where he'd be staying. Not that it mattered, since the kid was already tearing down the street as though his britches had been set on fire.

Nicolai walked out of the livery and stretched his legs. Apart from the slight commotion coming from the outskirts where the shooting had happened, the place seemed pretty quiet. He figured the wagon would be fine where it was until the kid's father got around to putting it away. Besides, he could always check in on it later just to be sure.

Turning his back to the sounds of excited voices, Nicolai started walking toward what looked to be a main street. It was his practiced eye and years of growing up in his father's trade that drew him to the end of a street that seemed quiet in a dreary, sleepy kind of way. The buildings there were well maintained, but still somehow looked abandoned. There weren't many folks walking the streets outside, and the few who were purposely averted their eyes from a particular storefront.

That storefront became Nicolai's destination, and when he got close enough to read the sign hanging over the door, he knew his instincts had once again pointed him in the right direction. It was the undertaker's parlor. Nicolai opened the door and stepped inside.

There was no bell over the frame to announce his presence, but it wasn't necessary. The room was tastefully decorated, smelled like flowers, and was just as quiet as the next place that most of its customers would be laid to rest. Responding to the sound of the door opening, which still echoed through the room, an old man wearing a dark blue suit covered with a white butcher's apron stepped through a door at the back of the parlor.

"Hello?" he said uncertainly as he squinted into the room and wiped his hands on the front of his apron. "Who's there?"

Nicolai stepped up to the man and held

out his hand, which was quickly enveloped by the old man's strong, bony grip. "I'm new in town. My name's Nicolai Graves."

"New in town and you came to see me? Must be here for the Eddings funeral. That won't be for a few days."

"Not exactly. I'm actually here because I heard you need a hand with things."

The old man scrunched up his face even more. "Well, there's a job for a man who's qualified," he said. Looking down at himself and holding his hands out, he added, "Not to mention you caught me at a good time to ask for it. I just found out that a man was killed nearby, and I've still got to see to Mrs. Eddings's marker. You know anything about wood carving?"

"Yes, sir. That's part of the job. That as well as some stone cutting, but I was always more partial to lumber."

The old man had yet to let go of Nicolai's hand. Just as that fact was becoming obvious, he glanced down and asked, "Were you a miner?"

Nicolai didn't have to ask what had brought that question about. Instead, he plucked his hand out of the undertaker's grasp and lowered it to his side.

Quickly, the old man's face turned sympathetic, and unlike most undertakers, the sentiment seemed genuine. "I didn't mean to offend. I just noticed you had the hands of a miner. You know . . . working with so many picks and dynamite and such."

Hearing the old man say that, Nicolai's left hand went reflexively to cover his right. The ring finger of his right hand was nothing more than a gnarled nub less than a quarter of its original length. The tip of his middle finger was gone as well. Even though he used his left hand to cover it up, that one wasn't without damage either. Half of his left pinky was gone, its tip having healed over into a patch of rough skin.

"I didn't mean to offend," the old man said once again.

Nicolai shrugged. "You didn't."

"So what do you know about the trade? My trade, that is."

"My father was a grave digger all his life. He taught me how to use tools by building coffins where I grew up."

"Really? Where was that?"

"Missouri and Kansas mostly. We traveled some, but only when he needed to move where there was more work to be found. He wanted me to learn his trade." Pausing, Nicolai added, "Your trade, that is."

The old man smiled and laughed while untying the apron from around his waist.

"I was taught how to build and decorate coffins," Nicolai continued. "I can engrave headstones and even prepare bodies for burial. More recently I've become a Mourner."

"A Mourner?"

"You must've heard of them."

"Of course. They help arrange funeral ceremonies and work with folks in their time of need." The explanation came out of the old man like a practiced sales pitch. "They also send out invites for wakes and . . . well . . . hangings."

Nicolai nodded and folded his hands in front of him, careful to keep his less damaged one over the other.

The old man fixed his clouded eyes onto Nicolai and looked him up and down. "We don't get many hangings around here, you know."

"Not many places do. That's why they're special occasions."

"Spoken like a true professional." Letting out a deep breath, the old man removed his apron and tossed it over Nicolai's shoulder. "I could use the help, and it sounds like you're more than qualified. I'm Dan Callum, by the way. When can you start?"

"As soon as possible. You know a good place for me to stay here in town?"

"There's some fine hotels, but they might be a little too close to the saloons for anyone who enjoys quiet like folks in our trade do. There's cabins to be leased, but I can put you up at my place until you get something arranged."

"I'd appreciate that, Mr. Callum."

"You wouldn't be lying about all them qualifications, would you? Not to insult your character, but a man'll say a lot of things to get steady work."

"You can decide for yourself when you see how I do. I'll even let you hold back on my pay until you're satisfied."

"Well . . . we can see how good you are soon enough."

The undertaker turned around and started walking back toward the door from which he'd emerged a few minutes earlier. "You look rattled, boy. Why don't you put that apron on, roll up those sleeves and get to work? That always clears my head. You can also tell me what you heard about that shooting. All I got was some stories passed by a widow who lives down there and was on her way to the store. Fill me in and we can get things squared away for the Eddings affair."

Already feeling more at home, Nicolai slipped the bib's loop over his head and tied

41

the apron around his waist. While moving from the front of the parlor to the workshop in back, his nose instinctively blocked out the smell of rotten flesh and decay. He focused instead upon the fresh, earthy scent of wood and stone that filled the other half of the parlor. The space was set up not too differently than his father's workshop. A little bigger and a little fancier, maybe, but plenty recognizable.

"You know what the only bad thing is about our business?" Dan asked once he was standing in front of a bench covered with tools. "We got to wait around so much for prosperous times. After all, it's not like we have much say in who lives and who dies."

Nicolai couldn't help but smile at that. In his mind, he could still see the face of that throwback gunman, the killer's expression a mix of shock and terror as he realized he'd somehow wound up on the losing end of a fight. Nicolai could still hear his bullet whipping through the air and punching into flesh and bone.

He could still feel the weight of his specially modified pistol that was specifically balanced to be gripped by fewer than four fingers and a thumb. The firearm's gnarled handle was actually expertly carved, even though it looked like it had been chewed on by some wild animal.

Dan Callum might not have had much say in who lived or died, but Nicolai Graves felt differently. He had plenty of say when that pistol was in his hand. And not only did he manage to keep himself from getting robbed or hurt by the throwback, but he'd also managed to throw himself a bit of legitimate business as well.

"Yeah," he replied. "But we don't have to wait around too much today."

"Nope. We sure don't. Today, we're in the right trade and — not that anyone else would understand this — I hope the lead keeps flying around here just so long as the right folks end up on that table."

Looking over to where Dan was pointing, Nicolai saw a rectangular table bearing the weight of a body covered in a black sheet. Apart from the fact that it was a grown person, it could have been a man or woman, old or young. The bodies tended to look the same at that point in their trip through this world. They deflated like an empty water skin and the eyes turned glassy once the spark of life behind them had been snuffed.

For a man like Nicolai, there was some degree of comfort to be taken from that. His father had taught him that all folks were the same once they were looking up at you from the bottom of their graves.

Stasys had called that the view from below.

"It all looks the same down there," Nicolai's father had told him more than once. "The only thing I know for sure, *spurgas,* is that what they are looking at, we cannot see."

As a child, Nicolai had often wondered what those eyes could see. Even as a grown man, he was still wondering.

THREE

Standing at one of two windows that faced out onto Fourth Street, Corey Manes kept his hands clasped behind his back and a calm, impassive look on his face. He'd heard the gunshots a few moments earlier, but didn't flinch at the sound. Instead, he'd rocked slightly back on his heels and let his weight draw him forward again as though he was listening to a melody being played on a piano.

He kept looking through the clean glass, listening until the only thing he could hear was the occasional rattle as the wind shook the pane in front of him. Light green eyes shifted in their sockets as a pair of figures crossed Fourth Street and headed straight for the front door of the building where Manes waited. He was still looking outside when the door beside him opened and both men stepped in from the cool autumn breeze.

"You're going to have to keep the shooting down to a minimum," Manes said as soon as he was certain both of the new arrivals were listening. "Otherwise, someone might expect me to do something about it."

The first man to step inside stood just over five and a half feet tall. His hair was a rumpled mess beneath his battered hat. Even though the wind was having occasional fits outside, the rat's nest atop his head looked the same even on the calmest of days. He didn't even try to pat it down as he took off his hat and gripped it in both hands. "You heard what happened?"

Manes turned on his heels and nodded. "I heard the shots. Kind of hard not to, wouldn't you say, Rich?"

The man with the rumpled hair shrugged his shoulders. Rich's smile was almost as messy as his hair and looked very uncomfortable on his face. His frame resembled that of a large rodent, with a prominent chin and jutting teeth to match. "I guess you're right about that."

Before Rich could get in another word, the second man who'd entered the building shoved past him so hard that Rich nearly lost his balance. This man was taller and somewhat more muscular, yet he carried himself with more confidence. Actually,

46

confidence wasn't the word for it. Arrogance was more like it. His name was Scott and he acted as though the title "Sir" belonged in front of it.

"Abe was stirring up some shit again," Scott said. "Happened on the other side of town near all them farmers' shacks."

Although he didn't smile, Manes seemed amused nonetheless. "Nothing new there, I suppose."

"Not really," Scott replied. "But what is new is that Abe ain't around to brag about what he done this time around."

Hearing that brought a definite shift to Manes's face. The change was something akin to seeing a painting scowl at an unsuspecting onlooker. Where Manes had been calm and sedate only moments ago, he now looked about one step away from jumping out of his skin.

This lasted all of two seconds, but caused the other men to take a few steps back and hold their distance even after the storm had passed.

"Tell me what happened," Manes said once the anger had been pulled back under his skin.

Rich lowered his eyes and glanced in Scott's direction. It wasn't the first time he'd been grateful for keeping his mouth shut.

Since he'd already started in on the topic, Scott knew well enough that he was the one to finish it. Letting out his breath in a grumbling rush, he said, "Some fella pulled into town and Abe was there to greet him."

Manes nodded, fully aware that the greeting would have been anything but friendly.

"Anyway, one thing led to another and Abe started getting rough with the guy."

"From what I heard," Rich said, stepping in against his own better judgment, "this man didn't have much more than a wagon and a few old nags to pull it."

Ignoring Rich, Scott went on. "Abe was laying down the law and then one of them farmers steps in on this other man's behalf."

"Farmer?" Manes asked. "Who was it?"

Scott shrugged as though he'd been asked the name of a bug he'd stepped on during his walk across the street.

Rich, on the other hand, wasn't caught unprepared. "Jed Arvey," he said. "He works a few acres outside of town."

Manes furrowed his brow as his eyes shifted toward the window. Nodding as though he could see Jed standing on the street outside, he said, "Go on. Let's hear the rest of it."

"There ain't much else to say," Scott replied without being able to meet the other man's glare. "That farmer stepped forward with a shotgun, and Abe must not have thought the fella had the sand to pull a trigger. Turns out he was wrong."

Manes took in the account in much the same way he might try to swallow a chunk of salt. It was hard to swallow and left a bad taste in his mouth. Still, he choked it down all the same. "So Abe's dead. This is what you're telling me?"

"Pretty much."

When Manes looked his way, Rich could only nod.

"I see. Abe wasn't one of the brightest I've ever met, but he should have been quicker on the draw than a farmer. What about this fella on the wagon? Did he just sit there and watch all of this happen?"

"That's what I heard," Rich replied. "Everyone talking about it says that Jed stepped up and dropped Abe in his tracks. They see it as a fair fight." That last part seemed hard for Rich to say, but he forced himself to get the words out.

"What about you?" Manes asked, leveling his gaze on Scott. "What do you make of all this?"

"I think Abe let his guard down and that

farmer got one hell of a lucky shot."

"I don't believe in luck."

"Well, that's the only way to account for it. Abe is spread open from that shotgun, and that damn farmer is out bragging about it. Luck's the only way to explain that kind of bullshit."

Rich shifted on his feet, obviously uncomfortable with what he was hearing and growing more so by the second. Even so, he kept his thoughts to himself and put up with Scott, like he always did.

Smirking, Manes said, "Good thing you're not a gambler, Rich. You might as well just write down everything on your mind and pass it around. Am I hearing everything I need to hear?"

"Yes, sir. Of course you are."

"Then what's bothering you?"

"Jed wasn't exactly bragging when I spoke to him. In fact, I got the impression he was surprised about what happened more than anything else. It's everyone around him building it up."

Manes pulled in a deep breath and shifted his gaze between the two men standing in front of him. His jaw clenched and relaxed as though he was literally chewing on what he'd been told. The longer he thought, the thicker the silence within the room became.

Despite the fact that there were plenty of pieces of furniture laying about, the room seemed strangely empty and untouched by any of those inside of it.

Like a ghost haunting the space rather than a man walking through it, Manes stepped around a small table and slid past a padded chair until he was standing in the middle of a thick, burgundy rug that covered a good portion of the floor. With his steps muffled by the rug, Manes seemed even more of an unnatural presence.

He came to a stop with his feet planted a shoulder width apart. His rigid posture made the simple yet well-maintained clothes he wore seem almost stately. The black boots covering his feet and shins glistened with a military shine.

"No doubt I'll be hearing plenty about this soon enough," Manes announced. "It sure didn't take you two very long to gather up some accounts and bring them to me, and I don't want you to do a thing that will discourage anyone else from stepping forward. Is that understood?"

Rich was the first one to nod in agreement, but Scott wasn't too far behind.

"The next thing I want to know about is this man who was driving into town. Is he family of anyone who lives here?"

51

"Not as far as I could tell," Rich answered.

All Scott had to offer was a shake of his head and a shrug of his shoulders.

"Is he still in town?" Manes asked.

"Yeah," Scott piped in. "He's around here somewhere."

Rich's voice wasn't as loud as either of the other two, but it piped up well enough when he knew what he was talking about. "He's over at Dan Callum's place. He asked directions from Jed when he came into town."

"Dan Callum?" More than just a question, the name seemed to be a genuine annoyance to Manes.

"He's the undertaker, sir."

"Oh yeah," Manes said. "That old man at all those funerals."

Manes caught some motion out of the corner of his eye and turned to look out the window where he'd been standing earlier. There were some locals gathering across the street, talking among themselves while occasionally pointing toward the building Manes occupied.

"All right," Manes said without taking his eyes from the window. "You two go about your business and do what I told you. And Scott?"

"Yeah?"

"Try not to get on the bad side of any farmers."

Scott choked back the impulse to spit out a few choice profanities, deciding to save them for Rich instead. He and his disheveled partner left the room the same way they'd entered it, allowing the wind to slam the door shut behind them.

That little bit of outside air was enough to drop the room's temperature a few degrees. Although Manes would rather die than let himself appear affected by something as common as the weather, his hands rubbed together out of a natural reflex to keep warm. He didn't have to watch Rich and Scott to know they were headed in the proper direction. His confidence in their ability to follow his directions was absolute.

Actually, his confidence in his own ability to shove them into their proper places was what truly inspired Manes's confidence. What didn't inspire one bit of confidence was the news that had been brought to his attention. Although that uneasiness was invisible to Rich and Scott, it would be more plain to the man Manes had to see next.

No matter how much he tried to tell himself otherwise, Manes knew better than to think he could show anything but the truth to the man who waited for him. It seemed as though that man was always waiting.

Waiting for everyone else to come running to him.

Waiting for death itself to come after so many years had left their ugly scratches across his worn, leathery flesh.

For a moment Manes thought the other man was already there, sitting at the back of the room like a ghoul lurking in the darkness of any available shadow. But the room was empty. Just to be certain, Manes took another, slower look.

Yeah.

It was empty.

Somehow, that didn't do much to ease his nerves.

"Son of a bitch," Manes said to himself. "Bastard." Like an uncomfortable whistle in the night, those words somehow boosted Manes's confidence until he was once again standing with his back straight and his jaw set in a determined line. To anyone who might have been watching, it would have looked as though Manes was cursing the locals screwing up their courage outside his window. He might have been referring to Abe, whose quick temper had finally flared up to place one last pain in Manes's ass.

But Manes's thoughts kept going back to that farmer, carefully staying away from the conversation that was looming closer and closer as the seconds ticked by. If it wasn't for that farmer, Abe would still be alive and the world would have been just the way Manes had left it when he'd gone to bed the night before.

Then again, Manes figured he did owe Jed and the rest of those farmers something when everything was said and done. They were the ones who allowed him to be something other than a farmer himself.

They were the ones who'd elected him their sheriff.

FOUR

Nicolai worked as he talked. While he wasn't used to too much casual conversation, he had to admit it felt good to be able to apply himself in a familiar way while talking in a familiar manner to someone who actually listened. All too often, folks tended to discount him the moment they heard his native accent, which bent his words in a fashion he'd never been able to shake. Each word was spoken correctly and precisely, but there was just a slight curl tacked onto the occasional syllable.

Having learned to speak like the Americans, along with his father, Nicolai had mastered the basics of English after his first few months in the country. It took Stasys a bit longer, but he'd gotten ahold of it as well. Even so, Stasys had stubbornly held onto his thick accent as if shedding it would have been a betrayal to the homeland he'd left behind.

For that reason alone, Stasys had always sounded like a stranger to his adopted country. And since he'd been raised the same way, it had taken Nicolai quite a while to sound any different. But throughout the years, he'd dropped all but that slight curl, and that was because of so many years of constant practice.

Dan Callum listened intently while he tended to work of his own. After the undertaker had returned with Abe's body, he and his new helper worked while talking about nothing in particular. Callum was busy making Abe a little more presentable, while Nicolai hammered together Abe's coffin.

"Pardon me for saying, Nick," Callum said from the workshop. Without any more sound to compete with him, Callum's voice carried powerfully through the propped-open door that led out to the back lot behind the parlor. "But you seem awfully pulled together for someone who entered town the way you did."

Nicolai chose to ignore the shortening of his name, which was something most people seemed to do after meeting him. Every so often, a stubborn streak inherited from his father made him want to correct those people. Then again, it made things a whole lot easier to just answer to Nick.

He shrugged and reached for another handful of nails. The hammer that filled his left hand moved through the air in a straight line beside his head; back and forth, each line punctuated by the sound of steel smacking against nail and wood. "A man sees plenty of bad things, Mr. Callum. Especially in our line of work."

"True enough. But even a man such as myself tends to flinch when a man dies right in front of him. My job isn't the prettiest there is, but at least the smoke's cleared by the time I get to my next customer. You've still got some of Abe's blood on you."

Nick stopped what he was doing and looked down at himself. His shirt was a simple collection of buttons and cotton that hung loosely over him like something that had been tossed onto the back of a chair. The sleeves were rolled up just past his elbows, to reveal a set of forearms covered with sinewy muscle and a layer of scarred flesh.

Sure enough, there were some flecks of dried blood on his arm that reminded Nick of flaking red paint. When he reached across to brush away the blood with the back of his hand, he spotted some more traces of crimson scattered over the row of buttons that closed the shirt around his neck. The stains must have come from the impact of the shotgun blast that had come after he had put Abe down.

"Guess I'll have to get another shirt," Nick said plainly. "Blood doesn't usually wash out too well."

"No, sir. It sure doesn't." Callum kept his eyes on the younger man. He wasn't much more than half Nick's size, but the brightness in his eyes gave him another kind of bulk, which seemed to make him seem taller when remembered by others. Although his skin clung tightly to the bones and veins of his arms and hands, he still worked with a steadiness that some gunfighters would have envied.

"You've been in this line of work for a while, haven't you?" Callum asked.

Nick nodded without hesitation. "All my life. I was born a grave digger's son."

"So your pa taught you this craft and carpentry as well?"

Looking down at the oddly angled, rectangular box he was building, Nick said, "He taught me how to build coffins. Carpentry came after that."

"Even an old-timer in this trade gets squeamish at times. Maybe not as much as other folks. Maybe not enough for anyone else to notice, but it's still there. It gets under a man's skin. Even I still feel it."

Nick had heard his father talk about the same sort of thing the first time he'd been shown what was inside those heavy, rectangular boxes. Even after all those years, Nick could still see the face of that first dead man. He hadn't known the dead man's name or even what had killed him, but that pale, waxy face would be with him for the rest of his days.

"I'd wager you don't even —" Callum stopped himself in the middle of his question. "Never mind. I don't mean to pry. It's just that there's not a whole lot of people who feel comfortable saying much of anything to a man in my profession. Usually, they pray they never have to see me coming their way."

Nick smiled and nodded. "Believe me, I know exactly what you mean. Every town has a boot hill, but most folks don't care to know how those holes got dug." What he didn't tell the undertaker was that he welcomed the way people averted their eyes from him. It made things a whole lot easier being the one who was commonly ignored.

Although Callum seemed a little more at ease than he had a few moments ago, there was still something in the back of his mind that kept him from relaxing completely. "I guess you're right about that. With your pa doing the work he did, I guess you got to see plenty of them boot hills for yourself."

"Sure did. When I was a boy, I used to toss horseshoes around some of the boots and such that were sticking out of the ground. That was when we'd first get someplace, though. My pa said leaving any man buried in those shallow graves was a shame against the Almighty. But I still remember those boots sticking out of the ground no matter how well my pa covered them up again."

In a strange kind of way, Callum took on a fond little smile as he thought about what Nick had said. "There are plenty of them boot hills around. I'll have to agree with your pa, though. It ain't right to toss a few handfuls of dirt on a man and be done with it. It don't matter what kind of wickedness he did in his life. We haven't ever had a boot hill in Jessup."

"That's good," Nick said with a darkness seeping into his voice. "I hope it stays that way. It seems like half my life was spent somewhere with those damn toes sticking up out of the dirt. I've had my fill."

Shrugging, Callum said, "Well, the main thing is what goes on here and now. It looks to me like you're doing a hell of a job over there," he pointed out, leaning over to inspect Nick's work. "I usually like to think a bit before I take on a partner, but I don't see why I can't just offer you the job straight out."

"I appreciate that. I'm sure you won't be disappointed."

"I'd better not. Pay starts off on the low end, but I can let you sleep in my spare room to make up for it. If your masonry work is any good, I'll give you a bonus for that as well. But don't get your hopes up too high. Folks around here prefer the wooden markers."

"I kind of figured that much."

Callum looked a little embarrassed, and he swiped away some beads of sweat that had been forming on his brow. "Yeah. I guess you would have, at that."

"Just tell me what needs doing and I'll do it. As for that extra room, I'd be much obliged so long as it's not a burden for you to let me stay there."

Smiling in a way that seemed to stop just short of sinister, Callum let out a short laugh and said, "Burden? Hell no. You might prefer to pay for one after spending a night in it, though. Check it out for yourself. It's right over there."

The undertaker raised one arm to point

with a bony outstretched finger in a way that reminded Nick of a book he'd read concerning a spirit of Christmases Yet to Come. When he looked in the direction indicated by that one outstretched finger, he saw a narrow door leading off of the workshop. The door was shut tightly and looked as though it was petrified in its place.

"That'll be fine," Nick said in a level voice.

"You'll have to get some linens and things from around here," Callum added. When he spoke, he seemed to be watching Nick carefully. "Just poke around in the closet and you should find some of the sheets I use for lining caskets or spreading under bodies at showings."

There was a little smile on the undertaker's face, hiding just below the surface. All that could be seen of it at the moment was a faint twitch at the corner of Callum's mouth, but he was ready to let it fly as soon as he had good reason.

"Much obliged, Mr. Callum," Nick said, knowing full well the older man was putting him through a few paces. "I'm sure it'll be better than some of the hotels I've been in lately. And this way, I don't have to walk too far to work in the morning."

After a few more moments of studying, Callum let the smile he'd prepared fade away and nodded to simply acknowledge Nick's response. "All right, then. When you finish up that coffin, come find me. It looks like I've got some business to tend to up front."

Nick thought the undertaker might be trying to stretch his legs or maybe even get away from him for a bit, but it seemed that the older man had been speaking the truth. Despite the fact that he hadn't even heard any steps himself, Nick could now see that there was indeed someone walking toward the parlor. He hadn't heard anyone coming or even seen anyone headed in their direction until after Callum had already spotted it.

The figure appeared to be a man, walking down the street and turning off toward the parlor. Callum had removed his apron and was straightening his suit by the time the approaching man spotted him.

Nick shook his head, smiled, and got back to work. Callum struck him as the type of man he could trust. There wasn't any real facts or reasoning behind it. Just the feeling in his gut after talking to the undertaker for a while and getting a good look at his eyes.

There was plenty that could be seen from a careful look at someone's eyes that could be hidden or overlooked after years of conversation. Words lied. Eyes didn't. Knowing that simple rule had seen Nick through plenty of hard times, not to mention a fair amount of poker games.

But there were no cards to be dealt just then. All Nick needed to worry about were the tools in his hands and the wood he was crafting. His muscles were warm beneath his skin as he once again slammed hammer against nail. The air seemed especially welcoming as it blew over his shoulders and cooled him off by rustling his hair.

It was a fine day, and Nick was happy being exactly where he was. He'd found some honest work and had even managed to pass some time with a friendly conversation. For a man who'd been forced to grow accustomed to so many unsettling things, those two simple things had become treasures indeed.

As much as his natural instincts told him to look up and watch the exchange between Callum and the other man, Nick decided to let himself get lost in some of the good things for just a little bit. He did enjoy talking with the undertaker, but hearing the wind rush around him like a flow of invisible water was a pleasure in itself. The prairie breeze was clean and full of bits and pieces of the wide open land that stretched out in every direction.

If he closed his eyes for a moment, Nick thought he could hear every blade of grass being pushed back and forth. He could feel the lumber bending to his direction with every blow of the hammer. Bits of dust and seed flew past him and landed on his cheek as another gust of wind churned on by.

Some people saw autumn as a time of death and the approach of cold. Nick's mother had seen it that way.

Even though he fought to hang on to them, Nick's memories of her were fading more and more each year. She'd died when he was very young, which made him hold on to the memories he did have that much tighter. But no matter how closely he guarded his mental pictures, they faded all the same. It was the unstoppable decay of time itself, and his memories weren't much more than rock being worn away by a constant tide.

He could lament what was missing, or savor what was left. In the end, Nick chose the latter and focused on one of the clearest pictures of her that still floated in his head from time to time. It had been sometime before the voyage to America, and he was a child living in the land of his birth.

His mother was more of a presence, really,

the way many dreams were, and she floated between one domestic task or another, always looking over her shoulder to watch over him. Even as he let himself drift back into his memories, Nick's arms still moved through their assigned motions of assembling the coffin.

A nail was hammered into place.

A board was straightened and set right.

Another nail was picked up.

That nail was hammered into place.

But his eyes weren't seeing the metal being buried into the wood. Nick was looking into his mother's eyes, even though hers weren't quite meeting his. He could feel the colder breeze of that day long past. He could hear leaves rustling against the dirt after falling from trees that were long since dead. He could see his mother's expression darkening as she wrapped her arms around herself and scowled at the changing of the seasons.

His mother never liked the cold. Everything about her would dim once the leaves started to die and fall to the ground. For that reason, part of him knew her spirit would never be able to rest in the cold water where the men had dumped her body during the voyage to America.

Nick loved the cold, and sometimes he

hated himself for that.

It didn't make sense if he thought about it long enough, the way dreams so often don't, but it was there . . .

. . . underneath the surface . . .

. . . where his mother still smiled, yet could never meet his eyes.

Nick tried not to think about her eyes for too long, or else his father's words would spring to mind. In dreams, he would wonder why she never could look at him. No matter how much he begged or pleaded, he could never get her to turn her face just that half an inch more so she could stare at him straight on.

When he got older, he told his father about those dreams, and Stasys had answered him so quickly that he must have had the same dreams himself.

"She's got the view from below now," he'd said. "That's what she sees. But don't take it to heart, *sunus.* She doesn't see me either."

It took a few more years for those words to lose their sting, but Nick eventually came to accept them. Now, after all the things he'd seen and all the things he'd done, he not only accepted them, but truly hoped they were true.

Even as the last nail was in place and every

piece of wood was fitted together, Nick kept pounding the hammer against the lumber. At first he sought out nails that weren't quite flush, but when he couldn't find any more of those, he just smashed the hammer against whatever he could reach.

When he was about to crack off a chunk from the side of the finished coffin, he stopped himself in mid-swing. The memories that had been keeping him company were fading and he was left with nothing but a tiredness in his bones and the cold wind blowing around him. Suddenly, the breeze wasn't comforting and it didn't feel good.

It just felt cold.

Nick got to his feet and was about to toss the hammer to one side when he decided to just let it fall from his grasp. Looking down at the work he'd done made him nod slightly in satisfaction. All it took was a bit of mental figuring using another set of more recent memories for him to know that the coffin would fit perfectly around what was left of the dead throwback.

At the moment, Nick couldn't remember the throwback's name or if he'd even heard it. That didn't matter just then. He'd worry about that when he was carving the marker.

Suddenly, something caught Nick's attention. It was a raised voice coming from the front of Callum's parlor. Nick looked that way and saw that the undertaker was still talking to the same man, only things weren't going as smoothly as they'd started. In fact, the other man seemed just about to take a swing at the old man in the blue suit.

Before Nick started walking, he clenched his fist as though still holding the hammer. His fingers closed into a tight bundle, he walked toward the parlor.

FIVE

"You want to say that one more time? I don't think I heard it quite right."

Dan Callum stood in the main room of his parlor with his hands clasped in front of him. His dark blue suit was a bit rumpled and dusty, but he still carried himself like a man who demanded respect. Unfortunately, the man talking to him wasn't giving him any.

Standing with one foot planted ahead of the other, Scott looked as though he meant to walk straight over the undertaker. His hands hung at his sides with fingers splayed. An ugly sneer twisted his upper lip.

"Perhaps you would have heard me," Callum said, "if you didn't insist on shouting. This is a place meant for reflection. It isn't proper to —"

Despite the fact that he seemed to be getting angrier, Scott did lower his voice. "I don't give two shits about what's proper. I just came here to make some arrangements for a man that was killed today, and you're the one that took a smart-ass tone with me. How proper is that?"

The parlor's main room resembled a smaller version of a church. It was a long, open room with a high ceiling. Much of the floor space was taken up by two rows of wooden pews. The altar at the front of the room was lower than something used by a preacher, however, and was wide enough to bear the casket of a full-grown man.

Although there wasn't currently anyone laying on display, the altar was covered with clean linens scattered with a few wrinkled flower petals. At the back of the room was a small, narrow door that opened to the workshop. It was from this door that Nick emerged, bending at the waist to keep from bumping the top of his head as he stepped through the opening.

Nick didn't say a word. He didn't have to. Both men were standing at the front of the room where wider, more ornate doors opened to the front of the building. The doors were flanked on either side by various cases used for display purposes and an easel used to hold announcements. Callum and Scott were standing closer to the easel, only a few feet away from the back of the last pew.

"Never mind us," Scott said as his eyes darted toward Nick. "We've got a bit of business to settle."

Nick walked down the row between pews and brushed the wood splinters from his hands.

When he saw his order hadn't been immediately obeyed, Scott straightened up and squared his shoulders so he could face Nick straight on. "You deaf or something? Move on out of here! Whatever you need to talk about can wait till I'm done with this old man. He'll be here when I'm through." Smirking, Scott shot Callum a glance and added, "So long as he plays his cards right, that is."

Slowly, Callum turned to look over his shoulder. Once he checked to make sure who was coming, he swiveled his head back so he could focus on Scott. "It's all right, Nick. Just get back to work and let me handle this."

Scott grinned even wider now, as if the other man's name was some kind of secret he'd learned. "Yeah, Nick. Go on and scat."

Nick didn't move.

His eyes remained fixed on Scott and his hands remained clenched at his sides. His stillness was so complete that Scott looked away from him as though he'd left the room altogether. The gun belt that Nick usually wore was in a corner of the workshop beneath his jacket. And even though he felt a yearning for the weapon to be in his hand, Nick was ultimately glad that it wasn't.

Sometimes it was best to do things the hard way.

"So are you gonna do your job or not, old man?" Scott asked.

Callum shook his head just enough for the movement to be seen. "I know my job, and what you're asking just isn't right. It's not —"

"You tell me what's proper one more time," Scott hissed as his hand snapped out to take hold of the front of Callum's shirt, "and I swear to God I'll see to it that you're the next one laying in one of them boxes you sell."

Something moved behind the undertaker, and when Scott looked up to see what it was, Nick was about ten feet closer than he'd been the last time he'd checked. Scott flinched so much that his body lurched back half a step. He hadn't seen Nick move or even heard his boots knock against the floor. One moment Nick had been too far away to care about, and the next . . . it was too late for him to know what he should think.

"Let him go," Nick said in a voice as cold as stone.

Before his higher impulses could kick in, Scott opened his fist and pulled his arm back. He didn't want to obey a man he'd never even met, but his survival instincts got the better of him.

"Who the fuck are you?" Scott snarled, over-emphasizing his anger to compensate for his actions. "And give me one reason why I shouldn't pull your head off."

Nick's lowered his hand onto Callum's shoulder and squeezed just enough to comfort the undertaker. When the older man looked around at him, Nick gently pushed him away from Scott.

"Please, Nick," Callum said urgently, "just let me handle this."

Shaking his head, Nick replied, "Go ahead and handle it, but there's no need for business to get physical." Although he'd never taken his eyes away from Scott, the tone in Nick's voice indicated that he was no longer addressing the undertaker. "Talk about your business or move on."

There was no mistaking that as a request. It was an order, plain and simple.

As if to make up for the back-step he'd taken, Scott squared his shoulders so he was facing Nick more than Callum. He straightened up to his full height and scowled beneath a few strands of hair that had fallen over his face. "It's about Abe's burial. I want him to receive a wake every bit as fancy as that one held here two weeks ago. He was a deputy, after all."

Nick still didn't look away from Scott, but the shadow was plain enough to see upon his face. The word "deputy" worked its way through him like a poison.

"Mrs. Overmeyer," Callum explained. "She was put to rest after a wonderful ceremony that was attended by most of the town."

"That's right. I want Abe to have a fandango just as big as that."

Nick didn't have to look at the undertaker to sense the distaste Callum was feeling. From the corner of his eye, he could see the older man shaking his head and starting to move a bit closer to the man who'd just threatened him.

"Mrs. Overmeyer lived here her entire life. She had children, grandchildren, even a great-grandchild that she would have seen had she held out for another month or two."

"So Abe didn't have a mess of kids," Scott spat. "So what? That means he don't get a proper burial?"

"I'm saying she had family. She had friends. She was . . ." Callum let his words trail off as though something inside of him had made him stop. Then, after taking a breath for strength, he finished his sentence anyway. "She was a valued part of this community and will be sorely missed. The man who was killed this morning will get a proper burial, but I cannot guarantee an event as grand as Mrs. Overmeyer's."

There was plenty more that Callum wanted to say, but it had taken most of his reserve steam to go as far as he'd already gone. The rest was needed to maintain his posture under Scott's burning scrutiny.

Scott's eyes flicked back and forth between Callum and Nick. His tongue snapped out to wet his lips, and rage built up behind his eyes. "See, now that's the part I keep thinking I didn't hear just right. Your job is to do what someone tells you to do. You don't tell your customers what they want or how they want it, do you?"

Callum didn't respond. He just didn't have the strength.

Seeing that bit of weakness put a spark in Scott's eyes. Nick spotted it right away and recognized it for what it was: the reflex of a predator. Even though there was the slightest trace of fear beneath it, that predator's eye could not be hidden.

"No," Callum responded, even though it was a visible effort to do so. "I don't."

"Then why should I be some big exception? Huh? Especially when I'm willing to pay you good money."

"You're willing to pay?" Nick asked.

Scott glanced back to Nick and nodded once. "Sure I am. You think I'm some sort of layabout?"

There was something different with the tone of Scott's voice. Something had changed in the last couple of seconds that boosted the man's confidence. Nick took a moment to look around and then thought about what could have happened to draw out a change like that.

It didn't take much thinking for him to come up with an answer. It took even less time for him to verify that he was right. In fact, all it took was a quick look through the open front door of the parlor for Nick to spot the other figure who stood just a pace or two outside the entrance. That second man was shorter and scruffier looking, but was dressed in a similar fashion to Scott.

When he looked back into Scott's eyes, Nick saw that his confidence had increased. And the smirk on Scott's face was wider and more arrogant. It turned Nick's stomach. For that reason alone, he chose to once again take the rougher path.

"If Mr. Callum doesn't want to serve you," Nick said, "he doesn't have to. And since this is his place of business, I suggest you leave. Right now."

Scott shook his head, reached behind him with one hand, pointed a finger toward the other man waiting outside, and hooked the finger back toward the parlor. Seeing that, the man outside began walking slowly toward the front door.

"Fine, fine," Callum said quickly. "There's no need for this to go any further. You're right."

Both Scott and Nick glanced toward the undertaker to see which one of them he was referring to.

Callum swallowed hard and nodded. "I'll put something together for the deceased."

Scott grinned victoriously as the other man entered the parlor.

"I'll put as much effort into it as I can, but you must understand that I simply cannot guarantee the same turnout as that of some of my . . . previous gatherings." The undertaker was picking his words carefully so as not to offend, but Scott was only half listening.

"There better be someone there besides

me and my friends. I want Abe to have a send-off just as good as anyone else."

"But you don't understand. If nobody else shows up then there's nothing I can —"

Stopping Callum with another touch on his shoulder, Nick spoke as though reading from a script. "There will be others there to mourn the loss of your friend. If this is what Mr. Callum wants, then I can guarantee that it will happen."

"Oh can you, now?"

"Yes," Nick responded. "I can. It's what I do."

Obviously, Scott didn't know exactly what to make of this. He stepped back, making sure to keep his eyes on both men in front of him. Stabbing a finger toward Nick, he said, "I'll be checking in on you. There's still some things we need to talk about."

The expression on Nick's face was unreadable. His posture was that of an unmovable wall. His hands remained where they were, hanging as heavily and as still as a man at the end of a noose on a windless day.

Scott stepped back and found the rest of his confidence once he was closer to his partner. From there, he whispered something to the other man and they both strode out of the funeral parlor. The door slammed shut behind them, bouncing off the jamb to swing out lazily before coming to a stop halfway between open and closed. Nick could see both men were strutting down the street with such arrogance that they didn't bother to look over their shoulders.

When Callum let out the breath he'd been holding, the rush of air sounded like a torrent echoing off all four of the room's walls. "Why did you do that, Nick? You could have set off something that . . . well . . . you just shouldn't have done that."

"Those men were wearing badges," Nick said plainly. "Why were they wearing badges?"

"Because they're deputies. That's why. And that's also why you shouldn't have stepped in the way you did. Those boys can do what they please around here because of those badges they wear."

"Who gave them badges?"

"The sheriff. Who else?"

Nick shook his head and walked up to shut the door, which had started banging against the frame at the insistence of a sudden gust of wind. "That's no way for a deputy to act."

"Yeah. Well maybe he's upset over the friend of his that was gunned down. You showing up here after being the last thing Abe saw probably didn't help things much either." Seeing the response that got from Nick caused the undertaker to nervously fuss with the easel and display cases near the front door. "Oh sure, I know what happened this morning. Most of the town knows it too."

"You want me to leave?"

"No. I want to . . ." He paused so he could take another deep breath and walk up to Nick so he could extend his hand. "I want to thank you for stepping in."

Shaking the undertaker's hand, Nick said, "For all the good it did. You still got stuck doing the job you didn't want to do."

"See, right there is where you're wrong. You're the one that's stuck. I forgot I had a Mourner on hand to take care of these things for me now. Don't tell me this is the first funeral you've ever arranged?"

Nick had to smile at the irony in that statement. "I've arranged plenty of funerals."

"Good." By the time he said that word, Callum seemed to have returned to his normal self. There was even a spring in his step as he walked down the middle aisle, flicking bits of dust from the tops of the pews as he went. "It's settled, then. You'll see to the details of the showing and make sure there's plenty of folks in attendance."

Just as Nick thought he might be able to give his arms a rest, his hopes were dashed by one last sentence from the undertaker.

"That is, of course, after you're done carving that marker."

Six

There was plenty that needed to be done. After all, a funeral was a complicated affair that nobody truly wanted to arrange. Unlike most other formal gatherings, most folks either never thought about wakes and funerals or outright dreaded them. That left the path free and clear for the professionals to step in and do their jobs without much in the way of outside interference.

Even for a simple funeral, there were arrangements to be made regarding the body itself, building a casket, carving a headstone, thinking of an epitaph, and picking a piece of land for the hole to be dug. There were eulogies to be written, considerations to be made regarding the choice of preacher and what day he was available to lead the services.

If there was to be a wake, and there usually was, a whole other set of matters came to the surface. In a strange sort of way, viewing the body was an affair much like a party or any number of social gatherings. There weren't many times for people to gather formally in most cities. Towns the size of Jessup had even fewer such occasions, since most people figured they crossed enough paths just tending to their own business.

But when someone in their community saw their last day, everyone who'd ever met that person's eye when crossing the street expected to pay their respects before the hole was filled. A viewing was more than just a chance for friends and family to close ranks around the deceased. It was a genuine event and needed to be treated as such.

Everyone loved a mystery, and death was one of the grandest mysteries of all. Folks gathered at funerals, wakes, even hangings. They were always on hand whenever a shouting match became a shooting in the street, and they would talk about such things for years, until the details blurred into tall tales and sometimes folklore.

A viewing had so many details that needed squaring away that some folks even made a living out of nailing each one down properly. Nick Graves was one such man. He wrote out the invitations and saw to their printing. He chose what food to serve and where all the guests would sit or stand.

When it came to the families or those closer to the deceased, there were more personal matters to address. Families didn't take too well to a poorly attended wake, and saw it as a personal insult to their loved one if nobody was there to view their body. Nick's job was to make sure there were people present to mourn, and if necessary he would stand in and mourn them himself.

He would not cry for them, but he would stand by and wish the spirit well while gazing quietly at their corpse. He would be there to comfort widows and console parents just as much as he was there to make sure everyone's drinks were topped off and that every possible seat was being filled.

It was a responsibility that most folks didn't even know existed. They just lived their lives and assumed a crowd would want to be there to cry over their dead bodies. The truth of the matter was something vastly different. People gathered for events and to catch up with familiar faces. A wake, a hanging, a fight in the street, these things were all events. Burials were not.

Most burials were small and poorly attended.

Most people were buried with little to-do and nothing but a few simple wooden planks to mark the pile of dirt under which their bones were picked clean by insects and their clothes decayed into brittle threads.

Nick felt that was a genuine injustice. After all, a burial was when that same loved one or friend was committed to the spot they would be in until there wasn't anything left. Yet, people pranced about and socialized at wakes and hangings. That seemed skewed in Nick's mind, which was probably why he became a Mourner in the first place.

He tried to be there for the whole process, knowing that if the deceased was aware of it at all, they would appreciate his efforts. As for everyone else, they would find out soon enough what death truly was.

When it came to what happened after someone's passing, Nick knew better than to try and figure out that one. As far as he was concerned, all that happened after someone died was a viewing, a funeral, and a burial. After that there was only the next job. The next death.

It looked like Abe's death was going to keep him so busy that he wouldn't have much time to contemplate life's bigger mysteries. Then again, he decided to pay more attention to Mrs. Eddings's arrangements. Even though he'd never even met the old woman, the fact that so many honest people missed her spoke volumes to a

Mourner. He would see that she was sent off properly and that her wake would be a time remembered fondly.

As for Abe, he would still be just as dead now as he would be later.

A good portion of the rest of Nick's workday was filled with seeing to dozens of minute details. Now he had two wakes to plan. Not only did he take care of what needed to be done there, he took his time while out and about to gather information on things more relevant to the living. While talking to the locals, however, he had to be careful to remain in his bounds. Since he'd wanted to garner trust as he'd gone about his day's work, Nick wasn't wearing his gun belt. He missed the familiar weight of the weapon at his side, but also knew that if he kept quiet enough he wouldn't be needing it anyhow. Folks tended to turn curious eyes toward armed strangers. Curiosity of that sort brought attention to him.

Too much attention turned his way was something he could not afford.

But he still had other questions to answer. He needed to know just what was going on with Jessup's lawmen. And there was also the matter of a certain person he'd been tracking since well before coming into Nebraska. That person was supposed to be in Jessup, and if he wasn't, then Nick knew he might just be sticking his neck out for no good reason.

As luck would have it, one of his stops that day covered a lot of ground. He needed to get to a printer's office, and the process of locating the place told Nick pretty much everything he'd needed to know about public opinion regarding the town's law. Everybody who didn't wear a badge was glad that Abe was dead. Getting folks like that to attend a wake would be a chore indeed.

Nick was a professional, however, and saw this obstacle as a challenge to be overcome. Standing at the counter of the small office that served as Jessup's printing press and newspaper publisher, Nick spoke to the man working there in a respectful tone while keeping his eyes warm and friendly.

The counter stretched across the front of the room. It came up a bit higher than Nick's waist, was missing several large chunks, and was smudged with enough ink to publish a special edition of the *Jessup Herald.* Another edition could be made from the numerous black smears on the face and hands of the young man on the other side of the counter standing within arm's reach of the monstrosity that was the printing press itself.

"I can save you some trouble, friend," the printer said. "Folks around here would take part in a tooth pulling contest before they'd bow their heads in the name of that asshole."

Nick smirked and nodded. "Yeah. I've been getting that impression."

The printer was tall and had a bulky frame, but there was something about him that put Nick at ease. It might have been the little round glasses, the eyes behind them that sparkled with a child's energy, or perhaps the easygoing manner in which he spoke. Whichever it was, Nick couldn't help but like the guy.

"You want another piece of free advice?"

Nick didn't say whether he wanted it, mainly because he figured his answer wouldn't matter much.

The printer hooked his thumbs around the apron straps that wrapped around the back of his neck. "You should steer clear of the subject altogether. While you're at it, keep away from the sheriff's office as well."

"I can't steer too clear of this matter. I need invitations printed for the deputy's wake as well as the gathering being held for Mrs. Eddings."

For a moment the printer looked confused. That faded quickly and was replaced by a dark red flush of his cheeks. "Oh yeah. The invitations. That's why you came in here. I sure am gonna miss Mrs. Eddings. She was a true angel. Her ceremonies are supposed to be held soon, aren't they?"

"Glad you remembered."

"Of course I remembered. If you plan on any services for Abe, on the other hand, I can guarantee you'll have plenty of empty seats at that one. On the other hand, I can give you a deal on printing up his invitations, seeing as how you don't need a lot of space to describe Abe's good points and all. That's fine, though. I can use my largest typeset. Come to think of it, you might not even need to print up more than a dozen or so. Besides the time and date, what else did you have in mind?"

Shrugging, Nick offered, "Free food."

"There you go! That should snag a few more interested parties, especially if they happen to be in from out of town. I'll print you up three dozen for a penny a word."

"Sounds fair."

"And a miscellaneous fee of one dollar." Judging by the look on his face, the printer knew he was pushing it by sneaking in that last part. "You know . . . for labor and paper costs."

"All right, but only if you print them so well that people snap them up as much as they do your newspaper."

"Done. You won't be disappointed."

After flipping a silver dollar onto the counter, Nick gave the printer the basic details that needed to go onto the invitations. He figured he could have gotten a better deal on the publishing rate but that the extra money could still be put to good use. And since there was no better time than the present to collect, he leaned one elbow on the counter and let out a tired breath.

"Oh," the publisher said with a quick snap of his fingers. "I damn near forgot. You don't have to worry about Mrs. Eddings's invitations because Mr. Callum already put that order in. They should be done real soon."

"Good. That's one less thing for me to think about. Let me know when they're ready and I'll pick them up."

"Will do. Then I'll get right to work on those other invites as well as some notices the sheriff requested."

"There's a lot going on in this town."

Smirking while pocketing the down payment, the printer said, "Not usually. Not until you pulled into town, anyway."

"So the sheriff usually keeps things pretty quiet?"

"Eh, pretty much, I guess. Of course, that's mainly because —" He stopped himself, eyes darting over to Nick as if to check on how much the other man already knew. "He does a fine job." This time the easygoing manner was gone from his voice. In its place was something verging on fear.

To a man like Nick, fear might as well have been a wave radiating from another person's skin. He sensed it just as easily as he would have seen waves of heat bending a street in the summertime as it slowly rose from the dirt. In response to that fear, Nick softened his mannerisms and leaned in on both elbows like a conspiratorial partner.

"Look," he said, "I was there when Abe was shot. There isn't a whole lot you could say that would go against my grain."

"That's great, mister."

"The name's Nicolai Graves."

The printer's face brightened a bit at that. "Matthew Niedelander. Just forget about trying to remember the last name. Everyone else in town has."

"Looks like I'll be in town for a bit, so I could use some help. Think you could point me in the direction of where I can find a good meal?"

"Try The Porter House. Steak's so good there, they named the whole place after it. Tell 'em I sent you." Straightening up proudly, Matthew straightened his apron as though it was a twenty dollar suit jacket. "I printed up their advertisements and reviewed the place in the *Herald*."

"Then I hope the crowd's not too big for me to find a seat."

With all the fear gone from his face, Matthew seemed completely back to his normally high spirits. In fact, he'd warmed up to Nick even more. "You might not even need my recommendation, though. Not after what you did for Jed."

Nick's eyes narrowed. "What do you mean?"

Leaning forward so he was able to drop his voice to a whisper and still be heard, Matthew added, "Not much gets past me, you know. I'm a journalist."

"I didn't do much of anything except ride away after the shooting stopped, and I was glad to be able to do that."

Matthew seemed stunned by the sudden shift in tone, and his eyes dropped down to the spot where Nick's pistol would have been if the gun belt was around his waist. "But I heard . . ." Even as the words were coming out of his mouth, Matthew seemed to be rethinking them. "Actually, I guess I should think before I speak more often. Give me a day and check in with me about Mrs. Eddings's invitations. If they're done sooner than that, I'll let you know."

"That would be great. I'm staying over at Dan Callum's place."

"His house?"

"No. His business."

A visible chill ran up Matthew's spine. "Oh. Well, then I'll know where to look. It shouldn't take much longer than a day."

"Perfect, because I'm on a schedule here." Nick turned and started walking toward the door, then stopped and glanced back over his shoulder at the printer. "By the way, I can count on seeing you at both wakes, right? Free food and all."

"Uhhh, sure. I guess I'll be there." The moment he said it, Matthew looked as if he wished he could take it back.

"I'll be looking for you."

Even before the door had shut behind him, Nick could hear the printer breaking out the tools needed to form the typesetting to spell out the invitations. He was fairly certain those invitations would be done as soon as possible, if only so Matthew could put them out of his mind. That was fine with Nick, since he'd gotten plenty out of the conversation without needing another guest for his list as well.

It was amazing what someone could learn by paying as much attention to what wasn't said as to what was. When he'd approached the topic of the sheriff, Nick felt a genuine nervousness creep into the otherwise easy-going printer. The fear that was mixed in went a long way to put together a helpful picture as well.

Throughout the whole day Nick had been getting pretty much the same kind of re-action from all the folks he met. What disturbed him even more was the fact that half the people were just waiting for him and Jed to be arrested. It didn't seem to matter why those shots had been fired anymore. It just seemed that someone had to pay for them.

The last thing he needed was an official visit from the law, especially now that one of its deputies had good reason to dislike him. The more he thought about everything, the more Nick felt his head start to hurt. He pressed the tips of his fingers to his temple and massaged some of the pain away, but there was still a long way to go.

What he needed was to give the matter a rest. As soon as he began to clear his mind, Nick realized that another part of him was hurting: his stomach. When he looked up from where he'd stopped walking, he found himself standing in front of The Porter House restaurant.

But it wasn't the heavenly aroma of cooking beef that drifted through the air that made him forget about things like possible run-ins with the law or the elusive person he'd tracked through three states, only to have him turn into a ghost after reaching Jessup. Something much simpler brightened Nick's mood. It was a smile warmer than any fire and pretty enough to make Nick forget about any and all of what had been troubling him before. That smile widened just a little bit as Nick struggled to remove the dumb, surprised expression from his face.

"Why don't you come in?" offered the striking brunette standing in the front door of The Porter House. "I'll bet I've got just what you need."

"Yeah," Nick said, suddenly forgetting about his empty stomach. "I'll just bet you do."

SEVEN

Following the smile that acted like a beacon to him, Nick made his way up the three stairs that led from the street onto the boardwalk and directly to the front door of The Porter House.

He hadn't been standing in one spot for more than a few seconds before he felt someone bumping him aside as they made their way past him.

"Excuse me," came the prescribed response as a squat man and his even squatter wife sidled past Nick.

It didn't matter how many times they apologized or how gentle the nudge might have been, Nick was always annoyed when folks jostled him for any reason. Perhaps that was a side-effect after having been brought up in the wide-open spaces and taking on such a solitary profession. Whatever the reason for it, a familiar scowl twisted his lips as he grudgingly stepped to one side.

When he turned to try and get away from the busy doorway, Nick was reminded of why he'd hustled into the restaurant so quickly in the first place. She was standing there waiting for him, dressed in a simple cotton dress that hugged her body nicely. That smile was still there, only this time it was even wider.

"Dinnertime turns this place into a madhouse," she said apologetically. She seemed amused at the way he was getting bounced around by elderly couples and even small children who were rushing in to sit down for their evening meals. "Why don't you come over here by me before you get trampled?"

Nick accepted her outstretched hand without hesitation. If he'd bothered checking the battered watch in his pocket, he wouldn't have been so surprised to find the restaurant so damn crowded. The woman's touch made him forget about things like that, however. Her skin was smooth and warm. When she pulled him a little closer, he could smell her scent, which was fresh, autumn air mixed with a touch of lavender.

The woman who'd caught Nick's attention only moments before a family of ten stampeded into the restaurant stood just tall enough to have to lift her eyes to look into his. Her skin was the color of browned, buttered biscuits, and her body filled out her simple blue and white checked dress well enough to hold his eye for an amount of time longer than what was considered appropriate.

Nick shook his head sharply as she lowered her light brown eyes and nervously reached up to brush away some strands of wispy hair. Despite her subtle shifting, she didn't seem to mind having his eyes on her.

"Sorry. I didn't mean to stare," she said quickly. "But we don't get a whole lot of new faces around here."

Instinctively, Nick shoved his mangled right hand into a jacket pocket and put on an easygoing smile of his own. "No problem. Hopefully I won't be considered a new face for too long."

The expression on her face reflected more gratitude than Nick would have hoped for. "Really? So you'll be staying for a bit?"

"I hope so. That is, if I don't starve first."

She rolled her eyes and covered her face out of embarrassment. "Oh my lord, sometimes my mind really does wander."

"There's nothing wrong with that," Nick said, reaching out with his left hand to ease her hands away from her pretty face. "Just so long as it wanders in the right direction."

Smiling, she said, "My name's Catherine Weaver."

"Nicolai Graves. Oh, and if it helps any, Matthew the printer sent me."

With a short laugh, she grimaced and shook her head. "Knowing Matt, he probably expected you to cover some of the bill he ran up the last time he was here. Besides, I don't think you need any help."

She let that hang in the air between them just long enough for Nick to start getting ideas in his head. "A table's opened up," she said before those ideas could turn into anything else. "Too small for any of the parties coming in right now, but it should fit you just fine. You look like a steak and potatoes kind of man," Catherine said. "It's our specialty."

"I'm sold. Just cook it long enough for it to stop kicking and put plenty of butter on the potatoes."

She nodded and gave him one more lingering smile. "I'll have some biscuits sent over first to take the edge off. I could even sit with you for a spell to keep you company. The owner doesn't mind if I socialize with the customers," she added with a playful wink.

More than anything, Nick wanted to ask

her to join him. Actually, he wanted to insist that she join him, but refrained. That wasn't due to any lack of confidence or shyness on his part. He just assumed she'd lose interest the moment she found out what he did for a living.

So as much as he hated to do it, Nick let the moment slip away. Part of him took some comfort from the fact that Catherine seemed disappointed when he didn't take her up on her invitation.

"Well, there's a lot of mouths to feed right now," she said. "I'll check up on you later. That is, if that's all right with you."

"That's just fine with me," Nick said before he had a chance to stop himself. "I'll be looking forward to it."

No more than thirty seconds went by after Catherine left before a kid in his early teens rushed over to Nick's table and threw down a napkin and a handful of silverware. The same kid reappeared another minute later with a tall glass of water and a basket of biscuits. When Nick reached for the bread, he noticed the kid's eyes widen at the sight of his mangled fingers. More than used to that response, Nick watched the kid to see what else he would do.

"What happened to your hand?" the young man asked.

Nick shrugged and noted the apprehensive yet polite tone in the kid's voice. Because of that, he decided to reply honestly. "I got into some trouble a while back," he said simply. "It may look bad, but it could have been a whole lot worse."

"What kind of trouble?"

"The kind that a man can get into if he doesn't think too much before he jumps into something." Pointing in a way that showed the halved pinky on his left hand, he added, "You'd do well to remember that, kid."

The server nodded vigorously and turned to answer a call coming from another table. Surprisingly enough, he didn't seem too eager to break away from the conversation.

Feeling that his civic duty was done for the day, Nick relaxed and started tearing into his biscuits. The first one went down so quickly that he didn't even get a chance to use any of the honey butter that had been provided in a small bowl. He took some more time with the next one and was glad he did. The biscuit slathered with sweet butter filled his entire mouth with a warm taste that made coming to Jessup, Nebraska, worth every step of the journey.

When his steak arrived and he took his first bite, Nick didn't even mind having to start his visit in town by shooting a man. In fact, he thought he might just have to shoot the first person who would try to take the plate away from him before he'd chewed up every last bit.

The steak was a cut of meat almost thicker than his table. Savory, red juices flowed out of it as he cut off each bite, and the meat melted in his mouth just as easily as the honey buttered biscuits. Nick was so wrapped up in savoring his meal that he nearly missed it when the front door opened and a group of men stepped into the restaurant.

He froze with his fork halfway up to his mouth. He could smell the tender meat, but refrained from biting into it. Catching himself before staring for too long at the new arrivals, Nick shoved the steak into his mouth and gnawed on it until he could get it down.

He didn't taste the food any longer. Instinctively, his posture decayed until he was all but hunching over his food. Nick didn't think he'd been spotted just yet, and he meant to keep it that way. As much as he would have liked to have gotten up and left, he knew it was too late for that. Standing at that point would have just drawn every eye in the place in his direction.

He hadn't met the sheriff of Jessup yet, but he recognized the badge well enough. The tin star was pinned to the lapel of a plain, yet well-tailored jacket. The man stood at just under six feet tall and wore a neatly trimmed beard that covered most of his face.

Flanking the lawman on either side were some familiar faces. Namely, they were the two men who'd come to visit Dan Callum in his parlor earlier that day.

From his spot in the back of the room, Nick watched as the sheriff was greeted by Catherine, who then led the three men to a table that had probably been reserved for him since he'd been elected to office. The sheriff seemed like a gracious enough sort, tipping his hat to anyone who looked up at him and smiling like a politician at nobody in particular.

The deputies, on the other hand, didn't seem half as courteous. In stark contrast to the sociable manner of the sheriff, the other two men sneered at everyone not wearing a badge. They acted as though they deserved every bit of the attention they got and would be more than happy to force it out of whomever didn't give it to them.

Having already figured what type of man Scott was, Nick knew the deputy would move his eyes over the entire restaurant but would be too confident in his own fearsomeness to do a thorough job. Sure enough, all Nick had to do was look down at the right moment and keep his head tilted so his hair fell down over his face. When he looked up again, all three of the lawmen were in their seats and no longer concerned with anyone else.

Of course, he couldn't completely blame the deputies for not spotting him. They'd been distracted by a very powerful force indeed. Catherine Weaver was standing at the lawmen's table, talking to the sheriff and smiling politely at the other two men.

Catherine stood in a rigid posture with her arms folded across her chest. Even after concealing her figure almost completely that way, she was still getting hungry stares from the deputies, who made no effort to hide the way their eyes slid over every inch of her entire body like slow, clammy fingers.

Nick knew he shouldn't stay in that room any longer than he had to. But despite the fact that he'd already spotted another way out, he made no effort to speed up his meal or move from his seat. It was that same, unreasonably stubborn streak that had caused more than one headache in his lifetime. He'd given up on trying to tame that part of him a long time ago. Doing so would have been just as easy as training his lungs to stop pulling in their next breath.

His body fell into a rhythm that kept his arms and mouth moving on their own accord. He fed himself without conscious effort, slicing off the next bite of food and scooping it into his mouth, to chew it up and swallow without enjoyment. Too much of his attention was focused on the lawmen's table for him to concentrate on his meal. Not only that, but they seemed to be holding Catherine at their table even as she tried several times to step away.

That didn't set well with Nick. Not one bit.

As if sensing his discomfort, Catherine shot a quick glance over to his table. The expression on her face was more than just concerned. She appeared troubled. As the sheriff looked up at her and kept on talking, the unease on Catherine's face only grew.

Scott and the second deputy were now looking over at Nick too. He could feel those eyes moving over him like sunlight focused through the lens of a spyglass.

This time, however, Nick didn't lower his eyes and he didn't shrink down any farther into his chair. Doing so at that moment would have felt like backing down. Besides, he knew it was too late to keep out of the lawmen's sight any longer.

Sitting up, he got back to his meal while giving the lawmen only a casual passing glance. He just caught a glimpse of the expression on Scott's face, as well as the cold, studying glare of the sheriff. Nick's view was interrupted by the young man who walked up to refill his glass of water.

"I probably shouldn't tell you this, mister," the server confessed, "but Sheriff Manes is talking about you."

"Is that a fact?"

"He'll probably be over here before too long."

Nick nodded. "Let him come." With that, he put another piece of meat into his mouth and felt as though he was tasting it for the first time. He chewed it slowly, savoring it to the last.

EIGHT

The sheriff didn't seem interested in coming over to visit him after all. Nick's brain was nagging at him to get up and walk out after paying his bill, but that stubborn streak kept him rooted to his spot. He was grateful for that when Catherine finally came over to his table and lowered herself into the chair across from him.

"Who are you?" she asked without hesitation. "And don't tell me your name again, because I already know that part."

"I'm nobody you need to worry about, but I am someone who would like to see you more after tonight." That last part had slipped out before Nick fully knew he was going to say it. The moment he saw her reaction to it, he was glad for the lapse in judgment.

Catherine's eyelids dropped just a bit, as her captivating smile reappeared. "Well, the sheriff was asking about you," she said

109

without bothering to address the flush in her cheeks. "He says you're not the type who should be trusted."

"And why would you come over here to tell me this?"

"Because the sheriff has a lot of things going that folks don't know about. His men aren't exactly the most trustworthy souls either, which is why it's not too surprising to have one of them end up dead. Hell, even the sheriff isn't too surprised about that. Besides that, you're not the first man to stop in here that Sheriff Manes didn't approve of."

It took a good deal of his willpower, but Nick was able to take his eyes off of Catherine and glance back at the table where the sheriff and his men were sitting. As if on cue, Sheriff Manes pushed away from his table and got to his feet, with both deputies quickly following suit.

Catherine looked behind her as well, and when she looked back to Nick, her face was darkened with the same concern he'd spotted earlier. "I tried to keep them busy so you could leave." Looking down at the table, which had been cleaned off so completely that only his water glass remained, she asked, "Why are you still here?"

"I was waiting for you."

"You still should have left. I would have tracked you down sooner rather than later."

"So what's the big hurry, anyway? Why would the sheriff be gunning for a worn-down grave digger like me?"

Catherine didn't seem surprised by what he'd just revealed. "I don't know. All I do know is that he was asking about you even more than that fellow who'd ridden through town a month or so ago."

Those words hit Nick like a hot poker that had been wedged into his gut. When he heard them, it was all he could do to keep from reacting in a way that would tip his hand. "What fellow are you talking about?" was all he asked, even though he could think of at least a dozen more important questions.

"He rode in by himself," Catherine replied. "Nobody thought too much of him, but the sheriff got it in his mind to keep an eye on him. There were some harsh words spoken at Mil's." Before Nick got a chance to ask her about it, she clarified herself. "It's a saloon down on Cavalry Avenue. Not exactly the type of place for a woman to spend her time, unless she makes her living with her legs in the air."

Although Nick didn't respond to that, Catherine still seemed embarrassed for having said it. "There was a couple of scuffles between the deputies and this other fellow before the sheriff got himself involved directly."

"What happened then?"

"The sheriff arrested him."

"So he's still locked away?"

Catherine's pause was enough to make Nick's entire body tense. He could already picture the gallows in his mind's eye, with a figure dangling from the business end of a noose. He knew that sight only too well, thanks to his profession. He was usually the one responsible for advertising when such a man would swing.

"I guess so," Catherine said after what felt like an eternity of thinking it over.

"And then what? Was he strung up?"

"Oh, lord no. We haven't had a hanging in Jessup since Jed Arvey's horses were stolen on Independence Day four years ago."

"I guess that explains why he keeps that shotgun so close at hand."

The emotion drained from Catherine's face, along with most of the color that had been in her cheeks. "Yeah, it does explain why. Especially since Jed lost his oldest boy to the son of a bitch that stole his horses."

"I'm sorry, Catherine. I didn't mean any offense."

She nodded and reached out to pat Nick's hand. "I know you didn't. You can't be expected to know the history of a place after being here for a day."

Now that most of the crowd had eaten their meals and left, The Porter House was empty enough for the sound of the sheriff's steps to echo throughout the room. Manes was making his way to the door, talking it up to the few people who were close enough for a handshake. Both deputies were waiting by the door with their eyes burning holes into Nick's forehead.

"I don't think they like me much," Nick said, nodding toward the lawmen.

"No," Catherine replied. "They don't. Is there a reason for that?"

"There must be. Nothing happens without a reason."

"Well, I'd better go see them through the door." Catherine got up and pushed her chair back in snugly beneath Nick's table. "He'll just come over here to get me if I don't." Even though she spoke with a lower tone of voice, Catherine didn't seem to care whether Manes heard her or not.

Nick liked that.

Watching as Catherine turned her back on him and headed for the men standing by the door, Nick did his level best to keep his attention focused on the lawmen and not the captivating motion of Catherine's hips. It was plain to see that he wasn't the only one enjoying the view.

Sheriff Manes made no effort to hide the fact that he'd practically undressed her in his mind before she'd taken three steps. The smile on his face made it obvious that he liked what he imagined he'd seen.

"A fine meal as always," the sheriff's voice boomed. "Too bad the atmosphere isn't as inviting as it normally is." With that, the lawman's eyes fixed directly on Nick. Seeing Nick returning his stare, Manes winked at Catherine and brushed the palm of his hand down her waist. "But don't you worry now. I'll make sure this place is back to its standards before that foul smell touches your pretty little nose."

Catherine lowered her eyes demurely, but there was nothing coy at all in the way she took hold of the sheriff's wrist and removed his hand from her body. "Thanks for stopping by, Sheriff. You and your men are always welcome."

After drinking in the sight of her for another second or two, the sheriff tipped his hat and left the restaurant.

One deputy was already outside, and Scott

was taking a few moments to take another look in Nick's direction. Catherine moved directly in front of him, herding the lawmen out with outstretched arms. Before she could say anything to him, Scott shoved the woman roughly aside so his view of the back of the room was no longer blocked.

But the man he was looking for was gone. All that remained at Nick's table was an empty water glass.

Shifting his eyes back toward Catherine, Scott started to snarl something but was cut short by a tap on his shoulder. The sheriff got Scott to follow him, and then the whole group was finally out of The Porter House. Their footsteps pounded on the boardwalk outside and could be felt even by Catherine as she stood at the window next to the door to make sure they were truly leaving.

Her skin tingled where the lawmen had touched her. It wasn't the warm sensation that she'd felt when Nick had brushed her hand or shoulder. Instead, it was a cold, itchy feeling of spider legs skittering over her flesh.

She tried to rub the feeling away with a few quick brushes of her hand, but knew the feeling would just have to pass on its own. Thinking of something that would ease her mind, Catherine looked back toward the same spot that Scott had been studying. She'd already thought of what she was going to say to Nick when she saw him looking back at her, but there was only that empty glass sitting on the table.

Suddenly, she was very aware that there were still a few other customers in the restaurant, and she prepared to use the assurances on them that she'd prepared for Nick. But they weren't even looking at her. What few customers remained were either too wrapped up in their own meals to notice what had happened or too absorbed in their own lives to care.

Not that Catherine could blame them. Unless Sheriff Manes was talking to you directly, it was a good choice to keep your nose down and ears closed. Going unnoticed by the likes of Jessup's lawmen was a kind of blessing. As if in response to what she was thinking, one of the few remaining diners looked up at her and smiled.

"You all right?" he asked with genuine concern.

Catherine nodded. "Yes, Billy. I'm fine."

With her nerves settling to a low rumble beneath her skin, she walked to the back of the room with growing curiosity. She couldn't find a trace of Nick. Then again, she wasn't too worried about it. In fact, she was glad he'd gotten out, and had to admit the confusion on Scott's face was more than a little amusing. Knowing the layout of the restaurant like the back of her hand, she made her way to the only place Nick could have used for an exit.

The door was wedged in a small space that was barely visible from the dining room. When she reached down to touch the handle, she swore she could feel the leftover warmth from Nick's skin as he'd pulled the door open and left. She was certain that he was gone because now that she thought back to it, she remembered hearing the distinct squeak of the back door being opened and closed.

"Did you use this door, Bob?" she asked the restaurant's head cook.

Bob shook his head and shrugged. The gesture looked almost funny for a big man who sported a shaggy, dark beard that would have been more fitting on a mountain man. "No, ma'am. It was that stranger who went through here. He said you told him it was all right."

As much as Catherine wanted to step through the door herself just to try and catch a glimpse of Nick, she held back. Partly, she didn't want to do anything suspi-

cious, in case any of the lawmen were still
skulking about. Another part was because
she knew he wouldn't be there.

NINE

When most folks thought of grave diggers, they pictured some ghoulish figure with a shovel in both hands, toiling in the shadows like something from a ghost story. For the most part, those notions were absolutely false. Grave diggers were hard workers who would rather be at home with their families instead of working after sundown. Anyone who spent time around such men would find that out quickly enough.

Those were the majority. Nick, on the other hand, was an exception. Much of what he did was in the darkness, and he was very much at home in the cool embrace of the shadows. He was no ghoul, however. He was just careful. Certain circumstances dictated that he be very quiet and very, very careful.

This was one of those circumstances.

The instant he'd seen his opportunity to leave The Porter House unnoticed, Nick had gotten up from his seat and moved toward the door he'd spotted when he took his first good look at the restaurant's layout. He kept his head low and walked on the balls of his feet so that the only noise he'd made was the rustle of his clothing.

The sheriff and one of his deputies had been walking out with their backs to him and Catherine was standing close enough to Scott to prevent him from seeing much of anything except for her own pretty face. With one hand on the door handle, Nick had opened it and walked through as he gave his quick explanation to the cook. Before any questions could be asked, he was gone.

The door opened onto an alley wide enough for a small cart pulled by one horse to ride through to the other side. With plenty of crates and other refuse stacked here and there, he had no problem finding cover as he made his way toward the front end of the restaurant while staying inside the thick darkness that filled the alleyway like ink.

Nick listened closely to the sheriff as he spoke to his deputy while leaving the restaurant. For a while Manes was just trying to get Scott to hurry up and leave the place. But once all three sets of footsteps were slowly walking down the boardwalk, the lawmen's conversation took a definite turn.

By the slurred and snarling sound of Manes's voice, Nick could tell the sheriff was chewing on a cigar as he talked. "That bitch knows something," he said, coming to a stop and lighting a match with a loud snap followed by the crackle of a small flame.

Knowing that Sheriff Manes was referring to Catherine, Nick's lip curled up from his teeth.

The next voice was one Nick didn't recognize, which meant it had to be the deputy that wasn't Scott.

"There's an easier way to find out, rather than eating at her restaurant."

"No," Manes replied. "Not just yet. There's still another matter that needs to be cleared up before anything else."

"Are you talking about that farmer?" This time it was Scott doing the talking.

Nick was crouched behind a stack of two crates and had to pull himself down into a tight bundle when the lawmen paused in the opening of the alley. His heart was pounding in his chest and he felt his next breath stop halfway between his lungs and his lips. The lawmen were close enough for him to smell the smoke when Manes let out a breath after puffing on his cigar.

"That's right," Manes said. "I sent Rich

and one of the others to have a talk with that farmer, but didn't get more than a few words when they got back."

"You should have sent someone you could trust."

"Yeah, well folks around here don't talk to the men I trust. They talk to Rich, though. At least sometimes they do. Rich still thinks Jed wasn't the one who killed Abe. That's the only thing keeping me from dragging that farmer in by his balls."

Scott let out a snort of a laugh and swiveled to stare into the alley. Even though the streets were only lit by the occasional lantern struggling to stay lit amid the cold autumn breezes, there was enough light to unravel a few of the shadows. From where he was crouching, Nick could see the lawmen's feet illuminated by a trickle of moonlight. His eyes were used to the dark, and that silvery light seemed like rays from the sun.

Even though he was crouched down too low to see anything but Scott's boots, Nick could picture the smug look on the deputy's face all too well.

"Next time, let me pay that farmer a visit," Scott said. "He shot a deputy, and that's a hanging offense where I come from. Maybe

I can get that chewed-up stranger to tie the noose."

"There is no next time," Manes shot back. "There's only now. Go check on that farmer tonight and ask him what he knows about that stranger. There's something familiar about that grave digger, and I still have a real hard time swallowing the idea that Abe was killed by some asshole with a hunting rifle."

"Familiar? But I didn't —"

"Just go! And don't forget to go easy on that farmer. He needs to talk. If he dies, he can do it at the end of a noose for the whole town to see."

"What about the family?" Scott asked.

There was a pause as Manes sucked in another lungful of smoke. "That farmer's the only one that needs to keep breathing. Anything short of killing him is up to you. I don't give a shit about anyone else in that house."

Despite the fact that all three men had resumed walking and were now past the alley, there were no other sounds to compete with their voices. Nick darted from one side of the alley to another, listening to what he could hear. Pressing his back against the wall of the building next to The Porter

House, he chanced a peek around the corner.

Scott walked beside the sheriff like an obedient dog as he asked, "And what about that grave digger?"

"I'll be calling on him tomorrow. If I don't like what I hear, I'll throw him to the dogs."

With the lawmen slowly walking away from where he was hiding, their voices started to get absorbed into the night. Nick couldn't be certain that he'd heard the sheriff correctly. The last portion of what Manes had said was washed out by the wind and his distance from the speaker, and the limit to how he was willing to stretch his neck. Whether he'd understood every word perfectly or not, however, wasn't the issue.

He had heard more than enough.

Once again his body acted instinctively. He turned his back to the opening of the alley and rushed down the cluttered passageway. Moving swiftly on the balls of his feet, he kept his head low and his hands tucked in close to his sides, where his fingers felt for anything that might get in his way or fall in front of him.

His ears were filled with the air that flowed around and past him. Deftly moving between whatever obstacles were in his way, he made it to the other end of the alley in a matter of seconds and was speeding through a series of back lots with the confidence of a Jessup native, even though he'd never seen this part of town until that moment.

It was desperation that made him move so quickly and so surely. He was desperate to keep something from happening that he'd unwittingly started. Even though he felt no remorse for drawing his pistol and firing the killing round into that throwback's chest, Nick regretted doing so in a way that put the blame on another man's shoulders.

Like many other chains of events, the steps leading up to Abe's death had come in a rush. Nick had been able to tell that Abe wanted trouble, and he could also tell that the farmer wanted to use the shotgun in his hands. At the time, Nick thought he was just making the best out of a bad situation.

He couldn't let that throwback hurt him or anyone else, and he couldn't act in a way that would draw too much attention. It all seemed so simple.

Nick was running toward Callum's parlor when he caught a glimpse of a water trough directly in front of him. His feet left the ground and came down running on the other side of the obstruction.

Simple as that.

Abe had died the same way.

Simple.

Nick had plenty of reasons for the way he went about things, and had just as many ways to push it all down so he could sleep through the night. What he couldn't simply push away was the thought of that well-meaning farmer paying with his life for shooting a man who was already dead. As he dashed silently toward the darkened storefront, he could almost feel the light smack of his father's hand against the back of his head.

"You know when you do something wrong, *sunus,* that you must fix it."

Stasys's thickly accented voice rolled through Nick's mind as always, pushing him in the right direction and scolding him in advance for things he'd done wrong even before he'd done them.

The funeral parlor was closed for the day. Callum was gone and the doors were locked, even though the townspeople avoided the place as if every board of every wall carried the pox. Nick hurried around the front of the building and turned the corner until he was headed straight for the back lot where he'd been nailing the coffin together earlier in the day. The fence swung open and he charged through, pointing himself toward the back door, which led to the workshop.

If a man didn't know any better, he would think the back lot was nothing more than a mildly cluttered yard. Callum kept it fairly neat, and had even managed to pick up some of the things Nick himself had left behind. Another thing Callum had done was leave the back door open so Nick could get to his room.

Not only was the door open, but a lantern had been left on to show Nick the way amid the benches and tools toward the spare room where his scant belongings had been placed on a narrow cot. The lantern's wick was burning just enough to keep the flame going, and compared to the pitch-darkness of the rest of the parlor, it seemed like a glowing beacon.

Nick's first impulse was to head for that beacon. Although it hadn't taken much to commit the workshop's simple layout to memory, he saw that enough things had been moved and shifted around to trip him up if he were to race around too quickly. Besides, it appeared as though Callum had brought all of his things into the spare room, leaving them there along with a flat pillow and threadbare blankets.

Reminding himself to thank the under-taker yet again for his hospitality, Nick stopped short. The expression froze on his face and his blood started to run cold. His gun was missing.

Letting out the breath he'd taken, Nick corrected himself and realized that his gun simply wasn't in that particular room on that stack of things. He took hold of the lantern, walked back into the workshop, then hurried over to the chair that had been used to prop open the back door, careful to check every other surface as he went. Sure enough, his gun belt was hanging over the back of the chair, right where he'd left it. Of course, the last time he'd been there, he had covered the gun with his jacket.

The jacket was sitting in the corner of the parlor's spare room now, so Nick knew that Callum had seen the gun. What the under-taker might have thought about the pistol being there was something else entirely, and it was something Nick was sure he'd hear about the next day.

As those thoughts moved through his head, Nick was already setting the lantern down and buckling the gun belt around his waist. With the back door ajar, and letting a thin stream of moonlight trickle onto the workshop floor, he twisted the lantern's knob until its light was gone, then headed for the door.

For a moment he seemed to be moving like something out of a dream. He slowed his steps until he was through the door, then strode away from the house filled with dead men and pulled his wide-brimmed hat down lower over his eyes. The jacket he wore was just long enough to cover the belt as well as most of the holster. Once he pulled it closed around him, the dark material eclipsed the lighter color of his plain cotton shirt. The darkness enveloped him like a hand from the grave, leaving only the cool glint of his eyes to break through the shadows.

Like an animal in pursuit of its prey, he headed through the alleys and toward the edge of town where he'd first crossed into Jessup. From there, he had a vague idea where to find the home of the farmer who'd come to stand with him against the throwback.

If he didn't find that farmer, Nick knew the man might very well lose his life either at Scott's hands or at the end of a noose. Thinking about that only made Nick run faster, his boots churning powerfully against the dirt.

TEN

The wind blew like a whisper from the surrounding plains, sending ripples through the flesh of animals milling in their pens and turning the metal wheels of windmills stuck into the ground. Dogs barked from behind doors and windows or from where they were tied to various stumps and posts.

All of these sounds were as integral to the nights in Jessup as the darkness that came with the passing of the sun. That was why it caught Jed's ear immediately when a good amount of those sounds came to a stop.

The wind was still blowing, but the animals were holding their tongues, and even the hinges of unlatched doors seemed to stop squeaking for a moment or two. Jed was a practical man, so he didn't believe in nonsense like spirits or demons, but he did believe that the Good Lord above helped out honest men every so often by showing them the way. When those noises stopped,

Jed could hear the sound of footsteps approaching his own front door, and the way that was shown to him pointed to another door leading out to his backyard.

If not for the fact that his wife and two girls were sleeping in the next room, he might have heeded the nervousness that stood the hairs on his arms on end and taken that way out of his house. But no matter how small his cabin may have been, his family couldn't get out fast enough to escape whoever was walking up to his home at that late hour, and Jed wasn't about to leave them.

He might not have been anxious to take on every danger out there, but he was no coward. The little house wasn't more than an oversized shack, but it was his home as well as the home of his family. Despite the nervousness that grew inside of him, he swallowed hard and moved to the front window. He would protect that shack and the souls inside it. He made that vow to himself right then and there. The instant his fingertips touched the curtains that his wife had sewn, Jed heard a knocking at the door that set every nerve in his body to jangling.

His hand pulled away from the curtains, but he'd already seen enough to justify the tension he was feeling. The men on his doorstep were wearing guns. Friends didn't come calling at improper hours, and they sure as hell didn't wear guns. Suddenly, Jed felt like a fool for not grabbing the shotgun that hung over his fireplace at the other end of the room.

"Who the hell is it?" he growled, doing his best to sound vicious.

Scott's face appeared in the window directly in front of Jed. "It's Scott and Jimmy. We're here on law business. Open the door."

"I told Rich when he came by here earlier that I shot Abe in self-defense. He was gonna rob that stranger and kill him. He's done it before and you all damn well know it!"

"Yeah, we know it. Now open the door so we can talk about it like civilized folks."

"Civilized folks come calling at a proper hour. I'm not going anywheres."

Scott rolled his eyes and moved back so he was standing at the door instead of leaning over to peek through the window.

Still wishing he could get his shotgun, but too nervous to move from where he stood, Jed pressed his side against the door and listened to what the two deputies were doing on the other side.

"That old piece of shit won't open the

132

door," came Scott's muffled voice through the weathered wooden slats.

The deputies shifted on the porch, their feet scraping loudly against the planks. Jed could hear them moving and talking among themselves, but the two had dropped their voices to a whisper that didn't make it into the house. After a few seconds, Jed was certain the deputies had actually given up, and he listened as their footsteps clomped away from the door.

Jed's mouth dropped open and started to form into a relieved smile. That smile faded quickly when he heard the footsteps pounding toward him. Although he could hear them coming, Jed wasn't quick enough to step aside before Scott's shoulder slammed into the door and smashed it inward.

The latch held for a fraction of a second, but snapped under the pressure of Scott's blow. Until this night, the farmer never would have thought he'd need the latch to stand up to anything stronger than a stiff breeze. It was too late to fix that now, however, and the door slammed against Jed's ear with enough force to rattle his teeth.

Heavy, dull pain surged through Jed's skull as the door pounded against the side of his head and Scott came charging in.

When he was finally able to collect himself, Jed found that he'd staggered within arm's reach of the fireplace, as well as the shotgun above it. Yet despite the fact that he was now in the place he'd wanted to be only moments ago, he didn't make a move toward the shotgun. He sank to the floor, his head still spinning from the knock he'd taken, and his blood pumping so quickly through his veins that he felt like he was falling through empty space.

In the time it took for Jed to shake some of the cobwebs from his skull, Scott and Jimmy had stepped into the modest home and started making themselves comfortable. Jimmy had a wiry body and moved like a snake as he reached around to put the door back in roughly the same place where it had stood. Once that was done, he took off his hat and tossed it onto a nearby table, revealing an uneven mess of brushy hair that he'd cut himself using the same razor he should have used to scrape the whiskers from his chin.

When he smiled, Jimmy displayed two jagged rows of yellow teeth and made a sound that was part laugh and part sneer. Moving away from the door, he headed toward the other end of the room, where a smaller door led into the house's only bedroom. Three sets of eyes were peeking out from the darkened room and shrank back as Jimmy stalked closer to them.

"Jesus Christ," Jimmy said. "This shack ain't big enough to squat in, and you got all them fine little women in here? You got two little girls, right? Oh, and that wife of yours too. Can't forget her."

"Wh-What are you doing?" Jed asked. Although his balance was still off as he struggled to his feet, the farmer could see well enough to tell that Jimmy was approaching his wife and two daughters. Seeing that, Jed snarled, "Get away from there!"

Scott hadn't stopped moving since he'd entered the house. The first thing he did was circle the living room and make sure the farmer didn't have any guests stashed away somewhere. As he checked the room, he swung his arms freely to knock over whatever he could reach. The sound of breaking jars and toppling furniture filled the room with more noise, adding another layer of chaos.

After making his way back to where Jed was lifting himself up off the floor, Scott reached out over the farmer's shoulder. Only after he saw the determination flash in Jed's eyes did Scott snatch the weapon from its rack and take it for himself. Seeing the disappointment in the farmer's eyes widened the grin on Scott's face.

"You really wanted to get your hands on this, didn't you?" Scott asked, holding the shotgun so its barrel was under Jed's nose.

The farmer didn't say anything in response to the question. The only movement he made was to lift his eyes so he could stare hatefully into Scott's face.

Scott met the other man's stare and nodded. "Yeah. I thought so."

At the other end of the room, Jimmy was forcing the woman and two little girls back into the shadows using nothing more than a mean, hungry stare. The females scuttled into the darkness, Jed's wife reaching out to gather up her children to make sure they were safely behind her.

Since he'd already circled the house before walking up to its front porch, Jimmy knew there was no way out of the bedroom. "I'll just save them for later," he said while slowly shutting the door. When the latch fell into place, he looked over to Jed and added, "Dessert."

The deputies' laugh was subdued, but still rumbled through the room. Scott shifted on his feet so he took up Jed's entire field of vision. "That's no way to treat guests, farmer.

Especially when we're here on official business."

With plenty of anger built up to make up for the fear and dread coursing through his body, Jed stood up straight and met the deputy's eyes. "State your business and then get the hell out of my home."

"That's easy enough. We're here to talk about how you gunned down a lawman earlier today. What've you got to say about that?"

"Lawmen don't bother innocent folks and them rob them of everything they own."

"Abe was robbing that stranger?"

"Yessir, he was, and you know damn well that he's done the same thing plenty of other times. The same thing and worse!"

"Do I?"

"Yes," Jed said without hesitation. "You've done the same thing yourself. I've seen you do it. That one too. Everyone around here knows what you do, and there's no reason for it. Sheriff Manes and that other one holed up in that jailhouse have enough money to buy this town and another one besides. There's no reason for them to —"

Jed was stopped short as Scott's hand snapped out and clamped around his throat. Holding the shotgun in his other hand, Scott pushed the end of the barrel up further against Jed's chin until the farmer's face was forced toward the ceiling.

"You talk like you know every little thing that goes on around here," Scott growled. "Are you trying to tell me that you're not just some asshole too stupid to do anything else for a living besides throw seeds on the ground and shovel shit from one place to another?"

Jed's mouth couldn't open much due to the gun barrel, and the effort of choking back the fear made it almost impossible for him to form words. But those words still came, pushed out by sheer will if nothing else.

"You say what you want, Scotty. I've known you since you were carrying feed for me so you and my boy could buy sarsaparilla and sticks of candy. I've watched you grow up into the man you are, and I've always known you wouldn't be half the man that my boy would turn out to be. But I never would have thought you could become an animal like this."

Scott leaned in so close that the scent of old steel mingled with the perspiration coming from Jed's skin. "I'm more of a man than your son ever was. Actually, by now I'd say I'm twice the man he is. What do you say, Jimmy? Shouldn't the worms have

138

eaten up at least that much of Jed's boy by now?"

"At least. Probably more than that."

"Yeah. I'd say there ain't even that much left of your boy. What've you got to say about that, old man?"

Jed kept his eyes intently focused and his backbone didn't waver in the slightest. But the deputies' torments had had the desired effect on him. There was no way Jed could hide that from the other two, and he knew it. So he kept quiet, part of him expecting to hear the shotgun's roar at any moment.

After a few seconds dragged by, Scott moved back and pulled Jed with him. "Why don't you have a seat before you piss yourself? We only came here to talk anyhow."

Still staring at the closed bedroom door, Jimmy said, "Speak for yourself."

"Yeah, well this can go a lot easier on you and your whole family if you just simmer down and talk to us nice and friendly."

Jed was pulled away from the fireplace and tossed toward a chair next to the dining room table. He only sat down once the shotgun was once again pointed at him. Besides that, he was now closer to Jimmy, and thereby closer to the rest of his family as well. "I already told you, just like I told Rich earlier today."

"Well tell it again."

"Abe was set to gun that stranger down and I told him to back away. I knew he meant to shoot me next, and there wasn't no reason for me to stand by and let it happen." Taking a breath, Jed tapped into that inner resolve that had served him well for most of his difficult life. "There's no reason for any of the good folks around here to put up with that. Not anymore."

"Well here's the problem," Scott stated. "I don't think you killed Abe. Tell you the truth, I don't think you got the sand to fire this here shotgun unless it's aimed at something smaller than a turkey."

"That's what Abe must've thought too, but I proved him wrong."

Compared to the way he spoke earlier, Jed sounded like a shell of himself. There wasn't any of the conviction that had been there before.

Scott and Jimmy picked up on the change in the farmer's voice even before Jed did.

"See?" Scott said in a voice dripping with self-satisfaction. "That there is why we were sent to talk to you in person. Rich is a friendly sort, but he's not good for much besides taking up space."

"He's a lawman," Jed interrupted. "The only one left in Jessup."

Jimmy glanced lazily toward the other two just long enough to spit out, "He's an asshole," and then shifted his hungry eyes once again toward the bedroom door.

Scott nodded. "True enough. And he probably swallowed your story and left. Am I right?"

Jed didn't have an answer, and Scott didn't wait long for one.

"So what really happened?" Scott asked. "You were there and you saw what happened better than anyone else. Was it that stranger? He started this whole thing, so maybe he was the one that finished it."

"I went out there to kill Abe." When the farmer spoke this time, his voice was strong and sure. "I pulled my trigger and he fell. That's what I did, and I'm not about to make some other man pay for it. I don't care if he's my neighbor or some stranger who Sheriff Manes is looking to hang. I did the right thing, and any lawman would see it the same way. Abe was an animal," Jed added, squaring his jaw and staring straight ahead past both deputies, "and I put him down like one."

When Scott looked at the man sitting in front of him, he saw a reminder of days when he'd been a weaker boy doing chores on Jed's land and scraping like a dog in the dirt. He saw the defiance that burned like a candle that wouldn't go out no matter how many times he tried to snuff it.

More than all of that, however, Scott saw a man who would not be intimidated. He saw a farmer so poor that he couldn't even afford a spread of his own, but who still figured he was good enough to look down at him and his badge. Scott saw a man who shot one of his partners and then bragged about it.

After letting all that flow through his mind, Scott couldn't see anything else but dark, angry red.

Scott thought those things in two blinks of an eye. The only visible trace they left upon him was the clenching of his jaw and the grinding of his teeth.

"All right," he finally said. "One last chance to tell me what else happened between you, Abe, and that stranger."

Jed shook his head. His time was running out and he could feel it. "I already told you. That's all there is to say."

"Then my job here isn't over. Get up."

"If you wanted me to turn myself in, I offered to go with Rich before —"

"You're not going to jail, but you are gonna be punished for what you done." Then Scott said the words the farmer had been dreading ever since he'd seen the deputies charge into his home. "Jimmy, go get those women."

ELEVEN

Jimmy was only too happy to follow through on the order he'd been given. In fact, he had been waiting to hear that single command, and sprung fully to life only after it arrived. Stepping forward, he reached out and pushed the door open before taking a second or two to truly savor the moment.

Having brought Jimmy along for this very reason, Scott watched as the farmer's face turned pale and he reflexively responded to his wife's urgent cries. Scott took Jed by the shoulder and roughly shoved him back into his seat. "No you don't. You'd best save your energy. This is gonna be a long night."

Since Jimmy had disappeared into the shadows of the next room, the house had filled with the sound of heavy steps scuffling back and forth as well as the scraping of smaller hands and feet racing in desperate circles. The children began to cry and Jed's wife started to curse violently at the deputy, but all three of those female voices fell silent once Jimmy's hand smacked against bare flesh.

"Son of a bitch!" Jed snarled, still fighting against the younger man's grip. "Cowardly son of a bitch, you call that dog out of there or so help me —"

"You'll what?" Scott asked mockingly. "Kill me like you did Abe? That was a fluke, but it's something you're gonna pay for. First," he said, nodding toward the bedroom, "they're gonna pay. And you get to watch."

The sound of fists on skin continued to emerge from the bedroom, mixed with the crying of both little girls. Through it all, Jimmy was laughing. Next came the sound of a belt buckle being undone.

Angry, hateful tears streamed down Jed's cheek. The more he fought to help his family, the less good it seemed to do. Scott had no trouble keeping him down, and finally restrained the farmer's arms altogether. Despite Jed's strength, it had all come from working a field and not from being in bar fights. That lack of experience had never been something he regretted until this very moment. Jed's eyes clenched shut and dread formed a ball of ice in his chest when he heard the shattering of glass and a gunshot erupt from the bedroom.

There were no more voices coming from the darkness. No angry curses or sobbing cries. The footsteps had dwindled down to a single set that were so heavy they could only belong to the deputy.

Scott's face twisted and he looked over to the darkened doorway. "You should have waited a bit before taking a shot, Jimmy. Now you're going to have to drag out the body and show the farmer here which one of his lovely ladies dropped first."

Jimmy came walking out, and both Jed and the other deputy watched to see who he was bringing with him. But when Jimmy stumbled back into the light, his hands were empty and his neck was covered in so much blood that it looked like he'd been splashed with a bucket of crimson paint.

"Jesus Christ," Jimmy said in a wheezing voice. "Holy . . . Jesus Christ!"

Scott snapped forward, but came to an abrupt stop like a dog that had been rudely introduced to the end of its leash. He wasn't about to let go of Jed, and so nearly wrenched his own arm from its socket. He noticed the blood on Jimmy's hand, then saw that the other man's gun was still in its holster.

"What happened to you?" Scott de-

146

manded.

Pulling in a wheezing breath, Jimmy reached up to the side of his face and instantly snapped his hand back with a painful wince. "Holy Christ," he shouted. "My goddamn ear's gone!"

Scott saw the blood and heard Jimmy's words, but scarcely believed any of it. Now he could see that blood was still spilling out from the messy pulp where an ear had previously been.

"Who's in there?" Scott asked his partner. With Jimmy distracted, poking around at the flaps of meat hanging from the side of his head, the deputy turned to the farmer he held in an ever tightening grip. "Who else is in there, old man? Does your bitch wife have a gun?"

Jed seemed just as surprised as either of the deputies. He shook his head and opened his mouth although no sound came out.

Frustrated and angry, Scott shoved the farmer away so harshly that Jed's chair tipped over and dumped the older man onto the floor. He grabbed the closest lantern he could find, twisted the knob as far as it would go, then headed into the bedroom to get a look for himself. The lantern's flame was jumping so high that it licked the top of the glass and heated the handle noticeably.

Scott ignored the heat soaking into his fingers and walked forward, his free hand snatching the Smith & Wesson pistol from the holster at his side.

Jed's wife sat huddled on the floor. The woman was in her mid-thirties, and she bared her teeth like an animal as she got ready to fight for her young. Her nightgown had been torn off one shoulder and ripped down a seam, exposing a full breast and half of her torso. She ignored her nakedness and kept her arms held out to shield the two girls, who kept poking their heads around her to see what was coming.

Scott lifted the lantern so he could illuminate more of the room. There wasn't much else in there apart from two beds and two small chests of drawers. A cross was nailed to the wall above the beds, and all three females were seeking shelter between the bulky pieces of furniture.

Jamming his pistol toward the woman, Scott shouted, "Where's your gun, bitch?" When he didn't get his answer right away, he thumbed back his hammer and lowered his voice in an even more menacing tone. "Hand over that gun you fired, or I'll splatter your fucking head all over them two girls."

He didn't need to hear her answer to

know that the woman didn't have a gun. Her hands were empty, and if she had been armed beforehand, she surely would have taken a shot at him by now. Something else caught Scott's eye at that moment: the broken bits of glass that were spread over one of the two beds.

He stepped toward the bed with the glass on it and looked up at a window set in the wall beside it. A square no bigger than two feet on either side, the window was a quarter of the way open, with a jagged section of glass missing from the pane. When he took a quick look through the window, Scott couldn't see anything but the open field where Jed's meager harvest once grew.

There was nobody standing outside the window and there were no other buildings facing that side of the house. Those things made the uneasy feeling in Scott's chest stretch out and tie his stomach into a knot.

"That's it," he said, more to himself that to any of the terrified females. Raising his voice so he could be heard by the people in the next room as well as whoever might be outside, he shouted, "That's it! I want that gun handed over and I want it right now, goddammit!"

As his voice echoed through the house and spilled out through the broken window,

Scott watched and waited for a response. What he got was a silence that only grew thicker and more oppressive, until even the frantic girls stopped sobbing.

With nothing to aim at, Scott pointed his gun out the window and squeezed off a shot. The blast roared through the room and rolled over the field outside, causing the woman and two girls to press themselves even farther back against the wall and floor. He was about to take another shot out of sheer rage when he was stopped by a voice from the next room.

"There you are, you bastard!" Jimmy snarled. "I got you now!"

Scott looked toward his partner in time to see Jimmy swivel and turn to the front of the house. Holding a rag against his head with his left hand, Jimmy drew his pistol with his right and took a quick shot.

At least, Scott thought that Jimmy took a shot. But in the instant he considered it, the gunshot seemed a little too far away, and there wasn't any smoke spewing out of Jimmy's barrel. Scott's mind had hardly put those pieces together when he saw his partner jerk back and the blood spray into the air behind him.

At that moment, Scott forgot about the woman and children huddling nearby. He could see what was going on in the next room as though it played out in slow motion. In that frame of mind, his reactions seemed painfully slow, as if he were moving through quicksand.

Wanting to see what had caught Jimmy's eye, Scott was instead distracted by the sight of Jed reaching up to make a grab for the gun in his hand. Having written off the farmer until it was almost too late, Scott delivered a savage punch to Jed's face, as though beating a misbehaving dog, before sending Jed to the floor with a swift boot to the old man's stomach.

Another shot sounded, this time from Jimmy's gun. Shouting out a string of obscenities, Jimmy lifted his pistol and pulled the trigger, causing a gout of smoke and sparks to erupt from the barrel.

"See there!" Jimmy screamed like a madman to his demons. "That's for what you did to my ear, you son of a bitch!"

Panicked, Jimmy fired again and again. Each shot seemed to flow into the next, turning the innards of the little home into a battlefield. With his blood coursing through his veins and the noise rattling his mind, he didn't need a specific target. Just knowing there was danger so close to him was enough to get the fire started. Scott stood close to

151

Jimmy. He lifted his pistol in one hand and the shotgun in the other. All he needed now was a target.

As his eyes turned toward the spot where Jimmy was firing, Scott saw that the front door had swung open all the way, to reveal the darkness beyond. A mist of dark gun smoke hung in the air, obscuring their vision and stinging both deputies' eyes. Before he could focus any better, a shower of sparks came from outside the front doorway. A sound like an angry hornet whipped through the air, ending in the wet slap of lead meeting flesh.

Scott reflexively tightened his fingers around both triggers, setting off both his own pistol and Jed's shotgun at the same time. The weapons kicked against his hands and let out a satisfying roar of their own.

Jimmy, however, wasn't firing back. In fact, he was lowering his hands and turning to look over at Scott with a strange, somewhat confused look on his face. The deputy's eyes searched for something, and they didn't even stop when his name was called out through the hot, smoky air.

"Jimmy?" Scott shouted over the ringing in his ears. "Did you see who's out there?"

But Jimmy obviously wasn't listening. Either that or he could no longer hear. The front of his shirt darkened with what appeared to be a black puddle that started as a nickel-sized smudge and quickly spread out and down toward his stomach. Although he tried to say something, the only thing that came from his mouth was a confused whine before he dropped down to his knees.

When his back hit the ground, Jimmy's entire body tensed and his hands clawed up as if to fight back the reaper himself. Scott looked down at the fallen man and saw the burnt hole in the middle of Jimmy's chest. Blood spilled from the wound until every muscle in his body relaxed and the final breath escaped from between his lips.

Not quite sure he believed what he was seeing, Scott dropped to one knee and took a closer look for himself. He'd seen a few dead men before, and there was no mistaking the fact that Jimmy was now among them. Even as Scott looked at the other deputy's glazed eyes and bloody torso, he still talked to him and asked him what the hell was going on.

But to find the answer to that question, Scott knew he had to turn his attention toward the front porch where Jimmy's killer still had to be standing. There was no way he could even be sure about that because the only thing he could see through the swirling smoke was the rectangular outline of the doorway itself.

Scott cussed every way he knew how while pointing his guns toward the door and squeezing both triggers again. The Smith & Wesson spat until its cylinder was empty, and over it all, the shotgun roared its final time. Every blast of gunfire made the inside of the house seem even more hellish, the burnt powder forming a gritty filth over Scott's face, hands, and inside his mouth.

The smoke was everywhere, but he was thankful for it. That smoke was the only thing potent enough to mask the pungent scent of human waste coming from the dead body at his feet. Scott stood his ground, flinching and shifting every so often since he expected a shot to punch through the gritty haze and bite into him at any second.

"Come on!" he shouted, trying to speed up the inevitable while fumbling for the fresh ammunition on his gun belt. "Come at me like a man, not some damn coward hiding out there!"

There was no response.

Suddenly, the deputy began to feel hope trickle back into his system like a cool drink of water. Maybe he'd hit whoever was out there with one of the shots he'd fired. Maybe the bastard who'd killed Jimmy was laying outside in a pool of blood. Maybe that son of a bitch was just about to kick off and he would miss it by standing inside the house one more second.

It was that streak of cruelty that boosted the deputy's spirits. Not courage or any strength of character. Just a jolt of sadistic energy that spurred him on and got him moving toward the front door.

The grin on Scott's face was forced and was trembling at both ends. His hands were shaking and sweaty, allowing the empty shotgun to slide through his fingers and drop noisily to the floor. He dropped several bullets while reloading his pistol, the full casings landing not too far away from the spent ones he'd tossed aside. The clatter of brass hitting wooden planks sounded distant and barely made it through the ringing in his ears.

"Where are you?" Scott hissed once he'd reloaded the Smith & Wesson and snapped the cylinder shut. He'd stepped through enough of the smoke to make out the doorway fully, as well as some of the details outside.

It was surprising how much he could hear, considering the circumstances. His entire body was straining to catch a glimpse of whatever it was that had descended upon that farmer's house. Scott caught himself thinking along those lines and shook the notion from his brain.

It wasn't some*thing* that had come at them. It was some*one*. A man. Not some monster or devil, but a man. He had to keep telling himself that because a man could bleed. A man could be killed.

Bolstered by his newfound courage, Scott nodded to himself and kept walking. He made it all the way to the front door without hearing anything but the voices of a few scared neighbors who'd heard the shooting but didn't want to poke their heads out from their hiding spaces. There was another noise that came like a tap on the deputy's shoulder. It spun him around, preparing for the worst.

It came from behind him.

It came from inside the house.

Not wanting to waste any more ammo, Scott hurried in a zigzag pattern through the smoke until he could get a look at where that noise had come from. The black haze was thinning out, and as soon as he cleared it, Scott saw several shapes moving at the back of the house. He recognized them immediately and quickened his steps to cross the room.

"Stop right there," he snarled to Jed and

his wife, who were herding their two girls into the kitchen and toward a back door. "Get back into that other room, or those girls —"

His threat was cut short by another blast of gunfire. This time it was a kitchen window that shattered as a bullet whipped through the air toward Scott's face, ripping through his cheek like an animal's claw and snapping his head back and to the side as it passed.

Still with no gunman in sight, it seemed as though the house itself was shooting at the deputy, spitting lead at him like invisible teeth. The blood felt hot as it trickled down Scott's cheek, but the pain was boiled away by the seething anger that filled him and made his muscles tremble.

"Get down."

Those two words came from nobody that Scott could see. Like commands from on high, they rumbled like a quiet undercurrent and were obeyed instantly by the faithful. Jed and his wife reached out for their daughters, who were close enough to the back door to feel the fresh air on their faces. Both parents dropped to the floor, taking their children with them and holding their anxious faces against the worn wooden planks.

But Scott was too worked up to notice any of this. All he knew was that someone was defying him once again from the shadows and it was probably one of the men skulking around outside. "Chicken shit assassin!" Scott screamed as he raised his gun and squeezed the trigger.

The explosion of gunfire filled the house, but it didn't come from Scott's gun. Rather, the shot from outside came a split second before the hammer of Scott's Smith & Wesson was able to drop. Sparks blossomed from the back porch, briefly illuminating a cold, angular face topped with a dark, wide-brimmed hat.

Scott only got a glimpse of the figure standing just outside the back door before the bullet from that unseen gun punched a hole through his flesh. The house teetered around him and the floor lurched out from beneath Scott's feet. It took a moment for him to realize that the bullet had drilled through his hip and the impact had sent him reeling in a tight downward spiral like a wagon that had suddenly lost a wheel.

The Smith & Wesson jumped in his hand one more time when his side hit the floor, but it was more of a reflexive response than any attempt to do damage. Once he was down, Scott had plenty of time to feel the pain of his wound. Light-headedness also started to overtake him as the blood poured from the gaping hole in his right hip.

Now that both deputies were on the floor, Jed stood up and herded his family through the door. Their footsteps bounced a few loose boards against the side of Scott's face, and then the house was quiet.

Scott thought he could hear the farmer talking to someone outside. After that, the air was filled only with smoke and Scott's grunting breaths as he tried desperately to get up and defend himself before the shooter walked up and put a round through his skull.

Pain stabbed through Scott's side, clearing some of the fog in his mind. He realized he was pulling himself up onto his feet, his body moving on its own accord. He clenched his teeth at the constant pain and tried to remember if his pistol needed to be reloaded or not. That concern flew from his mind the moment his vision cleared enough for him to see what was standing just outside the back door leading from the kitchen.

With the door still swinging after being pushed aside by the farmer on his way out, Scott could just make out the world beyond the house. Once the shooting had started, that world seemed to disappear, and now that it was back, it threatened to overwhelm him. The moonlight was still spilling out over the grass and buildings in a milky, gentle way that the sun could never master. And standing in a pocket of dark untouched by light from above, below, or any flame, stood a man.

The dark figure stood still as a statue, the details of his form too obscure for Scott to make out. A coat flapped in the breeze and the tops of weeds slapped against the leather of his boots. After staring for another couple of seconds, Scott could pick out a few pieces that weren't totally hidden from sight. The moonlight did manage to reveal the line of a jaw, a pair of narrowed eyes, and the cold steel gripped in one hand.

To see more, Scott would have had to get closer to the other man, and there was no way in hell he was going to do something like that.

"If you're gonna kill me," Scott said in a voice trembling with fear and pain, "just do it and get it done with."

The figure stared back at him and didn't move.

Somehow, Scott dredged up some courage. Either that, or he was getting even more light-headed from loss of blood. "Well?

What are you waiting for, asshole?"

Although he couldn't see it, Scott heard the metallic click of a pistol's hammer being thumbed back into firing position.

"You sure that's what you want?" came the low, rumbling voice that suddenly seemed vaguely familiar to the deputy. "Because I can sure arrange it."

Scott didn't have any more threats and he couldn't think of anything else to say. It was all he could do to keep from crying before his end came. And if there had been any more silence to contend with, he doubted he'd even be able to stop the tears that burned just behind his eyes.

"I'd much rather you collect your partner over there," the dark man said. "Take him back to your sheriff and leave this farmer alone. What's done is done, and if you insist on dredging up more business with Jed, then I'll come back and finish my business with you."

The dark man lifted his hand and held out the gun as if he meant to put a bullet right through Scott's forehead. Instinctively closing his eyes, the deputy held his breath and waited.

After a few moments he opened his eyes again, only to find that he was alone in the house and there was no man outside wait-

161

ing for him. Given that opening, Scott pulled himself up and got the hell out of there. It was amazing how fast a man who'd been shot in his hip could move when given the proper incentive.

TWELVE

Nick had only taken a few steps back from Jed's house when he saw Scott pull himself together and limp away like a scalded dog. His eyes never left the deputy as his hands quickly went through the motions of reloading his customized .45. The cylinder snapped shut as a smile slowly grew on Nick's face.

Being a poker player himself, Nick could truly appreciate a good bluff. When he'd nearly gotten Scott to piss himself, Nick had done it with an empty gun in his hand. Not only that, but he'd been standing close enough that Scott and the farmer's youngest child would have had a better than average chance of hitting him with one shot. But Scott hadn't tried his luck, and in the end Nick couldn't blame him.

That didn't make it any less satisfying to force the cocky deputy into retreat.

When he was sure the lawman was gone

and wasn't coming back again, Nick walked back to where the farmer and his family were hiding. The blood was still pumping quickly through his veins, and the smoke was still fresh in his nostrils, so Nick didn't think to soften his appearance before presenting himself to the frightened locals. "You folks all right?" he asked.

Jed was the first to nod and step out from behind the outhouse where they had all been hiding. Offering a hand in friendship, he said, "I don't know what to say, mister. You saved the lives of my wife and little girls."

Nick winced at that, thinking that Jed, his wife, and little girls would never have been in danger in the first place if not for his own actions. His eyes were drawn to the hand the farmer was holding out to him. It was open and waiting to be shaken. Jed's eyes were wide and earnest. Nick holstered his gun, held his hand out, but didn't grasp the one being offered by the farmer.

For a moment Jed's attention was caught by the gnarled, twisted handle of the pistol. At first glance the grip looked like a chunk of old, weathered root that had been sawed off at awkward angles and screwed onto a pistol. Then he saw Nick's ravaged hand and nodded.

"Friend of mine got two of his fingers bitten off by a mule," Jed said. "Had to fix up some of his tools, but he could still work well enough. I imagine the same thing goes for you." He reached out a little more and clasped Nick's hand, shaking it warmly. "Thank you, mister."

"My name's Nicolai. I was just setting things right, is all. It was the least I could do to make up for this morning."

The expression on Jed's face would have been just as easy to read in broad daylight as it was in the shadows. The farmer's strength was still there, but something else kicked in just beneath the surface. It might have been regret or it might have been something deeper . . . more spiritual.

"You didn't kill Abe," Nick confessed. "I shot him before you did. I didn't know he was a lawman."

"He's no lawman. Just some killer with a badge." Jed thought for a moment and nodded. "I thought I heard a shot before mine, but didn't see where it came from. Not at the time anyway. Funny, there was smoke and the sound of the first shot, but I would have sworn I did it. I did swear to it to the deputy who came to see me this morning."

"Well, put that out of your mind. You

didn't take any man's life. At least, not today."

"I probably won't be able to come back home anytime soon. That murderous son of a —" Jed stopped himself and glanced over to his two young daughters. Even after all they'd seen that night, he still didn't want them to hear their daddy curse. "That deputy will come looking for me. Probably the sheriff as well."

"Is there somewhere you folks can go for a while?"

A hand dropped onto Jed's shoulder and gave him a reassuring pat. It was his wife coming up from behind him, and her skin looked like smoothed out pearls in the moonlight. "My cousins live outside of Ogallala. They'll put us up . . . seeing as how we've got such harsh circumstances and all."

Ogallala wasn't more than three or four day's ride from Jessup. Possibly a bit more than that considering there were children to take into account.

"You might not have to leave town just yet," Nick said. "Just as long as you folks can stay out of sight for a day or two."

"It'll have to be longer than that," Jed said. "Trust me. I know most of those deputies, and they won't forget what happened here today. It'll be easier for us to move along and get a fresh start somewheres else. It's something I should've done a long time ago anyway."

"No it isn't. Your home is here. You're not the ones that should leave it."

"And what would you have us do?" Jed's wife asked. "Hide out while you gun down the sheriff, the rest of his deputies, and whoever else is living in that jailhouse?"

"Martha!" Jed scolded. "There's no need for that tone."

"The hell there isn't," Martha said with enough conviction in her voice that she got both Nick and her husband to back off a step. Grasping her children closer so that one of each of their ears was pressed against her skirts, she added, "Tonight was one thing, and we all thank you for it," she told Nick. "But I'd rather leave this town forever than wait around and watch it turn into a slaughterhouse."

"Who were you talking about?" Nick asked.

"My husband and family, we won't —"

"No. When you mentioned the jailhouse. Who were you talking about then?"

Martha looked at him as though he'd asked what country they were in or why water was wet. "We thought everyone knew

167

about that."

Nick shook his head.

"There's someone living in the jailhouse, and he ain't no prisoner."

"Martha, dammit." Jed's voice was quieter, yet even more insistent. "He don't need to hear about no stories."

"He's like a ghost," Martha continued. "Folks have seen him, but they don't talk about it. I've seen him." Looking over to her husband, Martha acted as though she'd only just then noticed how angry Jed was. "Well . . . I have."

Nick's brow furrowed as he mulled over the things he'd seen and heard that evening. There was a lot to digest and a lot more he would try to put out of his mind, even though he knew most of it would be with him for good. Killing a man was like that. Even if he'd never laid eyes on that man until pointing his gun toward him, Nick would never be able to forget that last noise or that last confused squint of the eyes as they glazed over.

The view from below.

Sometimes, Nick thought he'd seen it reflected so many times in the eyes of dead men that it would be no surprise to him when he finally saw it for himself. Then again, many of those dead men had prob-

168

ably thought that as well, and they still looked pretty damn surprised when their time came.

"We won't be able to leave for a bit anyhow," Jed explained. "We'll be staying with the O'Gradys until we've collected some things and scrounged up some money for the trip."

The youngest of the two girls appeared to be no more than four or five. She seemed content to keep her face hidden in her mother's skirts with her eyes clenched shut tight. The older girl looked to be about ten or eleven, and even in the dark of night, her hair looked like spun gold.

"Are we going away, Pa?" the older girl asked, her eyes wide open and the tears already drying on her cheeks.

"Just for a little while, angel."

"Will we ever come back?"

"Sure we will," Jed answered, in a way that couldn't have convinced even the youngest girl. "We'll come back just as soon as we can."

The older girl studied her parents for a couple of seconds before turning her eyes to Nick. To him, she said, "Thanks for helping us. I won't tell nobody about who you are or what you done."

Now it was Nick's turn to study the young

girl. What she'd said had been an earnest promise that didn't come from fear for herself or for anyone else. She'd simply kept her eyes open and put everything together as simply as only a child could. "Thanks," he told her. "I'd appreciate that."

Enough time had gone by for the neighbors to start poking their heads out their windows and venture out into their yards. After a few had gotten close enough to see the small group gathered behind the Arvey home, plenty more started following suit. Already, they were calling over to them, asking if they were all right or needed any help.

"You'd best get out of here, Nick," Jed told him. "Some of our neighbors aren't as opposed to gossip as I am." He couldn't help but shoot a meaningful glance toward his wife.

Martha shrugged and let out an exasperated breath. "I just told him what I saw."

When Jed turned toward Nick, he only saw the other man's back as he was walking away. With a downward turn of his head and a quick step, he went practically unnoticed down the narrow dirt path that meandered back into town. The neighbors who were nearby were too focused on the Arveys and their shot-up house to notice just another shadow moving among the rest.

■ ■ ■ ■

Somehow, the walk back to Callum's funeral parlor seemed a hell of a lot longer than when Nick had made the same trip about half an hour ago. This time, every step he took was heavier and more deliberate. Part of him felt drunk from all the adrenaline still coursing through his body, and part of him felt too tired to move. It was like that every time he killed a man. Those newly freed souls hung in the air heavier than the black gun smoke that he could still taste at the back of his throat.

He knew only too well that his body's wounds would heal. A good night's sleep would freshen his aching muscles, but the ghost of that deputy would be with him until the end of his days. Well, at least Jimmy wouldn't be lonely, he thought. There were plenty of other ghosts haunting Nick to keep him company.

As much as he wanted to go to bed, Nick passed up the intersection that would have taken him to his cot and little room. Instead, he kept on walking, following the sound of voices mixed with the tinny sound of an out-of-tune piano. Sure enough, those things led him to Cavalry Avenue, and the moment he turned that corner, Nick could see the large building marked by a painted sign that read MIL'S.

The saloon was just starting to fill up, which was a stark contrast to the quieter part of town that Nick had left behind. Of course, that part of town had become so chaotic that night that Mil's would seem like a kind of haven. That little irony was enough to bring a smile to his face just as he walked through the door, which was propped open by a satisfied customer serving a purpose while sleeping it off.

Several tables were scattered throughout the large main room, about half of which were set aside for card players and a pair of roulette wheels. What Nick was mainly interested in, however, was the bar, which ran from the front of the room all the way along the left wall to the back. From there, the bar turned a corner where some of the heavier drinkers could down their whiskey without having to see the outside world.

The floor was covered in sawdust, bits of broken glass, and the occasional tooth. Uneven and warped boards made it necessary for Nick to watch his step as he walked around the drunk doorstop and drew in a breath of air tainted by the combined smell of liquor and cigar smoke.

As Nick walked in, he was immediately spotted by several of the girls working the place. Their eyes sparkled at the sight of fresh meat, and they adjusted themselves accordingly to show off their individual assets. Even though he wasn't interested in renting a companion for the night, Nick was still a man and wasn't about to pass up the opportunity to let his hands wander over some of the more impressive figures that presented themselves for inspection. The girls quickly gleaned that he wasn't interested in anything more than a casual distraction, and by the time Nick reached a spot at the bar, he was alone once again.

Within a minute of standing with his elbows propped up on the chipped wooden bar, Nick caught the eye of the skinny, well-groomed man tending it. The barkeep wore a white apron over dark pants. A white shirt with the sleeves buttoned nicely around his wrists was accentuated with a set of brass cuff links. His short black hair was parted in the middle and his thick handlebar mustache was waxed to stay perfectly in place. In more ways than one, the bartender looked too good to be in a place like Mil's.

"Evenin'," the bartender said with a curt nod. "What can I get for you?"

"Vodka," Nick answered, ordering the

drink of choice that his father had introduced him to and had been damn hard to find ever since. Most saloons in smaller towns simply hadn't heard of vodka, and the bigger cities didn't really get enough of a call for it to order it themselves. Every now and then, however, Nick got lucky.

Judging by the second nod from the barkeep followed by the full bottle that was set onto the bar, this would be one of those lucky nights. In a way, it felt like a reward from the Fates.

"That's expensive stuff," the barkeep warned. "I only get a bottle or two in every year."

Nick dropped a silver dollar onto the bar. "Will this cover it?"

"For a drink or two . . . not the bottle."

"Then we're in business." Nick waited for the barkeep to top off a shot glass with the clear liquor and then lifted the drink to his lips. The vodka was potent and burned its way down his throat to settle like a warm ember in his belly. He then flipped some more cash onto the bar, removed a dented tin flask from a jacket pocket, and filled it all the way to the top.

After replacing the flask in his pocket, Nick took another sip from his glass. The warm, slightly dizzy sensation crept in at

174

the edges of his senses.
It was worth every cent.

THIRTEEN

The sun rose and shone upon Jessup, Nebraska, the next day as it had every other before it. There were plenty of changes in the town, as well as in some of its residents, but the sky still brightened first in the east and the world continued to turn without anyone's consent.

There was a definite tension in the air, which was felt by all of those who either knew what had happened at Jed Arvey's place or had seen Sheriff Manes when he stepped out of his house and glared angrily at the world around him. The lawman was not happy. His deputies knew it and kept their distance whenever possible. The rest of the locals tipped their hats and quickened their steps, hoping not to draw any of the sheriff's wrath.

As always, Sheriff Manes stopped in first at the jailhouse, where he would stay until almost noon. Normally, Jimmy would have been the deputy guarding the jailhouse door while the sheriff was inside, but there was a different man in that post this morning, as well as a fresh body in Callum's parlor.

The undertaker had been woken late the previous night to come and collect the body from Jed's house. He would have appreciated some help from his newest employee, but Nick hadn't been around. His bed hadn't been slept in, and what troubled Callum most was that his gun was no longer hanging over the chair where it had been the day before.

That had been nagging at the back of Callum's mind for hours as the rest of him had been kept busy by cleaning up Jimmy's corpse and starting in on the preparations for the deputy's funeral. There was still the matter of the Eddings affair, and when he thought about that, his head started to spin.

It was time for a break anyhow, since he'd gotten in almost a full day's work before most of the shops in town had even opened their doors. Callum set down the tools he'd been using and walked over to the little roll-top desk situated in his small office. Pulling open one of the desk drawers, he removed a cigarette case engraved with his initials which had served as payment for a burial several years ago. After fishing a few matches from the same drawer, Callum headed through the main room and outside through the front door.

He was just in time to see a figure separate itself from the rest of the growing foot traffic at the other end of Eighth Street and start walking toward his parlor. A cigarette was between his lips and lit before he could see any more than the fact that the approaching person was a female with a nice shape and short dark hair. It was the warm smile that gave her away, not to mention the round breasts beneath her white and pink striped blouse.

"Hello, Catherine," the undertaker said, making sure his eyes were pointed higher than where they'd been a moment before.

" 'Morning Mr. Callum."

He smiled back at her, resisting the impulse to ask her to call him by his first name since he knew she wouldn't come to see him often enough to remember. "What brings you by here so early this morning? I hope it's social."

Flinching at what a business meeting with Dan Callum would entail, she nodded her head. "It is, although I understand you've got plenty of business nowadays."

"Unfortunately, yes. I take it you heard

about what happened last night with Jed Arvey?"

"Only bits and pieces. Those bits were hard to believe, though."

"Well, if you're looking for details, I'm afraid I don't have any. The bodies can be viewed at the funeral, which is to be held as soon as possible."

"No need to send me an invitation, Mr. Callum. I don't want to pay any respects to either of those terrible, so-called deputies, and I don't think it's unfortunate that either of them are dead." Although she obviously meant every word that she said, Catherine didn't look proud of it.

Callum took another puff of his cigarette and held out the case to offer one to her. She refused with a polite shake of her head.

"Not to be rude, but was there something I could help you with?" Callum asked.

"Actually, I was wondering if Nick was available. If he's busy, I could come back later, of course."

Plenty of things went through Callum's mind at that moment. First, he thought about where Nick might be if he wasn't at the parlor or with a woman as pretty and interested as Catherine Weaver. Second, he thought about the gun that had been missing from that chair in his workshop, as well as the body that turned up last night. "Yeah," he said, making a decision using those things as a balance. "Nick's got his hands full right now. I'll send him over to you when he gets a spare moment, though. Would that be all right?"

"That would be fine. Do you think I could look in on him to say hello?"

Shrugging, Callum said, "That would be fine with me. You don't mind the smell and sight of blood, though, do you? It's a bit messy in there right now."

With those seeds planted, Catherine's imagination filled in all the empty spaces. Just as Callum had expected, the picture she'd formed in her mind's eyes was not at all a pleasant one.

"Umm . . . on second thought, why don't I just let him work?" Catherine said.

"Suit yourself. Does he know where to find you?"

"He should. Just tell him I'll have a nice lunch ready for him."

"Will do."

After giving Callum a friendly wave, Catherine turned and walked away as quickly as she could without offending the undertaker. The striped material of her dress hugged her backside nicely, accentuating the wiggle of her exit. Callum finished his cigarette and enjoyed the show, knowing full well that she wouldn't be turning around to look back at him.

Apparently, either he'd underestimated her politeness or he'd been staring at her a little too hard because Catherine did turn around to bid one last farewell. Callum's eyes snapped upward once again and he returned her smile, adding a wave of his own for good measure.

In all his years of living in Jessup, Callum had only talked to Catherine a handful of times when he'd stopped in to The Porter House for a meal. He'd always thought she was a nice enough girl, but now he realized that she was even sweeter than that. Any man would be crazy to spurn a woman like her, and he would be sure to tell that to his newest helper when he came back.

That brought another set of worries to Callum's mind. After the shootings last night, and with Nick nowhere to be found, he hoped his newest helper would come back at all. Just because the smoke was cleared didn't mean all the bodies had been found. The undertaker knew all too well that a man could catch a bullet and crawl off to die someplace where the crows and dogs would find him before anyone else.

Considering that the shootout had involved the sheriff's deputies added a whole other element to the mix. Sheriff Manes might have dragged him out of town behind his own horse and left him to die at the bottom of a hill somewhere. That bastard was capable of a good many things, and plenty of them weren't good at all.

Nick was a good man. Callum knew that much just from what little time he'd spent with him. But there was something in Nick's eyes that spoke of a great deal running below the surface. Counting a man like that out so quickly was never a smart thing to do. More than that, he couldn't imagine seeing the disappointed look on Catherine's pretty face if Callum failed to deliver her message.

Callum flicked what little remained of his cigarette to the ground and stepped on it as he walked toward Eighth Street. Realizing he was still wearing his apron, he went back and pulled it off and over his head before folding it neatly and setting it just inside the door. He then locked up the parlor and started his walk toward the busier section of town.

He'd suddenly gotten it into his mind to see if he could find out where Nick had disappeared to. The first thing he decided to check was if he'd simply headed out of town on his own. Although Nick's things were still in the spare room, Callum figured it somewhat likely that he could have taken off without them. That seemed especially possible considering his exit might have been very forced and very quick.

Callum remembered talking to Nick the previous afternoon about the forgetful kid who'd taken in his wagon upon entering town. That had to be Will. Dennis and Virginia's boy was funny and well-mannered, but tended to let a good amount of things fall out of that head of his. Will worked at the stable on the edge of town, which was where Callum headed.

The walk did him some good. He actually seemed to draw energy from the stretching of his legs and felt refreshed once he got close enough to smell the scent of horses and hay coming from the stables. One rap on the side of the barn door was all it took to bring the kid racing out from behind an old, clunky wagon like a shot of wide-eyed lightning.

"Need to put a horse up, mister?" the kid asked even before he got a good look at who'd come calling. His eyes narrowed and a good portion of the steam left his strides once he got a look at Callum. "Oh . . . you're the undertaker."

"I sure am."

"Do you . . . need a horse?"

"No, but I was wondering if you could tell me if you remember a man who left some horses here. He was a big fella driving a wagon and came in yesterday."

"Yeah," the kid responded as though he was going to win a prize. "That's his wagon over —" He stopped with his arm halfway extended like a chicken's wing. His hand curled up in a fist before he slowly lowered it back down again. "I wasn't supposed to say anything about it."

"You don't have to tell me where it is, but can you tell me if he's still here?"

Eyeing the undertaker suspiciously, Will shook his head. "No, sir. I shouldn't tell you anything else. He wouldn't like it."

That was all he needed. Nick's wagon and horses were still there, which meant he was more than likely still in town. "Well, I'll let you get back to work, then. Tell your folks I said howdy."

Will didn't say another word. Instead, he watched Callum like a hawk until the undertaker had walked down the street and turned a corner.

Stopping for a moment, Callum realized he didn't have the time or energy to scour the entire town looking for one man who could very well be . . . well, he decided to let that train of thought go, and instead put his mind back onto less troubling matters. He would be mad at Nick for not showing up for work on such a busy day, but he didn't like the thought of worse news than that.

The uncomfortable feeling in his gut only got worse when he saw one of the sheriff's deputies making his rounds. The sorry excuse for a lawman was checking in on the businesses as they opened their doors, asking brusque questions and poking around freely in each building he saw. Callum kept his head down and walked past the deputy without much problem.

There was one more place the undertaker decided to check. If there had been any problem the night before, Callum's best source of information would be the local gossip. And the best place to get some local gossip was where a good amount of the local gossipers spent their time. He didn't know where the sewing circle met, so he headed for the next best place. Besides that, Callum figured he could use a drink.

Mil's wasn't the type of place that the undertaker frequented, but it was the best known saloon in town. Besides that, Eddie Farrell, who owned the place, had enough

185

people spreading the word to visitors and locals alike that most everyone wound up at Mil's eventually. Callum pushed open the door to the saloon and was nearly knocked over by the smells, which hit him harder than those found in the stables.

It had been a long time since the old man had partaken of alcohol, and he was tempted to rectify that the moment he walked through the door. By the time he got to the bar, however, he'd found his inner resolve.

"Coffee, please," Callum said to the owner, who kept an eye on his place by tending its bar. He also recognized Farrell from the funeral he'd arranged for the saloon owner's second wife. Callum doubted his own face would be remembered so easily.

Farrell didn't say a word as he took out a tin cup and filled it full of strong coffee. He seemed to recognize the undertaker but didn't have anything to say to him.

Before he got a chance to ask about Nick's possible whereabouts, Callum heard a familiar voice at one of the tables in the other part of the room. He turned, looked for the source of the voice and had no trouble spotting it, since only a handful of the tables were occupied.

The most crowded table at the moment was one toward the back of the room with five men seated around it. Stacks of poker chips and playing cards were scattered on the table, vying for space among the bottles of liquor and drinking glasses. While all of the men were gesturing and talking among themselves, one of them in particular was making more noise than the rest.

"Sorry, friends," Nick bellowed as he pulled in the stack of chips that had been collecting in the middle of the table. "But if you've got a problem, you'll need to take it up with Lady Luck."

The other men at Nick's table didn't have one clean set of clothes between them. One of them, a fat pimp who lived at Mil's so he could be closer to his business, shook his head at Nick. "Lady Luck's supposed to be on my payroll. I'd say you've got a horseshoe stuck up yer ass."

"Maybe that's why he's sittin' so funny," chimed in the skinny drunk filling the space next to Nick.

But Nick laughed right along with the rest of them. "I'm sitting so funny because I'm sitting on a stack of all your money, Rob. How's that grab ya?"

Another round of insults went around the table as Nick grabbed a bottle and refilled all the glasses sitting on the table.

Callum watched this through narrowed eyes, wondering just how much longer he was going to go unnoticed. Perhaps he'd gotten the wrong impression of Nick after their first day of working together. Perhaps Catherine would like to know that she'd invited a drunken gambler to share her time. He knew she wasn't the type of lady who would appreciate that bit of knowledge.

The types of ladies that wanted a man who drank their breakfast around a card table were the ones hanging all over the card players at that very moment. They were the same ones who paid a percentage of their nightly earnings to the fat man currently tossing back the whiskey Nick had poured for him.

Callum didn't have to wait too much longer before he saw Nick's eyes come right to him. When he was spotted, the undertaker noticed an immediate change in Nick's face as well as his entire demeanor. At first he looked surprised to see Callum. But then his eyes snapped over to the front window, which was all but completely covered by a thick, dark red curtain.

Not a lot of sunlight made it through the curtain, but enough seeped in and trickled onto the floor to be spotted even at the back of the room. Suddenly, Nick didn't look surprised. He looked more like a man who knew he had some explaining to do.

FOURTEEN

Nick excused himself from his game, got up from the table and gathered up all of his chips. When he walked over to where Callum was waiting at the bar, his steps were much more even than what the undertaker had been expecting. Despite the reek of alcohol on Nick's clothes, he kept his stride balanced and his hands steady.

"Cash these in for me, would you, Eddie?" Nick said.

Compared to the way he'd treated Callum, the barkeep responded as though Nick was a long-lost relative. He accepted the chips and set a glass on the bar. "How about a drink on the house while I count these up?"

"Don't mind if I do," Nick replied as he waited for Eddie to fill the glass with a clear, potent liquid.

"So, how many does that make for you this morning?" Callum asked.

"This morning? One." Nick poured the shot down his throat and set the glass onto the bar while exhaling slowly. "What time is it?"

"Time for you to be at work," Callum said sternly. "Actually, that time was a few hours ago."

"Jesus, I'm sorry."

"You didn't sleep at all last night, did you?"

"Does it show?"

"Actually, it doesn't. That either tells me that you decided to spend the night in a room here or you're no stranger to sitting up and playing poker for days at a stretch."

Nick shook his head and met the undertaker's gaze. "I'm not as used to nights like that as I used to be, but it's a comfortable saddle to climb back into. At least, that's what my father used to say."

"And what would he have said if he knew you were playing cards with a whore on your lap instead of doing an honest day's work?"

Clearing his throat, Nick responded, "He would have said, 'You want to throw your life away, *jaunikaitis*? You do it where nobody can see. At least then they'll remember you as a better man than you ever were.' That's what he would have said."

191

The bartender came up to them and set a stack of bills in front of Nick. He smirked at the way Nick spoke in an exaggerated Slavic accent and then found something else to do at another end of the bar.

"Your father sounds like a smart man," Callum said respectfully. "A little harsh, but smart." He'd heard people talk about departed loved ones so many times before that he could immediately spot the shift in Nick's voice when referring to his father. He couldn't be sure that Nick was talking about a dead man, but there was definitely a loss there.

"What is that?" Callum asked.

"What's what?"

"Yow . . ." The undertaker shook his head while trying to wrap his tongue around the strange word Nick had mentioned when quoting his father. "Yow-ni-kie-tee. What's that mean?"

Nick laughed and stood so he was facing the undertaker directly. *"Jaunikaitis."* The sounds were similar to when Callum had said them, but the word flowed off of Nick's tongue like exotic wine, each syllable melding into the next. "It means young man."

"I see. Is that . . . Polish?"

"Not quite. It's Lithuanian."

"Really? You never mentioned you were

from there."

"That's because just about everyone I meet probably wouldn't have heard of it. Hell, most folks don't even ask. Usually, just saying the 'Old World' or 'overseas' is enough to appease them. Most folks don't care about much that doesn't affect them directly."

The undertaker wished he could argue with Nick on that point, but couldn't think of a way to dispute it. Most folks truly didn't care, and he knew that from firsthand experience. Rather than gripe about how he was all but ignored in the town he'd spent a good deal of his life in, Callum took a sip of his coffee and let the brew swirl around in his mouth. Like the coffee served in just about every saloon, it was made more as a tool for sobering someone up enough to get home than for anyone's enjoyment. As such, the stuff tasted about one step above mud, but acted like toothpicks that would prop his eyes open for at least an hour per sip.

"You're not drunk at all, are you?" The undertaker's words seemed less like a question and more of a statement. "But you smell like you've been rolling in whiskey all night long. How do you account for that?"

Nick smirked and replied, "Everyone at that table's been drinking whiskey. I can drink that like water and all it does is wet my throat. This is vodka. Not even the same animal. My grandmother gave me my first taste of the stuff when I was eight years old. She saw it as a tonic.

"Besides, I could always hold my liquor. My father was raised in the Old World, and over there, it's healthy to have a bit of alcohol in your system every day." Nick paused and stared down at the shot glass. "A lot of things go down easier as the years go by, and liquor is certainly one of them. Even so, I come by vodka so rarely anymore that it's about the only thing that can take its toll on me." Leaning back to give a friendly wave to the card table he'd left behind, he spoke to Callum softly enough so that he knew nobody else could hear. "You see them?"

"Yeah."

"They drank like fishes all night long while I poured half of my whiskey down my chin or onto the floor. What little I drank didn't do much more than slake my thirst. I've got my grandmother to thank for that."

"So why bother drinking at all?" Callum asked distastefully, thinking back to the way he'd instantly thought less of Nick once he saw the company he was keeping and smelled the reek of alcohol hanging around him like a noxious cloud. "Or why even bother pretending to drink?"

"You really need to ask that?" Nick said, tapping the stack of money the barkeep had set in front of him. "The more they drink, the worse they bluff. Apart from the real professionals, most card players are just as human as the rest of us and they get sloppy the more whiskey they drink. They'll just keep knocking them back so long as I sit there drinking with them, though."

"Well I'll be damned," Callum said. "I always thought gamblers learned how to cheat or mastered their games or found some way to get luck on their side. What you do seems so . . . easy."

"It is easy. Poker's an easy game. There are things to master, and that's what the professionals do. A real professional doesn't need luck because they're artists. Believe me, I've seen them work, and it's a thing of beauty just so long as it's not your life savings going into their pockets.

"The professionals earn a living playing cards, and the only real way to do that is sit in on the big games. I'm no professional card player. For gamblers like me, it's just a lot of simple tricks and nonsense."

By the time Nick was done talking to Callum about gambling, both men had finished their drinks and were leaning against the bar like a pair of old friends. Callum didn't know which shocked him more: the layers that he was seeing beneath Nick's surface, or the fact that he'd actually finished a whole cup of that godawful coffee.

Nick had ordered another cup of the thick coffee for Callum as well as one for himself. Now that his winnings were safely tucked in his pockets and the card game was back in full swing without him, he didn't have any more reason to put up a facade. Callum just wanted to get back to work now that he'd found his assistant, but didn't want to leave before he talked about one last thing that had been nagging at him ever since he'd heard about the shootout that had taken place the night before.

Before asking his question, Callum took a casual glance at Nick's waist. Sure enough, the gun belt was there. The pistol itself was mostly covered by the length of his jacket.

"You heard about what happened, didn't you?" Nick asked, as though he could read Callum's thoughts.

The undertaker nodded. "Yes I did. Most everyone's heard about it by now, I suspect. That deputy's body is already sitting in my workshop waiting for a coffin. That reminds me . . . you didn't sleep in my spare room."

Laughing once, Nick took a sip of his own coffee and winced at the potent, bitter taste of it. "A dead man laying on your table reminds you of me, huh? That's great."

But Callum wasn't laughing. "Maybe I'm not so far off."

"We'll all wind up on that table. If not here, then a table somewhere else."

"I was talking about *how* that deputy wound up on that table. He was shot last night at Jed Arvey's place. Plenty of folks thought Jed killed Abe, and for good reason, but not one of them is convinced he had anything to do with Jimmy getting killed."

"Good."

"Is that all you have to say about it?"

"If you mean to scold me," Nick retorted with a subtle edge in his voice, "then save your breath. It never did any good when I was younger, and my father was a hell of a lot better at it than you."

"People around here act like they don't see me, so I get to hear plenty of talk because of that. And when something like last night happens, everyone's dying to talk about what they heard to anyone with ears on the sides of their heads.

"They're talking about those two deputies shooting at anything that moved like a couple of squeamish youngsters. They were scared, Nick. Men as dangerous as that and with the backing they got don't get scared. Not without good reason."

Nick listened and sipped his coffee. The expression on his face was unreadable, giving a hint as to how good a poker player he truly was.

Leaning in closer and dropping his voice to a fierce whisper, Callum asked, "It was you, wasn't it?"

Nick's lips moved, but just enough for him to tip his cup back and let some more coffee trickle down his throat.

Undeterred by the other man's silence, Callum went on to say, "Everyone else is making things up as it suits them, but I know it was you."

Taking on a cold, stony demeanor, Nick set his cup down and looked once again at the undertaker. His eyes shifted in his skull, looking as unsettling as a marble gargoyle suddenly getting up and stretching its wings. Once his eyes focused on the undertaker's, Nick's head turned in that direction as well, moving so deliberately that the sound of bones grinding together could almost be heard.

"So what?" Nick asked. "If you're so certain about what you know . . . what happens now?"

"I can help you," Callum said, pushing the words out as though they'd been heavy burdens lodged in his throat. "Jessup was a better place when we had real law here. Hell, it was better than this when we didn't have any law. Jed's not the only one ready to do something against the sheriff. We're simple folk. We don't know what we can do."

Nick studied the undertaker's face. He stared deeply into the old man's eyes and saw right away that Callum was dead serious. He'd seen that same look in Jed's eyes as well, and several others before that. That look, that determination, could be a welcome sight or something from a nightmare. It all just depended upon which way those eyes were pointed.

"Come on," Nick said as he stepped away from the bar and tossed down enough money to cover both coffees and a tip besides. "We've got a lot of work to do."

FIFTEEN

Everyone had their morning rituals. Every lawman had another set of rituals. Sheriff Manes followed rituals that stayed close to any sheriff's while also subverting them just enough to suit his purposes. Like many other lawmen, he checked in on the residents of his jailhouse once a day to make sure everyone was where they needed to be.

The strange part about that was the fact that Jessup's jailhouse hadn't had a real prisoner in it for quite some time.

Even so, the sheriff paid a visit there every morning, and with an armed escort to boot. Everyone whose business took them within eyeshot of the old jailhouse noticed this eventually. But like so many other things that went on in that town, it was a whole lot easier to pretend that nothing out of the ordinary was taking place.

It was a whole lot healthier that way too.

Another deputy stood in Jimmy's old post

while Sheriff Manes went inside. The jail-house itself was as solid as a building could be. Its walls were stone, reinforced with thick timber beams placed at regular intervals. The windows were one foot squares lined up along both sides, each of them sporting thick bars of rusted iron.

The inside of the building looked every bit as oppressive as the outside. Eight cells were divided into two rows of four with a wide corridor passing directly between them. Being inside the jailhouse was similar to being inside a hollowed-out brick. Cold air came in through the windows and stayed there, seeping into the bars of the cells along with the bones of anyone inhabiting them.

Each cell contained a cot and blanket along with a small bucket that served as a toilet. They could dump their shit out their window or eat it for all the jailers cared. That was the standard line given to all prisoners on their first day inside their cell. But even though there was a single resident inside the jailhouse, there was no mistaking him for a prisoner.

Prisoners weren't allowed to keep their door open, and they most certainly weren't allowed to have whores keep them warm at night. Beyond that, the extra blankets and nicer furnishings were just further points leading to the same conclusion: the man living in that jailhouse was a guest.

Sheriff Manes made sure to make plenty of noise as he entered the jailhouse and slammed the door shut behind him. He figured that would give his guest plenty of time to prepare and get the woman sleeping with him a head start as well. Naturally, there was a bit of commotion down at the end of the row of cells. Bodies rustled on the cot and clothes were picked up from wherever they'd been tossed the night before.

The woman tried to pull on at least her slip by the time Manes started walking down the corridor. She didn't try to set any records, however, and just barely managed to pull one strap of her slip over her shoulder before the sheriff could get a good look into the cell. Despite the chill in the jailhouse, her skin was sweaty and the thin slip clung to her flesh in an even more provocative way than if she'd been completely naked.

Being accustomed to dealing with soiled doves like that one, Manes didn't take the lustful glint in her eyes personally. Being a man, however, he wasn't at all opposed to standing there and watching the attractive woman pull on the rest of her clothes.

The man inside the cell with the woman was still laying on his cot. Actually, it was two normal cots that had been pushed together and was still barely big enough to hold both his weight and the woman's. Letting one bare leg hang down from the blankets bunched on top of him, the man pulled his fingers through the tangle of steel-gray hairs on his head and cleared his throat like a consumptive having a fit.

"You run a hell of a good place here, Sheriff," the man said once he'd cleared enough of the filth from his throat to speak. "Ever think of going into the hotel business?"

The sheriff's mouth twisted into half a grin, yet he spoke without a trace of humor. "If I ran a hotel catering to the likes of you, I'd go out of business."

Letting his eyes wander to the whore wriggling into her dress, the man in the cell grinned and scratched the stubble on his neck. "Yeah, I see your point."

The woman did a good job of ignoring the two men as they spoke around her. Actually, appearing to be nothing more than an accessory was a big part of her job. She pulled on just enough clothes to be presentable to the outside world and leaned down to kiss the man sitting on the cot one more time. She was nearly pulled off her feet when the gray-haired man reached out and took hold of her to kiss her like he was about to pull off the clothes she'd just finished pulling on.

"All right now," Sheriff Manes said impatiently. "I let you have a visitor one night, but don't push it. Folks talk a lot around here."

The man on the cot pulled back from her and wiped his mouth with the back of his hand. His smile was so lewd that it would have made any respectable woman blush. The woman who'd shared his bed was used to seeing the worst of men, however, and pretended she thought it was attractive. Inside, she was already planning how many different types of salts she would use when she took her much-anticipated bath.

"Did you pay her something extra to keep her mouth shut?" the man in the cell asked.

Manes stepped aside and let her walk by. "That won't be necessary, will it, honey?"

She laughed without looking back and kept walking. "I know my business, Sheriff. We're even just so long as you keep throwing men like this one my way."

By this time the man in the cell had gotten up from his cot and was pulling on a pair of raggedy pants. He then reached beneath the mattress and pulled out a large, Army-issue Colt. With one hand he pulled on his suspenders, and with the other he took aim with the Colt.

Reaching out so quickly that his arm resembled a snapping whip, Manes took hold of the other man's wrist and twisted it upward so the Colt was pointing toward the ceiling. For a moment the man in the cell looked like he might turn his blood lust toward the sheriff. That storm passed once he pulled in an unsteady breath and let it out through clenched teeth.

"Are you insane?" Manes hissed as the working girl left the building and shut the door behind her.

The man in the cell kept his eyes focused on the closed door as though he could still watch the wiggle of the woman's hips through the obstruction. Licking his lips, he said quietly, "She don't know what she's missing." Stuffing his pistol into the waistband of his pants, he reached for a shirt that was hanging inside his cell. "What's all this I heard about shootings yesterday? Is someone causing you trouble?"

"Nothing you need to be concerned about."

"Oh, I think I'll be the judge of what it is I should be concerned about. Tell me."

"Two of my deputies were killed."

"Is that a fact? I suppose they were fighting to uphold the strict letter of the law and went down in the line of duty." He couldn't even make it through that sentence without busting into a wide, sarcastic grin. "Or did they just shoot each other over a card game?"

"No, they were gunned down. Any more than that, I honestly couldn't say."

"You want me to look into it for you? I could use a chance to stretch my legs."

"Stretching your legs like that kind of defeats the purpose of holing up in here, doesn't it?"

The gray-haired man leaned against the bars of the next cell and buttoned his shirt. "Yeah, well there isn't much purpose to me being here when you've got someone gunning down your deputies. I thought this place was supposed to be safe. That's what I paid good money for."

"This is plenty safe for you," the sheriff said in a stern tone of voice. "That other problem doesn't have anything to do with our arrangement."

Almost done with his tucking, the gray-haired man plucked the gun from his waistband so quickly that Sheriff Manes didn't even have a chance to react. He held it

206

pointed toward the sheriff for a moment or two, watching the lawman twitch nervously.

Satisfied, he lowered the gun and walked over to where his gun belt was folded up on the floor next to his cot. "That may settle your mind, Sheriff, but it don't do much for mine." The gun belt was off the floor and buckled around his waist in a few seconds flat. Only then did the Colt leave his hand, settling into the worn leather holster. "I think I'll have a look for myself. It'll make me feel better."

"Suit yourself. One of my deputies can —"

"Your deputies can stay the hell away from me," the other man shot back with a laugh. "Since they're the ones catching all the lead around here, I think I'll just stay back and let them fall without me."

The sheriff obviously didn't appreciate that. His eyes became angry slits and his breath hissed from his nostrils like steam coming from a train's engine. But he didn't move to stop the gray-haired man as he walked toward the jailhouse door. When the deputy looked at him from his post, Manes signaled for him to let the gray-haired man pass. The deputy was only too happy to comply.

Even though he could tell the deputy

wasn't about to move against him, the gray-haired man stopped and leaned forward until he was practically nose-to-nose with the younger lawman.

"You're not gonna follow me, are you?" the gray-haired man asked.

Although the deputy did his best to try not to look scared, he wasn't doing well enough to fool anybody. "I've got plenty of better things to do."

Turning to look back toward the sheriff, the gray-haired man said, "You've got a fine bunch of men here. Real good at coming to when their master snaps his fingers."

"They'll do plenty more than that," Manes replied. "Be sure to keep your nose clean when you're in my town or you'll find that out for yourself."

"Oh, I'll be sure to keep that in mind." Before he stepped through the door that was now being held open for him, the gray-haired man snapped a fraction of a step toward the deputy. Just as he'd thought, that quick bit of movement was enough to cause the younger man to flinch back and nearly bump against the door frame. Laughing, the older man kept walking and stretched out his arms out as if to embrace the sunlight that washed over the length of his body.

"Shut that door," Manes snapped.

The deputy did as he was told, stepping inside before the latch fell into place. He took a quick look through the slot cut in the door and shook his head. "He's walking straight for Cavalry Avenue, Sheriff. Someone's bound to see him. Hell, they've probably already spotted him coming out of here."

Manes walked toward the front of the jailhouse, putting the single occupied cell behind him. "Let him go. He's the wanted man. It's his skin on the line."

"You sure you don't want me to follow him?"

Staring at the deputy for a moment, Manes smirked the same way a professional boxer would when a five-year-old took a swat at his arm. "If you're feeling brave enough, then by all means. Follow him all over town and tell me how many drinks he downed at Mil's. That's probably where he's headed anyway."

Nodding, the deputy said, "You're right. No need to follow him if he's just going to get liquored up some."

Sheriff Manes opened the jailhouse door and stepped out into the bright sunlight. Rich was standing by outside, glancing nervously between Manes and the direction of Cavalry Avenue.

"I know," Manes said before the other deputy could say anything. "I saw him leave." Looking over at Rich, he saw the deputy fidgeting even more than usual.

Rich was the only lawman who had worked in Jessup before Manes had taken office. Normally, Manes put up with him because the deputy was at least good for doing the shit work of a normal sheriff, while the rest of his deputies were more than content to follow orders. The way things were going, however, Manes wasn't much in the mood to put up with Rich's judgmental stares and beady little eyes.

"Tired of guard duty?"

Rich responded to the question with a lopsided nod. "Yeah, you might say that."

Placing his hand on Rich's slouched shoulder, Manes said, "Tell you what. You know that man that just stormed out here and headed toward Cavalry Avenue?"

"Yep."

"Why don't you follow him for me and keep me up to date on everything he does and everywhere he goes?"

Rich accepted the job with gusto, happy to be doing a real lawman's task for a change.

SIXTEEN

Callum followed Nick straight back to Eighth Street and the funeral parlor at the end of it. The stench of whiskey still hung around Nick's shoulders like a circling vulture, but there wasn't the slightest hint of the whiskey's influence in the way Nick walked or even talked. It seemed that he hadn't lied about his tolerance for the stuff. In fact, Nick was ready to get to work. He'd already shed his jacket and was rolling up his sleeves as he walked around to the funeral parlor's back door.

Callum's eyes drifted over to the front door and his hand went reflexively to the keys in his pocket when something popped into the front of his thoughts. "Oh, I nearly forgot to tell you," he called out to Nick's back. Waiting until the other man stopped and looked back at him, Callum said, "Catherine Weaver came by here earlier. She wanted to invite you to have lunch with her."

The expression on Nick's face reflected definite interest, but there was something else that kept him committed to the task at hand. "I'll catch up with her for dinner instead. I'm sure she'll understand, seeing as how busy we are."

"If you want to see her before then, it's fine with me. You shouldn't keep a pretty lady like that waiting for too long."

"And I shouldn't have kept you waiting so long either. I lost track of time when I should have been here doing my job. Let me put in a good day's work to make it up to you."

Callum grumbled slightly as he slid back into his professional frame of mind. "However you cut it, I'll be behind until all these folks are laid to rest. Whether you were at work bright and early this morning or not, there's only so much a man can do." Nodding toward his helper, the undertaker added, "Only so much two men can do, I meant to say."

Nick returned the nod and headed around to the back of the parlor. From there, he walked in through the workshop and headed straight for the little room Callum had set aside for him. The gun belt was the first to come off. The jacket was dropped onto the bed on top of the pistol, and finally he removed his shirt so he could change into a few fresh articles of clothing.

The sounds of wood being stacked and tools being moved greeted Nick's ears the moment he stepped back into the workshop. Callum rattled off a list of what needed to be done and then got busy attacking his own set of chores. With the scent of gunpowder still hanging in the back of his nostrils, Nick was more than ready to set his mind to some honest labor.

The afternoon passed into early evening, and not only had Nick finished building the coffins for Abe and Jimmy, he'd also carved Mrs. Eddings's marker and paid visits to Matthew Niedelander, the printer, as well as a few other merchants to pick up some supplies for the approaching wakes. The invitations for Mrs. Eddings were simple and elegant. Matthew had even printed up a few announcing the deputies' wake, which weren't the best but were legible. That seemed good enough, considering how apathetic the locals appeared to be when Nick mentioned any of the dead lawmen.

The sun was already dipping below the horizon and dinnertime was swiftly approaching. Nick pulled in a deep breath of autumnal air and detected the scent of cooking coming from one of the nearby homes. He knew The Porter House would be filling up soon and that Catherine was undoubtedly waiting for him. Of course, he hoped he wasn't just being overly optimistic in thinking she would understand why he hadn't shown up for lunch.

Women weren't as easy to read as drunkards sitting around a card table. The ones that affected him as much as Catherine were even tougher to get a handle on.

Rather than weigh himself down with even more mental knots that needed untying, Nick decided to just tend to the matters at hand and find out what Catherine thought of him by seeing her in person. Already, it seemed as though he'd gone for a year without looking at her, and he was anxious to set his eyes upon that pretty face again very soon.

Just picturing her bright, warm smile pushed the echoes of gunfire farther back into Nick's head. He hadn't forgotten about his promise to Jed or about his own business in Jessup, but as Callum had said not too long ago, there was only so much one man could do.

For the moment, Nick knew he needed to keep his eyes open and watch what happened once the deputies started poking their heads out from their holes again. After two of their number had been taken down, the lawmen were definitely scarce around town, and the locals seemed all the happier for that fact. Still, that didn't mean he was free to do what he pleased. Judging by the fact that he hadn't had an official run-in with the sheriff after all this time, Nick figured a storm was headed his way.

Crooked lawmen didn't just sit by while their deputies were killed. There was no doubt in Nick's mind that the sheriff was up to something. The fact that he couldn't see what it was made the approaching storm seem all the more powerful.

Like any animal, those lawmen would certainly make their presence known soon enough. If territory wasn't continually marked, it was lost. That fact held true whether the predators were pissing on trees or snarling at locals while flashing the guns on their hips. Nick knew better than to be too encouraged by the peaceful day.

The storm would arrive in its own time. Until it came, he would go about his job and keep his eyes open. All he had to do was wait like a hawk perched on a cliff, and the mice would show themselves soon enough.

After dropping off the other miscellaneous supplies back at Callum's parlor, Nick took the invitations to the Eddings wake over to the stables where his wagon and horses were being watched over by that eager, forgetful boy. The moment he stepped inside the stables, he heard Rasa and Kazys start to whinny and scrape the floor with their hooves. Both horses were in neighboring stalls at the back of the stable. Nick was pleased to see that his wagon was in the back as well, covered by a dirty tarp.

"Can I help you, mister?" came a scratchy voice from within the stables.

Nick paused for a moment since he was unable to see who'd just spoken. His eyes caught some movement nearby as a man stood up from where he'd been cleaning out one of the empty stalls. He was about six feet tall and had a solid build. A black beard with an ample amount of gray strands threaded through it covered a round face and an amiable smile.

"The boy that works here," Nick inquired, "are you his father?"

The man nodded and stepped out from the stall. He was wiping his hands with a rag, but used the side of his weathered coveralls to finish the job. "Sure am. I'm Dennis and my boy's name is Will. Did he do something wrong?"

"Oh not at all. I just came by to check on

my horses and see if he was interested in another bit of work."

Dennis eyed Nick carefully and cocked his head slightly to one side. "What kind of work are you talking about?"

Holding out the stack of Mrs. Eddings's invitations, Nick said, "Delivering these. It's nothing too big, but I thought the boy would like to earn some extra money. He seemed like the eager sort when he took my horses in."

"Them your horses?" Dennis asked, tilting his head back toward the stalls where Rasa and Kazys were fretting anxiously.

"They sure are."

"And that'd make you the fellow who had that run-in with Abe and Jed yesterday morning."

"Yes, it would."

Just when the conversation was getting even more uncomfortable, Dennis took a few steps closer to Nick and held out his hand. "Jed's a good friend of mine and I'd like to thank you for what you done."

Nick shook the other man's hand, but shrugged his shoulders when he said, "I didn't really do much."

"You didn't run away neither, and there's a lot to be said about that. Besides that, I heard some folks talking about what happened at Jed's house last night."

"What happened? Is he all right?"

Not only was it obvious that the stable-man was trying to fish around for informa-tion, but he also seemed to know a little something of his own. He apparently didn't know enough to verify or deny whatever rumors had been circulating, because he seemed confused by the well-practiced look of ignorance on Nick's face.

"You know what happened," Dennis said.

"I know another deputy was killed. Ter-rible business."

Scowling, Dennis cleared his throat and spat a juicy wad onto the straw by his feet. "Yeah. Real terrible."

"What about Jed?"

"He disappeared. Word is he and his kin got out with their hides, but other than that, nobody knows."

The stableman was lying. Nick was as certain of that as he was that the sky be-longed over his head. Fortunately, this was one of those rare times when he was glad to know someone was lying to him. It meant that news of the farmer's whereabouts wasn't common knowledge circulating among all the other gossips in town.

"I hope he's safe, wherever he is." And when Nick said that, he was telling the

God's honest truth. Anyone could have seen that.

Apparently, the stableman saw it clearly enough himself and his manner lightened up a bit. "Jed's a tough old bird. He'll do just fine. Now about that job you had for my boy?"

"Here's the invitations. There's a dollar in it for him if he'll —"

"Will!"

Dennis's voice echoed through the stables and rattled the brain inside of Nick's skull. Thankfully, the boy appeared at the stable doors before his father let out another holler like that one. The kid's head popped around the corner, quickly followed by the rest of him as he bolted inside and came to a stop right at his father's side.

"Yes, Pa?"

"This is the fella you were telling me about," Dennis said. "He's got a job for you."

"Really?"

Holding out the invitations, the stableman waited until they were all safely in his son's hands before continuing. "Deliver these to . . ." He paused and glanced back at Nick. "Who's supposed to get these?"

"Well, pretty much everyone in town."

"You heard the man. Deliver these to

everyone in town and do it quickly. Job pays a dollar, so if you do it well enough, you can keep half of it for yourself and the rest will go toward the rest of the family."

If the boy was disappointed with not being able to keep the whole dollar for himself, he gave no indication. Instead, he held on to the invitations tightly and thought about where he would start delivering them. Smiling proudly, he took out one invitation from the stack and handed it up to Nick.

"Thanks," Nick said, accepting the piece of paper, folding it and then tucking it into a pocket.

Dennis stood looking at his son as if he expected him to do a trick. There wasn't any anger or discipline in the stare, but there definitely was something else beyond just a casual glance. The boy sensed it too and took a moment to try and figure out what he was supposed to do. Finally, he grinned and handed an invitation up to his father.

"Will, didn't you say you had to tell something to this man here?" Dennis asked while taking the invitation from his son's waiting hand.

The boy thought about it for another long couple of seconds before his entire face lit up once again. "Oh yeah! I have to tell you something, mister!"

In a strange kind of way, watching the kid go through his thought process was the most fun Nick had had in some time. "What did you need to tell me, Will?"

"You said to —" The boy cut himself off in mid-stride so he could shoot a loaded glance toward his father.

Getting the hint, Dennis threw his hands in the air and started walking toward the stable doors. "Fine. Just be sure to say what you need to say and finish your supper before doing anything else tonight." And with that, he left Nick and his son in the stables.

Will took another look around before saying, "You said to let you know if anyone came around asking about those horses."

Suddenly, Nick's amusement came to a halt. "I did."

"Well there was a man who came around here. He looked at the horses and then asked about you too."

"Do you know who it was?"

Will nodded. "It was Mr. Callum, the undertaker."

Nick let out the breath he'd been holding. "That's all right. He was just looking for me when I showed up late for work."

"Well . . . you said you'd pay me extra if I

told you about anyone asking about those horses."

"So I did." Nick started reaching into his pocket for some more money.

"I just remembered. There was another man asking about you."

At first Nick thought Will might have just been fishing for some extra payment. He knew that wasn't the case when the boy described the other man. He handed over some coins and thought about this turn of events.

"I can point him out to you if I see him, mister."

Nick's head snapped around to look directly into Will's face. "No. If he comes around again, you go straight to your pa, understand?"

"Is he a bad man?"

"Yes," Nick said without hesitation. "Yes he is."

SEVENTEEN

It wasn't very late, but the sun was already gone from the western sky. Nick looked at the horizon, which still had a few dark purple and orange smudges that were the last of the daylight. He always liked the autumn months because of the short days and cooler temperatures. Things always seemed better during that time of the year. In fact, he had savored cloudy days or even nighttime all the way back to his childhood.

"Why do you smile so much in the dark, *sunus*?" his father had always asked him.

Nick used the same answer the first time he'd heard that question and every time after that. "Because, Tevai, I like to look up at the sky and not have it hurt."

Stasys had gazed upward at the stars, reflexively squinting. But without the sun being there to burn his eyes and blur his vision, there was no need for precaution. It didn't hurt and he could stare at the heavens for hours on end. "You were always a smart boy, *sunus*. Always smarter than me."

Thinking back on those nights, Nick found himself looking up at the stars and feeling as though his father was still right beside him. But the only thing he had of Stasys at the moment was the older man's memory. As always, he cherished that memory for as long as he could before being forced to pay attention to the outside world once again.

He caught himself staring up at the sky a little too much while walking toward The Porter House. Someone headed in the opposite direction almost bumped into him and nearly lost his center of gravity when trying to compensate.

"Sorry about that," Nick said while reaching out to help steady the other man.

The local was about to say something else when he spotted the gun belt strapped around Nick's waist. Although his jacket had covered most of the weapon, the extension of his arm had opened it wide enough to reveal the pistol.

"My fault," the local responded quickly. "Sorry. I wasn't looking." And with that, he was already on his way. Each step was quicker than the last, until there was a good twenty yards between him and Nick.

Close enough to smell the familiar scents of The Porter House, Nick straightened his jacket so it hung properly once again and walked up to the restaurant's front door. The place seemed just as busy as it had the night before, with the only difference being that he didn't see Catherine right away.

Nick walked inside and took a look around. The main room might have been packed full of people, but Catherine had a way of standing out in a crowd. At least, she stood out very well in Nick's eyes. He waited until she turned toward him before giving her a smile and wave.

She moved through the crowd, dodging servers and wayward chairs and elbows like an expert rider navigating a slalom course. All the while, her eyes never left his and the smile got brighter as she approached him.

"Good lord," she said with an exaggerated gasp for air. "You always pick the busiest times to show up here."

"If it's a bad time, I can always —"

"No, no. Don't be silly. I'm just glad to see you at all."

"Mr. Callum told me you stopped by today, but we've been pretty busy over there as well."

"I know. The funeral for Mrs. Eddings is tomorrow. You just missed the boy delivering the invitations. Plus . . . well . . . all the other messes I'm sure you have to clean up."

He nodded and stepped sideways to avoid getting run over by a small child racing inside to dash over to a nearby table. "Still, I wish I could have let you know I wouldn't be here until supper."

"Well, now is all that matters," she said while reaching out to take hold of Nick's hand. "Come on. I've got a table waiting for us someplace we can sit and talk without all these distractions. It's time for me to take a breather anyhow."

Even though she was holding his left hand, which was only short by half of one finger, Nick still felt very conscious of the injury, which was already nearly a decade old. Catherine didn't seem to notice, however, and even squeezed his hand a little tighter once she'd taken him to a table set up in the back of the kitchen and away from the restaurant workers scurrying about their duties.

"It's not the fanciest table in the place," she said. "But nobody will bother us."

Nick pulled out one of the two chairs for Catherine. The battered little table was probably only used for cooks and servers to grab a quick bite for themselves. From the formal way they seated themselves, one might have thought that Nick and Catherine had put in a reservation.

That formal facade was dented somewhat when Catherine shouted their order to the closest cook and then batted her eyelashes at Nick as though she was the belle of the ball. The cook laughed at them both and got started on their food right away, putting their order ahead of several other customers.

"So what have you been up to lately?" she asked.

Nick watched her for a moment and smirked. "Why do I get the impression that you already know part of the answer to that question?"

"Only part? Maybe you're underestimating me."

"Maybe, but I doubt it."

The truth of the matter was that if she knew all of what he'd been doing, Nick figured Catherine wouldn't have wanted to be with him at all. And there was no way in hell she'd want to be anywhere vaguely private. Her warm expression and welcoming eyes told him that she did want to be with him and didn't mind being secluded one bit.

"So you came all the way to Jessup because Mr. Callum needed a helper?"

"Mainly, yes. There's not a big call for men in my line of work."

"I would think every town would need someone like you. Everybody dies, right?"

"That's what I've been told."

She cringed and laughed a little at herself. "You know what I mean. I'd bet that you could find work anywhere."

"Most towns need an undertaker, but most towns also already have someone that's been doing that work for years. It's not the type of job everyone's after, and the folks who know the trade stay in it. Just like any other profession, I guess."

"That makes sense. Tell you the truth, I've never really thought about it until now."

"Most folks would rather not think about it," Nick said. "Especially when they're about to eat."

"You must think I'm so crude."

"Not at all, Catherine." He reached out to put his right hand on top of hers, but paused and pulled back a bit, as though he'd forgotten about the mangled fingers.

Before he could pull his hand back under the table, Nick saw Catherine reach out for it and hold it inside her own smooth, soft fingers.

"You're a gunfighter, aren't you?" she

asked. "Or at least, you used to be. Am I right?"

Nick know he should have felt tense, hearing that particular question. It wasn't the first time it had been asked and it certainly wouldn't be the last. What set this time aside from the others, however, was that his defenses didn't go up and the normal double talk didn't come out of his mouth.

"Why do you think that?" he asked.

Her fingers traced lightly over the scarred remains of Nick's right ring and middle fingers. Although he couldn't feel her touch as well in the more damaged areas, he could tell she was trying to be gentle. The look in her eyes was one of simple curiosity and nothing more.

"There's a lot of old farmers in this town, Nick. You don't have to be a doctor to see people missing fingers or worse. My brother is a farmer and he lost some toes to a plow. I knew a man who got some fingers cut off by an axe. Yours look like they were picked off one by one. Maybe even shot off."

"Did you get all that from looking at my hands?"

"Not all of it." She let him hang for a moment before blushing and leaning back. "Farmers don't usually wear guns either. That kind of gave you away more than anything else."

"Plenty of people wear guns. And this one here," Nick added while removing his jacket and draping it over the back of his chair, "is just some piece of junk that I got for a good price."

"And why do you wear it to dinner?"

"Because a lot of folks are getting shot around here. It's better for a man to be safe than sorry."

Most of that was the truth. What little bits and pieces Nick kept to himself were hidden for a reason. Besides, there was no need to tell Catherine too much, seeing as how this was only their second real meeting. Nick felt his old defenses rising up, and he couldn't say for sure if having them there was a good or bad thing. For him, it was the only thing.

"Our food should be ready pretty quickly," she told him. "Have you had a chance to talk with our esteemed sheriff?" The last two words of her question were dripping with so much sarcasm that Nick thought they would leave a bitter aftertaste in Catherine's mouth.

"Actually, I haven't."

"You shouldn't feel too left out, because I heard he would be coming by here sometime tonight."

Nick tensed, but didn't show any outward trace of what he was thinking or feeling. "Really?" he asked, as though he almost didn't care. "Is that why you made sure we sat back here?"

"Not at all. I just wanted to get you to myself for a while so I could ask some uncomfortable questions and see how you'd respond. I thought you'd be more open to talking about something apart from the weather if we didn't have an audience."

"I'm not exactly used to having someone want to hear what I have to say."

"Well, it's not often that someone says something worth hearing. I hope you don't mind me bringing you back here and ambushing you like this."

"Mind? I'd have to be dead to mind a woman like you wanting me all to herself. Unfortunately, the sheriff might want to get me alone as well. Like, in a jail cell."

She shook her head and pushed away from the table as one of the cooks called out that their food was ready. "You won't go to jail," Catherine told him once she'd gotten the plates and set them onto the table. "I already told you about that."

"Yeah, right. There's supposed to be someone else in there. I guess I'll find out for myself once the sheriff comes for me."

"That won't be for a while. This place would have to be on fire for him or any of his dogs to poke their noses in here any time before seven. Except for Rich, that is. He keeps regular hours." From there, the conversation switched to a more casual track. Between bites of tender steak and baked potato, they talked about such mundane things as family histories and the approaching winter. Although the small talk would have been considered banal by anyone else's standards, Nick was glad to hear every word. He didn't get many normal dinners complete with normal conversations anymore. Besides that, Catherine had a way of making every story funny, and when their eyes met, there was a definite sparkle that each of them could see.

The food disappeared quickly, even with both of them filling the time with chatter. Before long, Catherine was getting up and clearing the table.

"You want any dessert?" she asked. "We've got some great apple pie."

"Now that's spoken like a true hostess," Nick said, leaning back from the table and patting his stomach.

Shaking her head, Catherine replied, "On the contrary. All my servers are selling the pumpkin pie because I've got a bunch of them about to spoil. The apple is the good stuff," she added with a wink. "You'd like it."

"Then how could I refuse?"

Catherine turned and walked to another area of the kitchen just as the door to the dining room flew open. One of the servers, a young woman with a troubled look on her face, took a quick look around and then headed straight for Catherine. Both women had a quick conversation, punctuated by frequent frantic gestures on the server's part. Finally, Catherine said something to calm the girl and sent her back into the dining room.

Walking back to the table, she said, "The sheriff's here, Nick. He insisted on talking to you."

"He knows I'm here?"

"It looks that way. I could always go out there and —"

"No," Nick interrupted. "You stay here. I don't want any trouble here in your place, so I'll do my best to get him to go outside."

Nick stood up, and Catherine moved close enough for him to feel the warmth of her body against his own. Her hands slid around his waist and moved up along the middle of his back. Once she could slip her fingers through his hair, she pulled his face down close so she could kiss him gently on the lips.

Even after the kiss was done, Nick could still taste her and could still feel the soft press of her flesh against his mouth.

"Be careful," she whispered.

As much as he wanted to stay there with her, Nick stepped back, got his jacket and slipped it on. She moved with him toward the door leading to the dining room, where he stopped, put his hand on her waist and pulled her in close to him for one more kiss, which lingered much longer than the first.

EIGHTEEN

Nick had to check his watch as he walked out of the kitchen and into the dining room. It felt more like he was going into the fire after having skipped the frying pan altogether. His meal had been so nice, in fact, that it had lasted the better part of two hours.

The dented little watch in his pocket said it was a quarter after seven, meaning that the lawmen were running right on the schedule that Catherine had mentioned. He had stepped into the dining room with his hat in hand, making him appear humble and cowed to put the sheriff at ease. Judging by the confident smiles he saw at the lawmen's table, his disguise was working.

Manes got up and motioned toward the only empty seat at his table, which was wedged in between two of his men. "Come on over here and take a load off."

Nick didn't recognize either of the deputies. He did, however, spot right away that they were armed. They were both about the same age, which put them somewhere in their late twenties. One of them wore a mustache to cover the way his upper lip came up over his teeth as though it was attached to a string. The second deputy had hair the color of straw, which was combed neatly and cut just over his ears. Both of them let their hands drift toward their guns as Nick walked up and stood behind the chair he'd been offered.

"If it's all the same to you, Sheriff," Nick said humbly, "I'd rather stand."

Manes didn't take his eyes away from Nick as his smile seemed to melt off his face. That false geniality was replaced by an expression that was all business. "Well, it isn't the same to me, boy. Take a seat and listen. I've got some things I want to say to you."

The sheriff spoke like a man used to getting his own way. When he called Nick "boy," he did so as if purposely needling him. His lips curled around every word, like he was spitting them into Nick's face, and when he didn't get a punch thrown at him, Manes actually seemed disappointed.

Nick swallowed what he truly wanted to say to the lawman and nodded instead while lowering himself onto the chair between the deputies. "All right, then. I take it this has something to do with what happened yesterday morning."

Once Nick was seated, Manes sat down again as well. Neither he nor his deputies said anything. Instead, they watched intently while Nick pretended to squirm.

"That deputy that was shot by the farmer when I was coming into town," Nick went on to say. "Is that what this is about?"

A basket of biscuits was sitting in the middle of the table. Manes snagged one, pulled it apart, and shoved a piece of it into his mouth. Nodding as he chewed, he finally responded, "Yeah. That's what this is about. That and other things that have been brought to my attention."

"I was going to pay you a visit on my own, but —"

"Yeah, I'll just bet you were," the harelipped deputy interrupted. Sounding out the B in the word "bet" was an effort for the younger man and caused him to spit when he talked.

Nick ignored the deputy's words as well as the spray that accompanied them and picked up where he'd been cut off. "But I've been very busy. I'm working for Dan Callum, the undertaker."

"I know who he is," Manes said sharply. "Two of my best men are laying stretched out on that grave digger's table right now."

"Mr. Callum is cleaning them up and seeing to their final arrangements," Nick said, feeling the edges of his humble act starting to fray. Meeting the sheriff's glare with one of his own, Nick put a cold edge into his voice when he added, "I'm the one that'll be digging their graves."

The sheriff didn't have any trouble catching the challenge buried in that simple statement. Although what Nick had said was true enough, there was still something in his eyes that was meant to act like a steel hook digging into Manes's open wound.

It worked.

Setting the rest of his biscuit aside, Manes placed both of his hands flat upon the table and kept them there. The tips of his fingers curled in as if they were forming claws, which scraped along the surface of the wood. His jaw muscles clenched and jumped beneath his skin.

"So tell me," Manes said, barely hiding the raw aggression he was feeling, "why shouldn't I just drag you out of here and string you up by your worthless neck?"

"Because riding into town isn't a crime," Nick answered. "And the only one who committed a crime was that deputy. He meant to rob me and hurt that farmer."

"And why would he do that?"

Nick shrugged. "How would I know? But I was there and saw what happened better than anyone else."

"Not better than Jed Arvey. He was there too, with a shotgun in his hands."

"Yes he was. Why don't you ask him about it? I'm afraid I don't have much else to add to the story." Nick's poker face was on securely and didn't leave enough of an expression for anyone to read. All the while, he studied the sheriff closely, especially when the lawman was about to talk about Jed.

"He's gone," Manes replied. "Disappeared. Probably on the run."

Nick would have bet good money that the sheriff was telling the truth. After seeing that, it was a real effort to keep the smile from coming onto his face.

The sheriff nodded, maintaining his own hardened expression fairly well now that his initial anger was receding. "So I guess that just leaves you to answer for Abe's murder. By the way . . . where were you last night?"

"Working. You can ask Mr. Callum if you don't believe me."

"No need for that. My guess is that he'll

lie for you no matter what I ask."

"He's got no reason to."

"Perhaps," Manes said, in a tone that was drifting further from the control he was trying to exert over it. "And what if I told him who you really were? What do you think he'd have to say then?"

Nick didn't flinch.

Inside, however, he was racing to pin down if he knew this lawman from somewhere else. Although Manes talked as though he had some vital piece of information, Nick couldn't decide if that was real or some kind of bluff. The possibility was just as strong either way, and he wasn't about to put his money on one or the other.

Sheriff Manes was obviously enjoying what he was doing. Sensing the discomfort within Nick, he leaned forward, tipping the table a bit more toward himself. "You came to fetch that fella that came into my town a month ago. Tell me that isn't so."

Nick said nothing.

"I'd wager that you're the one that's supposed to meet up with him, so that would make you that killer from Montana. I heard plenty about you, all right."

There was no reason in playing a part any longer. The sheriff did know something. Nick had seen enough within his eyes to be sure of that now.

Tilting his head to one side, Nick's entire expression changed. The false innocence was gone, and there was enough intensity to cause both deputies to slide away from him and move their hands toward their guns one more time. "You like doing all the talking," he said. "So you can tell me what you've heard about me. I'll bet it's only half the truth, whatever it is."

"Oh yeah? What makes you think that?"

"Because if you knew the whole truth, you'd know better than to keep digging at me like this."

"Ooooh, now I guess we're all supposed to be scared?" It was the first time the blond deputy had spoken. After the look he got from Nick in return, it would be a while before he'd speak again.

The sheriff sat back in his chair. As he dragged his hands over the table, his palms made a dry scratching sound, like wood being sanded down. "So what business did you have with that fella you're looking for? Was he a partner? He owe you money? Did he fuck your sister?"

But Nick was beyond being pushed by simple profanities. He returned the lawman's glare without any further emotion. His eyes were like balls of lead that had been wedged into his skull. They reflected nothing. They felt nothing. They gave away nothing, yet they seemed to see all.

"Where is he?" Nick asked. "Your jailhouse?"

"Oh you know about that, huh? Well, he isn't in there. If you want to check for yourself, I can arrange it."

Nick shifted his eyes from one of the deputies to the other. He could tell both men were just waiting for the word from Manes before they moved in on him.

"Now what have you got there?" Manes asked, his eyes focused intently on Nick's gun. The longer he stared at the weapon's handle protruding from the top of its holster, the more intrigued he appeared. "Let's have a look at that."

Without needing to hear another word, both deputies lurched into motion. The harelipped one reached down to remove the gun from Nick's holster while the blond one took hold of his own sidearm to cover his partner's play. Rather than appearing nervous, both deputies actually seemed anxious for Nick to give them a reason to fight. Judging by the look in their eyes, any reason at all would have sufficed.

Nick allowed himself to smirk when he looked at those two. "Youth," he thought while shaking his head.

Instead of giving either deputy what they wanted, he allowed one to look tough while the other took his gun from his holster. Even after they'd disarmed him, the younger lawmen paused for a few moments, as if thinking the task couldn't have gone off so easily.

It was hard for Nick to tell if the deputy who took his gun was snarling or if it was just the deformity in his lip making it look that way. As soon as the man saw that he wouldn't meet any resistance, he smiled crookedly and placed Nick's pistol on the table.

"Here you go, Sheriff," he said proudly.

The blond one smiled as well, beaming as though he'd actually done something worth bragging about.

For all of the deputies' posturing and smug expressions, Sheriff Manes hardly seemed to notice a thing. He only looked away from Nick once he heard the gun clunk onto the table. The deputies might as well have been shirts stuffed with cotton and propped up in the seats for all the attention he paid them.

Then, looking down at the gun his deputy had taken, Manes seemed genuinely perplexed. "What the hell is that?" he asked, reaching out to take hold of the weapon the way someone might try to pick up a dead animal before moving it out of sight. Although his hand went instinctively toward the gun's grip, he only gripped it with his thumb and two fingers. His other hand came forward to take hold of the barrel, which appeared somewhat more familiar to the lawman.

Manes shook his head as he put the gun's cylinder in the palm of one hand and lifted the whole thing up closer to his eyes without touching the barrel at all. The longer he looked at it, the more he shook his head. Overall, he seemed like a disappointed teacher going over something a dimwitted student had turned in.

Looking up at Nick, the sheriff repeated, "What is this?"

"That's about all I could afford. I don't even really know why I keep it around. If I didn't travel so much, I'd probably just sell it to a junk dealer."

"That why you're carrying it with you tonight?"

Shrugging, Nick said, "This is a tougher town than I thought it would be. If there's a law against being armed in certain places or times, I didn't know about it."

But Manes appeared to only be half listening. Nick's gun was still doing a good job of holding most of his attention. "Is this a Schofield?"

Nick nodded. "Started out as one. At least, I think the firing mechanism did. The barrel is from another model than the cylinder, though. It might have been damaged somewhere along the road."

"It looks like it got run over by a team of mules," the blond deputy said.

Oddly enough, the younger lawman wasn't too far off. Even to the untrained eye, the barrel of the pistol was obviously not in its original condition. There were grooves that ran along its length, turning in a spiral that ended at the tip. Overall, the barrel looked as if it had been melted down and sloppily twisted into something vaguely resembling what any other gun should look like. There was no sight at the end of the barrel. Instead, there was just a smooth patch along the top of the twisted metal that looked as if some kind of animal had chewed off the sight and continued gnawing on the steel.

Sheriff Manes turned the gun so he could take a closer look at the cylinder and hammer. Compared to the rest of the piece, those two things were the most normal looking parts of the entire gun. The hammer didn't protrude like most Schofield models, which told him that it could have been filed down. Upon closer inspection, Manes saw that the hammer wasn't even the original, and was instead something that had been fitted into the mechanism later on.

The cylinder itself could have come from anywhere, but Manes guessed it was a part of the original Schofield. The trigger, its guard, and a few other bits and pieces looked familiar, but seemed out of place where they were. "Did some of these parts come from a Colt?"

Once again, Nick put on the expression of someone who'd been asked to explain how a steam engine worked when they'd never even seen a train. "Maybe. I just know it was fitted together from other pieces. That's why I got it so cheap."

Manes was becoming more comfortable with the gun in his hand. In fact, he held it like he would a child's toy. The confused smile on his face truly blossomed when he tried to take hold of the grip and put his finger on the trigger. The gun's handle was a gnarled mess of wood that twisted and turned in a way more like an old root.

Instead of flaring out to the traditional shape of a pistol's grip that was made to fit in a man's hand, the handle of Nick's gun tapered down almost to a point, which looked like the tip of a cane when protruding from the top of his holster. Manes started to laugh when he tried to hold the gun using that handle and could barely get his finger through the trigger guard without accidentally firing off a shot.

"Now this is one sorry excuse for a weapon," he said, sounding like a disapproving Army officer. "Let's see what you think." And with that, he tossed the gun through the air toward Nick.

Both deputies jumped back in surprise and tensed themselves to be ready for whatever happened once that gun found its way back to its owner.

Nick reached out his right hand and barely caught the weapon before it bounced onto his chest. His gnarled fingers had trouble getting a firm hold of it, but finally did manage to find some sort of purchase on the twisted handle. Once he had the gun, he looked at the sheriff with a mix of anger and embarrassment.

"I guess you do what you can with whatever you got left, huh?" Manes asked.

Nick's expression left embarrassment behind and turned fully into anger. "Yeah. Something like that."

"One of you two take that gun away from

him," Manes ordered his deputies. "It may be a chunk of shit, but it can still fire live rounds, and I want to finish my talk with this fellow without a distraction like that close at hand."

"Yessir," the blond deputy replied before reaching over and roughly pulling the gun out of Nick's grasp. Nick reflexively tightened his grip around the gun's handle, but all it took was a twist of the younger deputy's wrist to pull the gun through the gap left by Nick's missing fingers.

Holding out the gun to Manes, the deputy asked, "You want to keep this?"

Manes didn't take his eyes away from Nick when he answered, "I'd rather dig a turd out of your ass than touch that sorry excuse for a gun again. You keep hold of it and make sure he don't get it until we're through talking."

When the sheriff and both his men got up from their seats, Nick glanced at each of them in turn. "Where are you going?"

"We're all going outside for a bit, and you're coming with us. Like I said, I'm not done talking to you yet." Looking around at the other customers in the place, Manes tipped his hat to them. He then turned toward the kitchen and tipped his hat that way as well. "He won't be long, ma'am."

Nick saw that Manes had said that last part to Catherine, who was standing in the kitchen doorway, nervously wringing her hands. The way she watched the lawmen lead Nick out of her restaurant, it was plain to see that she didn't like it one bit.

Unfortunately, Nick was feeling the same way.

NINETEEN

Sheriff Manes didn't say a word as he led the other three men to the door. Nick was forced to walk behind the sheriff, with the deputies taking up escorting positions around him. Harelip was to Nick's right and Blondie brought up the rear. The entire restaurant seemed quiet as a grave, with each set of eyes in the place fixed on the little convoy that stepped outside into the darkening evening.

Nick didn't much care about any of those watching him except for one set of eyes that seemed wide as saucers. Catherine had started to walk outside behind them but stopped when she caught a stern warning glare from Nick. Even then she looked ready to defy him and follow him outside anyway. Only the nervous questions that came from the customers after the last deputy had left the restaurant kept her from stepping out.

With the slam of the door still echoing

ominously in her ears, Catherine turned back and tried to calm down the diners. She assured them everything would be just fine, even though she didn't believe a word of it.

Thinking about it made her wonder if there was anything she could do to help or if it was too late to save Nick at all.

The door slammed behind them with a solid sense of finality. Although Nick had been fairly certain he would have to confront the sheriff face-to-face, he didn't think the man would drag him out into the street and shoot him like a dog. With Manes's back to him, it was difficult to tell what he was thinking. For the moment, however, Nick figured there still was something the other man wanted to say or do. If killing him was the sheriff's main concern, he certainly could have done it before now.

Manes strode to the space directly between The Porter House and its neighbor. The alleyway was just wide enough for Nick and the deputy assigned to him to keep walking side by side. Once he emerged from the alley, Manes took about three more paces before stopping and spinning around sharply on the balls of his feet.

"Bring him right here," he ordered. "Right in front of me."

251

Manes waited until his deputies had pushed and shoved Nick into the designated spot. When he spoke again, he looked directly into Nick's eyes, using a menacing tone that wasn't anything like the voice Nick had heard in the restaurant.

"This is better," Manes said. "Out here we can have some fresh air and don't need to worry about anyone listening in on what we have to say."

Playing up the fear that he was supposed to be feeling, Nick put just enough of a waver in his voice to appease the lawmen. "Those people back there saw where you were taking me."

Blondie gave Nick's back a rough push as he stepped around to where he could be seen. "So? It don't matter who the hell saw you. They won't say shit because they know they might not see you again."

Despite the fact that Harelip seemed to find that hilarious, Manes merely leveled his stare and watched every move Nick made.

"What my deputy is trying to tell you is that folks around here don't know you. They know me, and I'm the one that's been running this town for a good while before you got here. I'm the one they trust to keep the streets clear of scum like you, and I'm the one they pay to keep doing that."

"You pay your deputies to rob people just trying to pass through?"

"My deputies do whatever the hell they want. If they get out of line, then I'm the one who handles it. So unless I say so, my deputies can do no wrong. Everyone around here knows that and they don't have much of a problem."

"Sounds like they don't have much choice," Nick retorted.

"They've got a choice, all right. They can do what I say or they can pay the price. If they keep their noses clean, there's no problem anyway."

"I'm working an honest job," Nick said. "Ask Mr. Callum, if you don't believe me."

"I believe you about that. But I've also heard some things about you that I don't like too much. Things like you killed upward of half a dozen men in Montana and that you were a bloodthirsty monster that can't even show his face to a lawman out of fear of being recognized."

"Who told you this?" Nick asked.

"Why? Am I hitting a bit too close to the mark?"

"If I'm to be accused of something, I should have the right to know who's doing the accusing."

Manes stepped forward so quickly that it was surprising he didn't butt heads with Nick before he stopped. The sheriff's face had lost all trace of civility, and his teeth were bared like an animal when he spoke. "I'm the one accusing you! Me! That means I'm the only one you have to worry about."

Now that he was close enough to stare straight into Nick's eyes and down into his soul, Manes didn't follow through with another threat. Instead, he studied the face in front of him, carefully soaking up every last detail. Taking a step back, he was nodding as he reached into the inner pocket of his jacket and removed a folded piece of thick, yellowed paper.

Slowly, he unfolded the paper and studied it, his eyes darting back and forth between that and Nick's face. "Yeah," he said finally. "I can see the resemblance." The sheriff turned the paper around to reveal the very thing that Nick hoped he wouldn't see way out in the prairies of Jessup, Nebraska.

The wanted poster wasn't the same kind as those put out by the Union Pacific for train robbers and such, but it had the one element that usually caught the most attention. Across the top, printed in large block letters, was the word reward. Below that was a drawing of a younger, more fresh-faced man, but it was most definitely the man who called himself Nick Graves.

"That's you," Manes said with a laugh. "It looks to me like you've been chewed up and spit out since then, but this sure as hell is you, isn't it?"

Nick didn't answer.

"What do you think?" he asked, turning the notice so Blondie and Harelip could see it. "Do you think this could be him?"

"Hell yes, Sheriff," Harelip answered, without bothering to take more than a passing glance at the sketch on the old notice. "I'll bet that reward's still good too."

Nick heard the sound of boots crunching against gravel approaching from behind. The sheriff's eyes darted in that direction, looking past Nick until he saw something that made him smile. Both deputies took a quick glance for themselves, but seemed to be more on guard after having gotten a look at that poster.

"Sure it's still good," whoever had made the newest set of footsteps said. "Not only that, but the price may have even gone up a bit over the years."

At first Nick had been too occupied with the lawmen to pay special attention to this new arrival. When he'd heard the steps coming up behind him, he figured it was just

255

another deputy or two coming over to watch the show. But with the last couple of words, Nick had heard enough to draw his interest.

He recognized that voice. He just couldn't quite believe he was hearing it.

"Didn't I tell you, Sheriff? This here ain't just some grave digger. He's a goddamn gold mine on two legs."

All three lawmen chuckled at that, although the deputies still didn't seem quite at ease.

If Nick had had any doubts about who was speaking, they were gone now. He let out a breath. "I never thought I'd live to see the day when you'd be working with a lawman, Skinner."

The gray-haired man who'd been sleeping in Jessup's jailhouse stepped around so he could be seen by everyone in the back of that alley. His face seemed less leathery in the dark and more like the visage of an animal. That image only intensified when he smiled and his mouth took on the wide, toothy expression of a hungry wolf.

"Hey there, Nick. Even someone as thick-headed as you should know that these boys ain't the law. There ain't no law. This here's an open town. Just like in Montana." Staring intently into Nick's eyes, the man named Skinner said, "Why don't you boys take hold of my old friend here? I'd like to say howdy."

One nod from Manes was all it took for Blondie and Harelip to each grab one of Nick's arms. They pulled in opposite directions, stretching his body taut.

Skinner walked around the sheriff, massaging his knuckles and savoring every moment. "You see, Nick, what I have here is an arrangement with Sheriff Manes. The circumstances aren't the best, but I've been making the best of them for a while."

"You still on the run?" Nick asked.

Skinner shrugged. "Yeah, well you know all about that, don't ya? I'd say I've been more comfortable than you or those others that made it out of Montana. I told you to stick with me and you'd be taken care of, but you never listened."

Without so much as a flinch or change of expression, Skinner tightened his fist and sent it stabbing straight out until it slammed into Nick's midsection. His bony knuckles were knotted and callused after years of fighting in saloons.

Nick felt the punch plow straight into his innards, pushing all the breath from his lungs and replacing it with pain. If the deputies hadn't been holding him up, he would have dropped to the ground as his knees buckled beneath him and a wave of nausea threatened to spill his dinner onto the ground. Nick hadn't seen the punch coming. Skinner always did have a damn good poker face.

Nick squeezed his eyes shut and shook his head to air it out a bit. When he opened his eyes again, Skinner was looking straight at him.

"Damn, Nick. It feels like it's been a coon's age since I saw you last."

Knowing Skinner the way he did allowed Nick to tense before the next punch came. Even so, he was barely able to prepare himself before the man with the steely gray hair twisted sharply at the waist and placed a stiff uppercut just a bit lower than the first.

This time his punch caught Nick square in the stomach, making it impossible for him to choke back the vomit that had risen up after the previous impact. His body convulsed in the deputies' arms, and when he opened his mouth, a foul stream came spilling out and drenched the ground at his feet.

Hopping back just in time to avoid the splatter, Skinner put an arm around Sheriff Manes and leaned on him like they were both old drinking buddies. "I don't know what happened to him, Sheriff. He used to be able to stand up to a lot more than this back when we used to raise hell together. Maybe this isn't ol' Nick Graves after all."

Skinner stepped up close to Nick and stood right in front of him. Placing the edge of his left hand under Nick's chin, he lifted it up until he had Nick looking toward the stars. With a distasteful scowl, Skinner said, "Nah. That's him all right. He's got his pappy's big fuckin' nose."

It was as though Skinner was calling his shot in a marksman contest. Even though he could see it coming, Nick didn't have the time or the leverage to brace himself before Skinner's hamlike fist came crashing into the middle of his face.

Nick's entire head filled with the sound of bone pounding against bone and the wet snap of breaking cartilage. Blood welled up into his sinuses just like the puke that had welled up from his gullet, spilling out much the same way in an uncontrollable rush. He coughed up a breath as the bottom half of his face became slick with warm fluid that gave off a coppery reek.

Watching with wide, happy eyes, Skinner shook his hand and wiggled his fingers in a cruel mockery of the pain he'd given to Nick. "Oh, I just know that one hurt."

The deputies tightened their grip on Nick

when he begun to struggle and they felt his arms slipping out of their grasp. Both of them planted their feet solidly against the ground and dug their fingers into his arms as he bucked and pulled against them.

As pain washed through his skull and torso again and again, Nick managed to push it back down. He stopped struggling, concentrated on breathing through his mouth, and managed to pull enough air back into his lungs to clear his blurring vision. As he'd expected, Skinner was still there . . . watching.

"What took you so long to get here, kid?" Skinner asked. "I been waiting around in this shithole town wondering if you'd ever show."

"I just came here to work," Nick said before spitting out a mixture of spit and blood that tasted like a dirty penny. "I'm moving on with my life."

"Yeah. I am too. Only men like us don't just move on. It ain't that easy. Not after what we been through." Tilting his head to one side, Skinner looked at the hand dangling from Harelip's grasp. He reached out and twisted that hand until he got a good look at Nick's damaged fingers. "Especially you, boy. There ain't no way in hell you could go through this and just move on. But then again, it ain't exactly like you can be the way you were either."

Memories flashed through Nick's head. They were more like nightmares that didn't wait for him to sleep before ravaging his mind. Not only could he see and hear the visions, but he could feel them as well. He could see the flashes of gunfire, hear the laughing and taunting, feel the blinding pain as his fingers were picked off one at a time like bottles from a fence post.

Those memories hung in his brain, just behind his eyes, blurring his senses momentarily as Skinner watched and drew back his hand one more time. In a way, Nick was grateful to those memories. Their familiar agony dulled the pain of Skinner's fists being driven into his sides, cracking ribs and stealing even more of Nick's breath.

"Ease off there," Sheriff Manes said, laying a hand on Skinner's shoulder. "We'll be able to get more money for this one if he's alive."

Skinner pulled away from the lawman's touch as though it burned him. "Take yer fuckin' hand off me! Whoever's offering that reward won't give a shit if he's alive or dead. Besides, if it wasn't for me tellin' you, there's no way you'd even know who he is. You'll get yer payment. This here's mine."

"I'm still the law around here, and you'll do what I say."

Reeling around to face the sheriff directly, Skinner stared Manes down and stepped up until he was standing toe-to-toe with the other man. He was sweating from the labor of pummeling Nick and his knuckles were dripping with blood. "You're gonna turn this into a pissing contest now? I scout this town out in one afternoon, find this here wanted man hiding right under your nose, show you how to get rich off his hide, and now you want to start slinging orders?"

Sheriff Manes had been watching intently and taking everything in, waiting for his moment. Now that he'd decided to assert himself, he wasn't about to back down. Doing so in front of his own men would have been something close to suicide.

"I took this town for myself without the help of any scum like you or him," Manes said, jabbing a finger toward Skinner and Nick respectively. "And if it wasn't for my protection, you would have been strung up for that man you killed outside of town."

"Man?" Nick wheezed. "What . . . man?"

Although Skinner had been getting more enraged with every word that came out of the sheriff's mouth, hearing Nick's question seemed to pick up his spirits. "Oh, nobody's told you? Your old buddy Red Parks is dead. Isn't that really why you came here, Nick? I've been tracking him for months because I knew you wouldn't be far behind. Ol' Red never was as good at hiding as you."

It was hard to talk with a mouth full of blood, an aching rib cage and broken nose, but somehow Nick managed. "Where . . . is . . . he?"

"You'll see soon enough," Skinner grunted. "In fact, we'll plant you in a hole right next to him."

TWENTY

Nick let his body slump, allowing himself to be dragged farther back, out of the alley and into a lot filled mostly with broken crates, old wagon wheels, and lumber too busted up or decayed to be used for much of anything. The two deputies doing the dragging were eating up the fact that they were in control of him after the struggle he'd put up earlier. Behind them, Skinner and Manes were talking to each other. Even though they kept their voices down, the night was too quiet for any noise to go unnoticed.

"So who is this fella?" Sheriff Manes asked. "It sounds like you two go back a ways."

Skinner's laugh was more of a breathy grunt. "Yeah. We sure do. I knew that one when he was just some punk kid trying to get away from his pappy's shack in Missouri. The funny thing is that now he ain't much different from his old man. Back to digging in the dirt and planting dead men."

"And Red Parks?"

For a moment Skinner seemed to have forgotten he'd even mentioned that name. "Oh him," he said before too long. "He's that card cheat who came to you asking for an arrangement. You remember. The skinny fella with the scars on his face."

"That's not what I meant," Manes said, his voice interweaving with the four men's footsteps and the sound of Nick's boots dragging against the dirt. "Who exactly is he? Was there a reward for him too?"

"Maybe, but I doubt it. Red's face wasn't nearly as well known as this one's. Ain't that right, Nick?"

Nick heard the question through the pounding in his head but didn't reply. Apparently, he looked bad enough that it was no surprise to the others that he might not be able to hear what Skinner had said.

But that was no problem for Skinner. He was perfectly happy to go on without any encouragement from anyone else. "Nick's been looking for Red even after the price was put on his head. He stuck his neck out more'n once to find Red after they both got out of Montana with their worthless skins. I don't know why he'd bother. Myself, I would've left Red to the dogs. It would've given Nick a better head start if nothin' else."

The deputies came to a stop at the back of the cluttered lot. A tall fence surrounded the area, leaving the alley as the only way in or out. From what Nick could see through his swollen, downcast eyes, there might have been a building in the lot at one time or another since there were several posts protruding from the ground at oddly spaced intervals.

Nick was straightened up, spun around to face the sheriff, and slammed against the wall. The impact sent a shockwave through his back, which came around all the way to the front part of his torso, rattling the cracked ribs as it went. Although the pain was enough to rob Nick of his next breath, it also told him that the injury wasn't quite as bad as he'd thought earlier.

He'd been busted up and knocked around more than enough times to have learned a thing or two. His ribs were aching and sore as hell, but he didn't think any were broken. Still, cracked ribs were more than enough to make part of him wish he'd just pass out and be done with it.

"And don't worry none, Sheriff," Skinner went on to say, even though he was speaking more in Nick's direction than to Manes. "Red didn't have nearly enough money to pay for your services like I did. He served his purpose by bringing Nick here to me. I mean . . . us. That should be worth the price of a few of your men."

"You saying this one killed my deputies?"

Skinner nodded. "I'd bet on it."

Manes watched over the group with cold, dispassionate eyes. "Then I want more than a cut of the reward. Even with what you paid me to stay here, it's not enough to make up the losses I've had since this one came to town."

"You can keep *all* the reward money. Hell, I bet there's more'n one party interested in seeing Nick dead, and they'll all pay the man who killed him as a thank-you." Skinner kept his eyes on Nick and nodded like a proud papa. "Oh yeah. He's been a busy boy. I should know.

"Most real bad men don't know how to stay busy and stay alive. They're either too busy killin' and robbin' to know when they need to lay low or they're too chicken shit to come out once they manage to let the storm pass them by. But not Nick. He's one of the rare ones." Straightening his posture and jutting out his chin, Skinner added, "Just like me."

Manes looked over to Nick, studying the way his deputies had pushed the man against the wall with his arms stretched out on either side. The image struck a chord in his mind, almost as if they meant to nail him to that wall and leave him for the vultures the way they did in ancient times.

Perhaps it was that picture in his mind or a bout of conscience, but Manes suddenly started to feel uncomfortable. He shifted on his feet and let out a breath that formed a white haze that hung in the air in front of his mouth. "If we're going to do this, let's just do this."

"What's the matter, Sheriff?" Skinner asked. "You getting queasy?"

"No. I just prefer conducting this type of business quickly and a little farther away from town. Either that or he should be hung in a proper manner."

Skinner laughed. "Hung properly, huh? You lawmen sure are a hoot. Pin a badge on your shirts and even the crooked sons of bitches like yourselves tend to get all high and mighty. Well don't worry none. This won't take much longer. I just thought I'd like to take my time and enjoy myself a bit, that's all."

"If this is how you enjoy yourself, then you're a sick man."

Nick could sense the growing tension in the deputies holding him in place. Their fingers twitched and squirmed where they were digging into his arms, and their feet shifted uneasily against the ground. Since he wasn't putting up much of a struggle anymore, he knew they weren't squirming because of anything he'd done. On the contrary, he had let his head loll forward to give the impression that he was either unconscious or well on his way there.

Even with his eyes nearly closed and his chin drooping against his chest, he could see nearly everything around him. All this time, he'd been focusing on what was going on and where everyone else was positioned partly as a way to form an accurate mental picture and partly to divert his thoughts from the pain Skinner had inflicted upon him.

Skinner was an expert in taking a man apart. Nick had seen the man break every bone he could break in another person's body before finally snapping the poor bastard's neck. He knew damn well that Skinner could draw this out for hours, maybe even days. The only thing that kept Nick going was the stubborn streak that flowed through him just as surely as the blood flowed through his veins.

Even stronger than the desire to live, Nick wanted to keep his eyes open just because Skinner so desperately wanted them closed. He knew it wasn't rational, but it was there all the same. Hell, plenty of things he had done in his life didn't stand up to reason. This would just be another one to throw onto the pile.

Skinner and Manes hadn't spoken for a good couple of seconds. The silence seemed to drag out, and Nick cursed himself for not catching it sooner. Perhaps he was passing out despite his efforts to hold back the cold tide of unconsciousness. His window of opportunity was closing fast, but if he didn't wait for the proper time, he wouldn't be able to get to it no matter how stubborn he was.

It was a lot like a poker game. What mattered was walking away with the most. All the other hands, wins or losses, just led up to the big one. Of course, the biggest trick was staying in the game long enough to make it to that one, glorious hand.

There was one heavy footfall followed by the rush of something sailing through the air. The sound was like a thick axe handle being swung, and it ended with the blunt thump of Skinner's fist pounding against his chest.

The gray-haired man let out a satisfied grunt as Nick thrashed against the punch to his heart.

Bright spots of red exploded in Nick's field of vision and the blood in his veins ignited with a painful fire. When he tried to take a breath, Nick came up dangerously short, causing the world to teeter precariously around him. It was a mixed blessing that he could hardly feel much of his body anymore. At least that way, the follow-up punch to his left side was just a vague discomfort that rumbled in his aching torso.

"Jesus Christ," whispered the deputy holding Nick's right arm.

Those two words echoed in Nick's ears somehow, even though he could barely hear Sheriff Manes's voice, which was much louder than anyone else's.

"Just finish this already!" the sheriff ordered. "We don't have the time to muck around here any longer. Someone's going to stumble in here, and then I'll have to keep them from spreading it around the whole goddamn —"

Once again Skinner laughed. This time it came out of him in a more strained manner since he was actually getting winded from beating Nick like he was tenderizing a slab of beef. "Looks like you were right, Sheriff.

I . . . may have been . . . just a little too loud."

"He's right, Sheriff," said one of the deputies. "Someone's coming." The words sounded messy, so Nick knew it was Harelip doing the talking. "Looks like one of them cooks from the steak house."

Manes turned around and slapped his hand against his holstered gun loud enough for Nick to hear.

"What's the matter, Sheriff?" Skinner asked in a mocking tone. "Isn't this your town? Can't you do anything you want?"

"Shut up, goddammit!" Manes said, looking toward the alley opening. "I can do what I please so long as the worst things stay rumors. Other lawmen pass through this town, you know, and some of them are a little stricter than I am." Turning back to Skinner, Manes added, "And since you're relying on me staying in my office, I'd suggest you do something to help."

One of the figures in the alley turned toward the street and shouted, "Get away from here, Catherine!"

Skinner grumbled something under his breath and turned around to take a good look at whoever the lawmen had spotted. "My my. What have we here? Looks like Nick's sweetheart sent someone to check up on him."

Those words stabbed like icicles straight through Nick's chest. They were sharp and cold, sending spikes of frost that acted like a splash of water upon his face. Skinner was grinning widely when Nick lifted his head to take a look for himself. It didn't matter how Skinner knew about Catherine or the people working at The Porter House, just like it didn't matter how a disease knew how to eat a man from the inside out.

The cluttered lot stretched out in front of him like a forest of broken posts and piles of refuse. At the other end, which seemed a mile away, in the opening to the alley, stood two familiar figures. One of them was the cook who'd prepared the meal Nick had shared with Catherine less than an hour ago. The other man, standing next to the cook was one of the servers.

"Yeah," the gray-haired man chided. "I thought that would wake him up." But there was something else in his eyes as he looked at Nick. Skinner seemed to be studying the captive closely, sizing him up. "Why don't I just go fetch those two and bring them back here? Maybe that little sweetie is out here too."

Without another word, Skinner turned and stalked toward the alley. His hand reached around behind his back to remove a Bowie knife that had been sheathed there. The sharpened steel glinted in the moonlight as Skinner hid it from the two he was approaching and quickened his steps toward them.

"Run!" Nick managed to say through a thickening fog of pain.

Both people in the alley backed away, heeding Nick's advice without turning their backs on the scene they'd discovered. Skinner sped himself up to keep them from escaping him, bolting through the darkness even as the burly cook took a swing at him.

Sheriff Manes stepped between the back wall and the alley, blocking Nick's view. "Damn fool," Manes hissed. "I should never have let him out of his cage."

"You want me to go after him?" Blondie asked.

"No, let him have his fun. If Catherine Weaver did send those two to interfere with us, we'll just have to see that something happens to The Porter House. I can't have folks thinking they can slap me in the face and get away with it. A fire should do nicely. I'll have to make sure the bodies wind up in there as well. Tragic, but a necessary message to keep this place in line."

Blondie strained to get a better look at

what Skinner was doing to the two he was after. "Yeah . . . real shame. I loved eating in that steak house."

"Then I'll make sure to take up a collection to have another one built. It won't be enough to make up for the tragic loss of that sweet little hostess, but it should go a ways in making me look better to the rest of this goddamn town."

The sound of footsteps in the alley was growing weaker. In their place, however, came the noise of a close quarters scuffle. One of the voices in the distance could have been Catherine herself, yelling something, but her voice filled with more anger than pain. Nick knew that could only mean that Skinner hadn't gotten hold of her yet.

His head dropped completely forward and his entire body became heavier in the deputies' arms. One last breath flowed from his lips and his knees buckled like a marionette whose strings had been cut.

"Shit," Blondie said. "He's out."

The sheriff made a questioning sound, as though he'd already forgotten Nick was there. Next came the sound of his pistol being drawn and the hammer being snapped back into position. "Hold him up better so I can get a clean shot. Too much gunfire will just draw more people this way."

Blondie cinched his fingers in tight enough to make a row of gouges in Nick's flesh, and Harelip moved his hand up closer to Nick's shoulder so he could strengthen his grip.

It was just the moment Nick had been waiting for.

TWENTY-ONE

Harelip's grip loosened for only a fraction of a second. In that time, Nick forced his eyes to open all the way and dredged up every last bit of strength that his body could muster. The effort felt like his body was being torn apart from the inside out, but was more than worth it. His arm flexed out and quickly snapped in again, coming free from Harelip's fingers before the deputy even knew what was going on.

Not only did Nick figure that Blondie would tighten his fingers even more, he counted on it. So rather than try to break free of him, he twisted his arm in a tight circle until his palm was facing up rather than down. From there, Nick reached out with his free hand, plucked his own pistol from where Harelip had been keeping it, and bent his elbow, pulling Blondie in closer so he could drive his gun's barrel into the deputy's stomach.

Blondie stared into Nick's eyes as if waiting for him to say something. The deputy felt the gun pressing against him but couldn't truly believe it was there. That was the problem with overconfidence. Once that was shattered, it had a tendency of taking a hell of a lot along with it.

Nick's mind raced in the next fraction of a second. He wondered if he was letting a darker part of him have too much sway. He wondered if part of him wanted Manes to take his shot rather than just stand slack-jawed in surprise at his prisoner's sudden burst of movement. But in the end none of those things mattered much. He knew what he had to do, and his finger tightened around his trigger before he had a chance to think otherwise.

The specially modified pistol went off with a muffled thump as it spat its lead directly into Blondie's torso. The impact of the bullet lifted the deputy partially off the ground and would have knocked him completely from his feet if Nick hadn't been holding him up. Nick put another hole into his target for good measure, but still didn't allow Blondie to fall. Instead, he held him between himself and Manes before the sheriff could squeeze his trigger.

Nick then turned toward Harelip, know-

278

ing that the second deputy would be shocked for another moment or two after seeing his partner's insides sprayed through the air. But the uglier lawman wasn't as taken aback as he might have been and was launching an attack by the time Nick met him head on.

Rather than burden himself with Blondie's weight, Nick tossed the deputy toward Manes. The sheriff fired a shot into his own deputy out of pure reflex before he was knocked over by the incoming body and both of them toppled over. Dead before he hit the ground, the light-haired deputy thrashed like a fish on dry land while spilling his blood into the dirt as well as onto Sheriff Manes.

Reacting instinctively, Nick ducked down low and fought his way through the stabbing pains the motion caused within his battered body. Sure enough, Manes had been taking aim for a quick shot from the ground. Between Nick's movement and the awkward weight on top of him, the sheriff was barely able to aim before his target ducked completely out of his sight. Manes struggled to get out from under Blondie's corpse as Nick and the remaining deputy charged toward each other like rams about to collide.

Nick's fingers slid into place on the handle

of his gun. Whole and wounded alike, each digit found the groove that had been expertly carved for them in the wooden grip. Since he didn't have enough fingers to wrap around a conventional grip, the tapered shape of his gun's handle made it possible for him to keep hold of the weapon and move it with even more precision than a gunfighter with a normal hand using the most expensive store-bought model.

More than that, Nick's pistol was so perfectly balanced for his unique style that it felt almost weightless to him. It not only completed his hand, but felt like an extension of it. Once his shoulder impacted with Harelip's torso, he pointed the barrel like it was one of his own fingers and squeezed off a shot, though he was too close to his target to see where he was aiming.

The gnarled, twisted barrel spat a gout of sparks and smoke, throwing out its lead and drilling a hole through the hip of the deputy. Harelip let out a pained snarl and went down as his side exploded in a crimson splash. Although he'd been fast enough to draw his gun, the shot to his hip shifted his body downward, and when his finger jerked against his trigger, Harelip only managed to punch a hole into the ground not too far from his own feet.

Nick hadn't forgotten about Manes. Just when he knew the sheriff would be getting back on his feet, he turned his body to one side so he could drive the steel barrel of his gun deep into Harelip's gut like a club. That folded the deputy in half and took him completely off his feet. Staying low, Nick felt the deputy's upper body drop over his shoulder, and from there he swiveled so he was forcing Harelip back toward where Manes was standing. That's when the sheriff's gun went off. Nick could feel the impact of the bullet that had been meant for him as it burrowed into Harelip's back instead.

Sheriff Manes swore out loud when he saw he'd hit his own man instead of Nick. With shots still echoing through the air, he knew the time for discretion had passed. That only made the sheriff angrier, since he'd always wanted to keep his killings somewhat private. The locals could gossip all they wanted, but real evidence or eyewitnesses could bring down more trouble than Manes was prepared to handle.

Taking a few steps forward, Manes raised his pistol and sighted down its barrel, waiting for a clean shot to present itself as Nick wrestled with the deputy.

The adrenaline pumping through Harelip's body as well as the pain from his wounds added fuel to the fire in the deputy's gut. With desperation thrown into the mix, Harelip had become more of a dangerous animal than a man. He gritted his teeth and let out a string of barely decipherable curses while slamming his elbows and fists into Nick's back and sides again and again. He could feel the other man weakening, and with a sharp, upward knee, the deputy broke away from Nick and brought his gun around to take a shot.

Nick staggered back a few steps, reeling from the impact of a knee to his chin.

Gunfire roared through the air and smoke rose up directly in front of Harelip's ugly face. He smiled and tried to speak, but simply didn't have the strength. The pain from his hip was gone and the aching in his stomach where Nick had clubbed him was gone as well. In fact, he couldn't feel anything at all. That was when his vision started to cloud over.

Nick looked into the deputy's eyes and saw them widen into blank, glassy orbs. The shot that had just been fired came not from the deputy's pistol, but from Nick's. He'd taken it the moment Harelip's knee had put a little bit of space between them.

One bullet had drilled a hole clean

through the deputy's heart, exploding it in his chest while Harelip's brain tried to wrap around the fact that he was about to die.

Another soul to scream in his nightmares, Nick thought.

Another man gazing upon the view from below for the first time.

But he didn't have time to dwell upon it. He had to worry about the sheriff before the next bullet from the lawman's gun might drop him onto the ground beside Harelip. Twisting on the balls of his feet while crouching down, Nick lowered himself in a tight downward spiral until he was facing in the sheriff's direction.

The moment he came to a stop, he saw the lawman's gun spew its fiery breath, sending a bullet whipping through the air beside him. It was getting hard to make Manes out through the gritty smoke, and since Nick was already halfway through his ammunition, he kept moving rather than squeeze the trigger again.

His eyes seeking out the edge of the smoky curtain created by the gunfire, he spotted the area where the veil wasn't so thick and moved slowly in that direction. Another bullet hissed through the air as he pushed off to the side with both feet and leaned his head into a partially controlled fall.

Still keeping his pistol in front of him and ready to fire, he threw himself as far away as he could from Harelip's corpse. He prepared himself for the impact of his body against the ground, but was unable to stifle the pain once it came. His ribs screamed for mercy and his muscles strained but he still managed to keep from crumpling up into a ball as he dropped and slid for a couple of feet along the packed dirt.

While his mind dealt with the pain of cracked ribs grinding against each other, and his broken nose brought tears to his eyes, Nick's body burst into motion again before he'd even come to a stop. His feet scratched at the ground, pushing him onward as the sheriff's gun barked again and again. The first bullet to find him nipped a small piece from Nick's outer thigh. Another would have punched a messy hole through his kneecap if he hadn't reflexively tucked his legs in and twisted his lower body around behind the rest of him.

The bullet he'd managed to dodge kicked up a mound of dirt not far from Nick's body at the same time that he finally found the view he'd been looking for. In the darkness, the thickening smoke might as well have been a black velvet curtain dropped directly in both men's line of sight. Without it, the fight would have gone a lot quicker, but an experienced fighter knew how to deal with such inconveniences.

For his part, the sheriff kept shooting through the curtain, hoping to get lucky. Nick, instead, found a way around the curtain until he could get a clearer shot. Both men had responded to the situation in their own way, and Manes had damn near succeeded. Now it was Nick's turn.

A breeze kicked away some of the smoke, and Nick could finally see where the last several shots had come from. "God dammit!" he snarled.

Not only was the sheriff no longer in the same spot, but Nick couldn't see him anywhere. And Skinner was already gone, which left the lot eerily silent for the moment.

Nick jumped to his feet and almost fell over again as pain lanced up through his hip and spiked out in every direction once it reached his rib cage. The one thing that kept him going was the fact that he now could see the sheriff running toward the alley, darting from one shadow to another as he abandoned the cluttered lot.

Unwilling to be suckered into more unfamiliar territory, Nick jogged after the sheriff without committing himself to a full run.

Stopping at the mouth of the alley, Manes turned around to look, and saw Nick standing no more than ten paces away. Both men had been more concerned with running and keeping their balance, so when they finally faced each other, their guns were held down at their sides rather than pointed up and ready to shoot.

Although they both had their weapons drawn, with the barrels pointing to the ground as they faced each other, it made that short bend of an elbow seem like a long way to go. Nick stared at the sheriff and Manes stared right back.

There was no turning back now.

TWENTY-TWO

Catherine was standing outside the restaurant after asking her two coworkers to check up on Nick. She was worried enough that he'd been taken away by the lawmen, but when they forced him outside and out of her sight, her worries turned into cold fear. Those fears were far from unjustified since there had been plenty of times when people were taken away by the sheriff and never heard from again.

While not overly anxious to take on armed men, the two men who'd volunteered to check up on Nick had assumed that the sheriff or his deputies wouldn't do anything too drastic with eyewitnesses present.

But they hadn't figured on having to deal with the likes of Nathan Skinner.

The cook and server had made it just over halfway down the alley when they spotted the group gathered in the lot that had once been a dry goods store. Only the barest of bones remained of that store's skeleton, making it easy for them, with help from the bright moon, to see what was going on out there. Both men were in their mid-twenties and had muscular builds. The confidence that came from their physical strength and youth quickly faded when they saw Skinner turn his fierce eyes upon them like a hungry tiger.

"Get away from here, Catherine," the cook said while backing away. He'd almost forgotten about the knife he'd taken from the kitchen on his way out. Now, his fingers clenched tightly around the handle as he heard Nick shout from where he was being held.

"Run!"

Catherine didn't hear much more than a faint echo of that warning, but recognized the voice. She started to head toward the alley, but slowed her steps when she heard the sound of scrambling feet coming from the opening between buildings.

Inside the alley, the cook and server were more than willing to keep whatever was in the shadows away from her. They backed to the end of the alley before they stopped, saw that Catherine was still nearby, and decided to hold their ground. The cook took a breath to steel himself as he held his kitchen blade in front of him. The server wasn't quite so well prepared and only managed to grab a piece of lumber that was on the ground nearby.

Skinner charged through the darkness like a bull, ducking effortlessly beneath the hasty swing that was taken at him. Gaining speed, he cocked his Bowie knife back until the hand he held it in was against his ribs. Once he was close enough to the nearest man, he planted his left foot, pivoted forward and snapped out with his right hand.

The Bowie knife sliced through the air as though Skinner's arm was spring loaded. It made a deadly hissing sound, followed by the shredding of fabric and flesh. Even before his arm had come to a stop on the tail end of its swing, Skinner managed to flip the blade in his hand so the steel edge ran down over his wrist and partly along the length of his forearm.

The cook didn't even know he'd been cut until he felt the warm trickle running over his skin. When he looked down, he was surprised to see that half his right arm was covered with the slick crimson sheen of his own blood flowing from a fresh slice in his flesh and dripping off the end of his fingers.

"You've got sand," Skinner said as gunshots sounded beyond the alley behind him.

"I'll give you that much. But I'll bet the only thing you've ever cut in your life is a celery stick."

The cook didn't know what to say. Luckily, he didn't have to say anything before his companion came charging at Skinner from the side. The makeshift club hit the gray-haired Skinner, driving into him with everything the younger man had. But Skinner, expecting to take a hit from the second man, rolled with the momentum of the blow.

Spinning himself a full 360 degrees, Skinner brought himself all the way around to face the back of the man who'd plowed into him. With his arm now curled in close to his body, he took a moment to pick his target before unleashing a strike of his own. His left hand closed into a fist and back-handed the server's temple, causing the younger man to stagger to one side.

Blackness swirled into the man's vision, and he swung blindly with the board he'd picked up. He could tell he was a bit off target, and was barely able to keep himself from stumbling over while shaking the cobwebs from his head. The board was still cocked back near his head like an axe when he felt the stabbing pain of steel sliding into his exposed belly. It dug in deep and low, missing his groin by only a few inches. From there, the blade traveled upward and the pain became his entire world.

Catherine couldn't believe what she was seeing. Her breath caught in her throat and her hands went up to cover her mouth, but she still couldn't take her eyes away from the horrific spectacle. She'd known the server for several months and had counted him among her friends at work. She even knew that he was sweet on her but hadn't worked up the nerve to approach her about it.

Now, that same man was being eviscerated in front of her.

With a sharp, upward pull, Skinner kept cutting until his blade dug into bone. Then he removed the knife with a satisfied grunt, using nearly enough force to sever the younger man's sternum. Using his free hand, Skinner slapped the server away as guts started pouring from the gaping wound he'd created.

Looking over to Catherine, Skinner smiled so widely that it seemed to cut his own face in half. "Nick's got a soft spot for you, don't he? I wonder if it's as soft as the spot in this boy here?"

Catherine's muscles froze as pure horror flooded through her brain. Barely able to pull in a breath, she did the only thing her petrified body would allow and let it out in a terrified scream.

Skinner seemed to like that a lot. He'd been walking toward her, but now he moved faster, drawing the blade up and back in preparation for a sideways strike aimed for her naked throat. With his eyes focused on her jugular and his ears filled with the shrill sound of her fear, Skinner felt a powerful rush of pleasure course through him as his knife hand slashed out and the blade whistled through the air.

Never before had Catherine been so completely sure that she was going to die. In the course of her life she'd been sick, hurt, and had felt plenty of pain, but not until that moment did she ever believe that her life was less than a second away from ending.

The blade swept inevitably toward her, and she was too terrified to do anything but watch it come. Her muscles were already tensing and her mind beginning to wonder what the afterlife might hold.

When the steel bit into her, she couldn't help but notice that it wasn't as painful as she'd imagined. She also noticed that the ear-to-ear smile on Skinner's face was gone. He wasn't even looking at her now, but seemed confused by something he couldn't see. His body lurched in an awkward way, but that knife kept sliding on its course across her throat.

TWENTY-THREE

When he was facing Sheriff Manes, Nick could still see Skinner running off after whoever had appeared in the alley. He knew only too well that Skinner wouldn't just check to see who was there and what they were doing. Blood was going to be spilled.

Lots of it.

But before he could worry about that, Nick had plenty to keep him busy right where he was. Both he and the sheriff had their sights fixed on each other as though there were nothing else in the world. By simply blocking everything else out, each knew that the other had had plenty of experience behind a gun. Any wild dog killer could pull a trigger. A professional knew how to turn his entire body and mind into a weapon.

Each man thought about every move they made before they made it, as if standing on top of a powder keg with matches in their hands. Their breathing couldn't be too deep and they couldn't afford to risk shifting their feet. Anything they did could set the other one off. And once one of them was set off, the other would have to follow.

Nick could hear the sounds of a fight coming from the alleyway now. There were voices and plenty of movement, but he couldn't see what was going on. Sheriff Manes was standing between him and where he wanted to go. By the looks of it, the lawman didn't have any intention of moving until he was damn good and ready.

"I'll give you a chance, Nick," Manes said, careful to pick the right words. "Turn yourself over to me and I'll see you get treated fairly."

"Yeah. I got a taste of your fair treatment while I was up against that wall. I think I'll decline."

"I'm not the only one after you. Not with that reward on your head."

"I know," Nick said plainly. "I've been living with that reward for a while now."

"I've got other deputies. They'll come after you if you get away from me. Drop that gun and I'll keep you away from Skinner. I'll see you stand trial and have your day in front of a judge."

"Save your justice talk, Sheriff. And as for

the rest of your offer, keeping away from Skinner is the last thing I want to do right now."

Nodding, Manes said, "All right, then. That puts us right where we started."

Nick was sick of talking. He could already hear more disturbing sounds coming from the alley and knew Skinner had found someone to occupy his special attentions. Although he didn't much like the idea of gunning down a sheriff, he didn't see where he had many other options. Besides, Manes was hardly much of a lawman by the stretch of anyone's imagination.

The modified pistol hung from Nick's hand, moonlight glinting off its oddly shaped surface. Across from him, Sheriff Manes stood without moving a muscle. The lawman didn't even appear anxious as he held his ground and stared straight into Nick's eyes.

More than just cool under pressure, Manes looked more like a man who'd already seen how things would turn out. His confidence was so complete that it made Nick wonder what ace was tucked away up his sleeve.

"You've got one last chance, Nick," Manes said. "Come with me or die where you stand."

It wasn't the first time Nick had been offered that choice. He knew from experience the only way to answer it was through actions. Letting out his breath, Nick set his jaw in a grim line and readied the muscles in his gun arm.

Only Sheriff Manes's jaw moved when he said, "Fine. Take him, Scott."

If Nick hadn't been so completely focused on every sight and sound within the range of his senses, he might not have heard the faint metallic click of a fresh round being levered into a rifle barrel behind him. Unfortunately, there was no possible way he could have seen the moonlight glinting off metal within a nearby shadow without taking his eyes from the sheriff.

Fortunately, Nick didn't need to see the hidden figure, because he'd already launched himself into motion based on the sound alone.

The instant he threw himself straight down and to one side, he was pulling his trigger. That was the moment Manes had been waiting for, and he made his own moves as well, twisting his body to one side and dropping to one knee while taking his shot.

Three gunshots were fired simultaneously. One came from Nick and another from the sheriff, while the third came from the deputy who'd taken position behind a stack of crates in one corner of the lot. Since his hip was still hurting, Scott wasn't up to taking the more active jobs, but was certainly well enough to act as the sniper Manes preferred to have covering his back at any potentially dangerous meeting.

The rifle bucked against Scott's shoulder and lit up the entire front of his face and body as fire sprayed from the barrel. Cursing under his breath, Scott already knew he'd missed, and he levered in another round before it was too late.

Manes knew better than to stay put when someone was shooting so close to him. If he didn't hit with his first try, the sheriff wasn't about to stick around to try again. After all, that was what he was paying his deputy for. Jumping to his feet, Manes pointed his gun toward Nick, his finger already tightening around the trigger.

Nick could feel Scott's sights on him like a spider crawling under his shirt as Manes's sent a shot in his direction. It hissed through the air over his head. By then the sheriff was retreating into the alley, apparently unwilling to see the game through since his ace in the hole hadn't been enough to win it already.

There were two shots left in Nick's gun. If he had been standing or hadn't been in such a damn hurry, he knew he might have put Manes down instead of just clipping the side of Manes's neck before the sheriff turned and ran. But his shot wasn't completely wasted since the sheriff was running completely out of the fight.

Frustrated with the way things were going, Nick didn't feel like wasting any more time while Skinner was still out there no doubt having his way with that knife he liked to use. Nick pulled in a quick breath, turned quickly on his heels and fired at the spot where the rifle shots had come from.

His shot came just as Scott was aiming at his chest. Rather than try to dodge the shot that was coming, Nick let out his breath and fired again.

All of that took place in less than a second, and ended with one final crack as Nick's pistol sent its last round through the air.

Still unable to see much in the shadows, Nick opened his pistol and emptied the shells from the cylinder as naturally as he might scratch the side of his nose. The next sound he heard was something heavy dropping to the ground and a grunt as Scott wheezed one last time into the dirt.

Nick raced into the alley. Loading the

pistol would have taken more time than he wanted to lose.

It had gotten quiet in that alley.

It had gotten quiet throughout all of Jessup.

At that moment, Nick felt as though the entire world was closing in around him like a pair of leathery bat wings. He ran as if he was in a nightmare and his feet weren't really taking him anywhere. Already, he could make out the still form of a body on the ground at the other end of the alley, and he knew it wasn't Skinner's.

Nick could only hope that he wasn't too late.

TWENTY-FOUR

Even the sound of gunshots in the distance couldn't shake Catherine out of the panicked haze that filled her mind. The knife slashed across her throat, making its cut and starting the flow of blood down her chest. She felt her knees weakening. Part of that came from the loss of blood, and another part came from sheer terror.

Instinctively, she lifted her hands to her neck so she could feel the damage. Her fingers became slick with blood when she touched the shredded skin, and that single touch was accompanied by a sharp pain that resonated through her flesh in all directions.

Although the wound was clean and ran all the way across her neck, it didn't seem to be bleeding as much as she might have thought. In fact, just thinking about that made her senses come back to her, and she found enough strength to regain her balance as she staggered back toward the steps leading up to the front door of the restaurant. Emboldened by her newfound strength, Catherine touched her fingers to her neck once more.

The cut was tender, but surprisingly shallow. Although no expert on knives, she figured the blade must have just barely scraped over her skin to open the top layers of flesh without damaging anything too vital. The first thought that entered her head then was that she'd had a miracle worked upon her.

Unfortunately, the act was far from divine and had been bought at a hefty price.

Skinner teetered off balance for a moment or two after completing what should have been a killing blow. He gnashed his teeth and almost fell over backward before finally managing to shift his center of gravity and regain control of his stance. He could still feel the grip on the back of his shoulder, and knew then that someone had come up from behind to pull him back just as the knife had been headed for Catherine's neck.

Wheeling around with a vicious snarl, he swiped his left arm ahead of him, delivering a backhand to whoever had interrupted his kill. Skinner felt the knuckles of his left hand smash into flesh and bone half a second before he got a look at the other person's face. Just as he'd thought, it was the cook who'd grabbed hold of his shirt and pulled him away from Catherine.

"That was a big mistake," Skinner snarled as he swiped his right arm around and sent the knife's sharpened edge into the cook's bicep. "Now instead of just killin' you, I'll have to carve you up." The blade slashed out at the cook's arm, sending an arc of wet crimson through the air. "And cry as much as you want. I like it when my turkey dinner cries first."

The cook still had his knife and meant to drive it into Skinner's back when he had the chance. But aside from wanting to pull the madman away from Catherine before he cut her open, he found that he simply couldn't stab another human being in the back.

In his mind, there was all the justification he'd needed and then some. The problem was in his body and soul. In his heart, the cook was a father and a God-fearing Christian. He wasn't a killer. He'd never taken a human life, and found it impossible to start even then.

He had two realizations the moment he got a look at Skinner's face up close. First, the cook knew he should have risked damnation to kill the other man when he'd had the chance. And second, Skinner didn't seem to have any of the reservations that had stayed his own hand. In fact, Skinner barely even seemed human.

Human beings were good at heart, weren't they? The cook thought this odd question as Skinner's knife tore so deeply into his right wrist that it nearly severed the hand from his arm that was still grasping his cooking knife. The pain was so intense that it bordered on the sublime. The agony became so overwhelming as Skinner's blade was driven straight up into the cook's groin that his sight was washed away in a brilliant white light.

Was it the light that came before dying? Hardly.

As much as he wanted to die, the cook's body simply wasn't there yet. As much as he wanted to fall over and curl up into a ball, he was being held up by Skinner's strong free hand as the blade dug into him again and again.

By the time Catherine realized that her cut was superficial, Skinner had already started in on the cook who'd saved her. She watched for a moment, stunned by the horror of what she saw, and when she started to run toward Skinner's back to get him to stop, she caught a glimpse of the cook's face.

His mouth was bloody from Skinner's backhand and he was in so much pain that he seemed detached from the entire situation. The cook still spotted Catherine, however, and begged her with his eyes to back away. It was too late for him. The darkness was already overtaking the light.

Catherine saw the blood soaking into the dirt like a black pool. She saw Skinner's knife arm moving so quickly that it was just a blur of motion accentuated by the occasional flash of steel. What stopped her from trying to save the cook was when Skinner stabbed him with so much force that it lifted the other man off the ground and drove the last breath out of him.

It was too late.

Knowing that she couldn't save anyone but herself, Catherine choked back the tears, turned and ran to the end alley, toward where she knew Nick had been taken.

Skinner was too enraptured by the frenzy of death to notice her hasty exit. Although done in a matter of moments, he'd felt each slash as if it was a creation unto itself. He'd selected each target carefully and had listened to every inarticulate sound the cook was able to make.

Now that it was over, he let the twitching body drop and gave it one last blow to the stomach, using the toe of his boot. Only then did he think about what he wanted to do to Catherine. When he turned to find her, however, she was gone.

It wasn't much of a surprise, but it angered him all the same.

The blood was pumping so quickly through Skinner's body that he was feeling light-headed. There was nothing to compare to that special feeling. Nothing else could give him the particular kind of euphoria of opening up another person and seeing what they had inside of them.

Not liquor. Not even sex.

A few deep breaths brought him down enough for his common sense kick back in. There were people watching, and some of them would be screwing up their courage to come and see what all the screaming and commotion had been about. Skinner lifted the blade and took a look at the blood dripping all the way down the steel edge to form rivulets that ran down its carved bone handle.

The cook had stopped thrashing, but Skinner knelt down beside him and reached toward one of the wider wounds in the other man's gut. Dipping his finger into the blood, Skinner used that same finger to trace a few markings on the stretch of boardwalk closest to him. He had to dip his finger a few more times like a pen into an ink well, but he'd finished his scrawling before too long and lifted himself back to a standing position.

People were starting to poke their noses out and look from nearly every window and doorway. There were some footsteps rushing from the nearby alley, but Skinner turned his back on them and started walking slowly down the street. His eyes moved back and forth, meeting every disbelieving gaze he could to send that person scuttling back into the shadows. There were still too many folks around for his tastes, however, and murder was always better if there was enough time to savor it.

"I'll see you again, girl," Skinner hissed, picturing Catherine. "When there ain't so many people sticking their noses in."

Nick burst from the alley, missing Skinner's departure by only a few seconds. His eyes were drawn immediately to the shredded corpse on the ground, but his ears were filled with the wrenching sobs coming from a figure directly in front of him.

"Catherine?" Nick said, recognizing her even in the darkness. "What happened? Are you all right?"

She looked up at him as though she didn't truly believe Nick was there. Her eyes were wide with terror and filled with memories that were as fresh as the blood on the street, yet would haunt her for the remaining years of her life. She moved as though she just had enough steam to keep herself upright after getting out of Skinner's sight.

"Nick? You . . . you're alive?"

Before he knew it, Nick was next to her and scooping her into his arms. When he felt the warm slickness of her skin against his face, the bottom of his stomach dropped out and a cold knot formed in its place. "Oh my God, Catherine, what happened to you?"

Nick was already lifting her chin with the edge of his finger and examining the cut running crossways over her throat.

"It's not as bad as it looks," she said, wincing at the pain brought on by even the slightest upward movement of her head. "It's just a scratch, really."

Even though he was listening to what she told him, Nick wasn't satisfied by her words alone. Once he saw for himself that the blood had stopped flowing, he gently embraced Catherine as though shielding her from further attack. "I won't let him hurt you again," he whispered. "I promise. I'm so sorry I couldn't stop this from happening."

"He . . . killed them." Catherine's voice was so weak it barely made it past her lips. If Nick's face hadn't been pressed so tightly against hers, he might not have even heard her at all. "They're dead," she whispered. "He killed them both."

Nick shifted his eyes toward the bodies laying in the dirt nearby. Still holding Catherine close to him, he began walking toward The Porter House. Thin wisps of chilled air slowly drifted out through his mouth as he took in the grim sight before him.

The terrible thing was that he wasn't surprised at the carnage. Being familiar with Skinner's work, he wasn't shocked to find the bloody mess that was barely recognizable as a human's remains. Even though he didn't know either of the men personally, Nick cursed himself for not being able to keep them from falling into Skinner's hands.

"Where did he go?" Nick asked.

Catherine looked panicked for a moment and snapped her head first one way and then the other, which started the blood flowing once again from her neck. "I think he's gone. I hope to God he's just gone." With that, she'd reached her limit and broke into a fit of sobs that wracked her entire body.

If Skinner was still around, he would have struck by now. Nick knew that and had made sure to make himself a target by presenting his back to anyone nearby. Even while comforting Catherine, he'd been waiting to hear Skinner's voice or footsteps rushing toward him.

But there was nothing.

Nothing but pain that filled his body. Nothing but the sound of Catherine's cries, which filled his ears. Nothing but the coppery smell of blood filling his nostrils.

Reaching The Porter House steps, Nick spotted something smeared over the edge of the boardwalk where the steps led up to the front door of the restaurant: 3-7-77.

Despite the fact that it looked as if the numbers had been written in dark, wet paint, Nick knew better.

They'd been scrawled in blood and left there specifically for him.

Twenty-Five

Everyone in the vicinity of The Porter House and the nearby alley were running around in a panic. A few shouted for someone to fetch the sheriff, but those voices were quickly silenced by the locals who knew better.

"You need to find someplace to hide," Nick said to Catherine once she'd had a chance to calm down. "Someplace where nobody knows you'd be. Do you have a place like that?"

She thought for a moment and nodded. "Yes. It's —"

Nick stopped her by placing his fingertips on her lips. "Don't say it here. Come with me and you can tell me where it is in a bit."

With that, Nick helped her walk away from the chaotic scene. Although they'd met a horrific end, the two men who tried to save Catherine had done a world of good. They'd saved her life. They'd also provided enough of a distraction for her and Nick to slip away in the shuffle. With everyone focused on the bodies and the violence that still rumbled like a distant echo through their minds, nobody much noticed two figures stepping around a corner and disappearing from view.

Plenty of people would ask about Catherine and Nick once they got their wits about them, but by then it was too late. Nick was gone. He wasn't completely sure where he was going, but let his instincts guide his way as he took Catherine deeper and deeper into the quiet shadows several streets over.

Once they were far enough away from the restaurant and he was certain nobody had followed them, Nick took Catherine in his arms and rubbed his hands over her back. She was trembling. Right down to her core, she was shaking as if she'd forgotten how to stay still.

"Shhh," Nick whispered into her ear. "It's all over now. You're safe."

She had things she wanted to say. She wanted to tell him the animal with the knife had gotten away and that it couldn't be over. She wanted to say that she couldn't be safe anymore; not with men like Sheriff Manes and Skinner walking around in the world. She wanted to pray for forgiveness for getting her two friends killed.

"I know how you're feeling," Nick said. "There wasn't anything you could do to help those other two. If you tried, you would have only gotten yourself killed as well."

The tears hung at the corners of Catherine's eyes, but did not fall. Instead, they burned right where they were and she didn't wipe them away. She figured it just wouldn't be right to feel any comfort after what had happened. Not yet anyway.

"How do you know so much?" she asked.

Nick shook his head. "I only know some things because I've seen them before. When it comes to that killer you saw tonight, I know plenty."

"Is he after you?"

"I guess you could say that. Him and some others."

"But why? Why would someone like that be after you?"

The hackles rose on the back of Nick's neck, making him feel like a dog who'd just caught another predator's scent. "We don't have time to talk about this now. Take me to that place where you can hide."

As much as Catherine wanted to get some answers to her questions, she felt the same tension that was making Nick so uneasy. Taking him by the hand, she led him toward a row of smaller houses not too far away from Jed Arvey's home.

The place wasn't much bigger than a shack and appeared about one good gust of wind from falling over. Catherine pushed open the door and it swung back with a rattle and a rusty shriek. They both walked inside, and Nick quickly shut the door and started looking for a latch or some way to lock it. But there was no lock. There was only one hinge that looked nothing close to solid, so he grabbed the first large piece of furniture he could find and pushed it against the closed door.

"I guess that'll have to do," he said grudgingly. "Is this your home?"

"No. It . . ." She had to take a deep breath before finishing. "It's Bob's house. He's . . . he was a cook at The Porter House. He won't be coming home."

"I wish I could . . . I mean, I didn't want to . . ." Nick gritted his teeth and made a noise similar to a wounded animal. It started in the back of his throat, but was under control before it could become much louder than a menacing growl. Although he kept himself from making too much noise, he still felt the tension building up inside of him and knew it had to come out.

His fist curled up tightly and he slammed

his knuckles into the wall beside the door frame. The rickety shack felt the impact of the blow almost too much and dust began trickling down where it had been loosed from various nooks and crannies.

"I didn't want any of this to happen," Nick said. "None of this was supposed to happen."

Catherine felt as though she'd gotten a bit of a release as well after Nick had let out some of his frustration. Either that, she thought, or she was too damn tired to let herself get any more frightened than she already was. Even the questions she'd wanted to ask faded a bit in their importance. All that she wanted was be closer to Nick and try to take away some of the pain both of them were feeling.

"It's all right," she said, reaching out to place her arm over his shoulders. "Nobody would think to look for me here. I don't know if anyone but the owner of The Porter House even knows that he lived here."

Nick turned so he was facing her. Although he started to place his hands on her hips to draw her closer, he pulled them back again before he could get her fully into his grasp. Her body moved toward him anyway, responding to a touch that wasn't even there and closing the distance between them until

315

she was resting against his chest.

When Nick closed his eyes, he could still see the faces of the men who'd wanted to kill him. His ears were still full of gunshots. The stench of blood and gun smoke still coated the inside of his nostrils. There was so much from that night as well as from an entire lifetime's worth of fighting that he felt like he would choke on it.

But before those memories could wash over him into a full, waking nightmare, he was brought back into the present by a sensation that reminded him of how good things could be. It wasn't much more than a flutter of movement against his skin.

Catherine was kissing him.

Gently, almost tentatively, she kissed his neck and rubbed her hands against his sides. She felt him tense when her hands moved over his ribs, and lightened her touch so he could just tell that she was touching him at all.

Nick's bones still ached and his nose was throbbing with pain, but it was worth it all to feel her hands moving over his body. He realized she must have felt the same way because she pushed back the pinch of the cut on her throat and kept moving so she could kiss him some more.

Catherine had nearly forgotten her wound.

The blood had hardened into a shell and the pain was minimal compared to everything else that had happened.

Her lips felt like moist silk being lightly dabbed against his skin. Somehow, even after all that had happened around her, she still managed to remind him of a fresh breeze that had blown in from the open prairie. Ignoring the scent of blood and gunpowder, Nick could detect the scents of leaves and autumn mingled with the distinctive scent of her flesh and hair.

When her kisses stopped, Nick looked down at her. Catherine was looking up at him, her expression a mixture of trepidation and deep longing.

Her lips were so full and soft, they glistened in the weak bits of light coming in through the nearby dirty window. Before he knew what he was doing, Nick was kissing them in a renewed flurry. The moment his mouth touched hers, the passion between them became a roaring flame. Breathy moans came from the back of Catherine's throat and were expelled directly into Nick's mouth. The sounds and movements they made, even the thoughts running through their minds, were translated directly by their most immediate impulses. Despite the pain that came with just about every move he made, Nick wouldn't have stopped himself from making them, even if he could.

In fact, the pain even started to fade as he focused more of his attention on any part of himself that was touching her. He could feel her fingertips and the palms of her hands moving over the back of his neck and up over his shoulder. Her breasts were pressed against him and his legs brushed against her thighs. He could feel the heat of her body through every layer of clothing separating them.

She rubbed herself against him, moaning softly when she felt his body respond.

Her hands drifted through his hair and then down again, traveling all the way over his arms and then down to his waist. Every part of Catherine's body and soul wanted him at that moment. She wanted to feel his bare skin against hers before allowing him to enter her body where he could fill her up and make her whole.

She couldn't believe that she was thinking those things, but they were there all the same. The more she let herself dive into the moment, the less she could think about what she'd seen and experienced earlier that night. It was as though Nick could take her away from it just as he'd taken her away from the animals stalking the night.

Letting herself fall even more deeply for him, Catherine was suddenly brought back to the surface like a sleeper who had been roughly shaken out of a dream. Her hands stopped their exploration of him and were resting on the worn leather gun belt around Nick's waist.

He could feel the same jolt that had gone through Catherine's mind. Perhaps it was even more powerful for him. Suddenly, the gun seemed heavier around his waist, and the familiar holster became an anchor tied around a drowning man.

Like that drowning man, Nick slid down against the wall until his backside hit the floor. Without a word, Catherine knelt down beside him and then curled up on the floor as well. His arms opened reflexively and she fell into them, pressing her cheek against the solid strength of Nick's chest.

"Does this hurt?" she asked. "I could move if it hurts for me to sit like this."

It did hurt, but in response to her question, he said, "Don't move. This feels better than you could imagine."

Closing her eyes, she let her body rest for the first time since she'd seen Nick taken out of the restaurant and said, "I don't have to imagine."

They fell asleep right there on the floor,

holding each other within spitting distance of a perfectly good if somewhat broken down bed. All that was left for Nick now that the battle was over was to get some rest, savor the feel of Catherine's weight against him, and appreciate the fact that they were both still alive. Still, he kept his head against the wall so that even as he slept he might hear any sound that came from the other side.

Though he knew Skinner could creep as silently as any other animal stalking its prey, he also knew there wasn't much he could do about it. Once Skinner didn't want to be found, he might as well be removed from the face of the earth.

The blood still flowed through Nick's veins.

The blood still flowed through his heart and through his head. As long as that would happen, he knew everything he was and everything that was a part of him would remain alive.

His father. His mother. His childhood and all the mistakes that he'd made after those youthful years were over, all were alive inside of him and wouldn't die until his blood stopped flowing.

The blood flowed through his dreams as well.

Tainting his nightly visions a sickening shade of red that he could never shake, the blood in those dreams still flowed out of the bodies of all the men he'd either killed or had been unable to save.

Those ranks had grown by five additional souls since his last meal.

A few fitful breaths caused Nick to stir in his sleep, and when the swirl of his thoughts settled, he found himself back in Montana. In the dream, he inhabited a more youthful version of himself. And despite the fact that he knew where he was headed, his younger self kept walking along the same damn path that would open the door to the same damn nightmares.

The bloodthirsty cries of the mob echoed throughout his sleeping mind. Those voices had once belonged to a group of rational men. Some members of that mob had even been his friends, but now they were something else.

They were killers.

As soon as the first among them had spilled the first drop of blood, they'd been bonded together in the worst possible way. And like the damn fool that was his former self, he kept walking among them even as he wanted to scream at that vision from the past to just ride away.

Looking back on it in hindsight, he knew he should have left that place when he saw where things were headed. But there was no way he could have known how bad they would get. There was no way he could have seen where the trail led until he'd walked it at least once. When he'd been that younger self that he now only visited as a ghost, he hadn't seen things as bad as they'd been the night his entire life was changed.

He'd never seen death in such a raw, naked form as when he'd walked into that house and saw those men dangling from the rafters like grotesque decorations. Five bodies swung from five ropes, each of them with their hands tied behind their backs and their feet kicking like dogs fretting in their sleep.

Nick had wanted to look away from them, but in the dream his eyes had no lids and his head was unable to turn. Taking in a sight like that for even one second was one second too long. It wasn't just the hanged men. Many children were exposed to as much at a town's gallows when a killer or horse thief had reached his final morning.

It wasn't just the sight of death. Nick had seen death once or twice even at that early time in his life.

What made that moment a glimpse into

hell was the fact that he had known all those hanged men personally. There was no justice in their execution. What he'd seen was no hanging. It was a slaughter, and there was no law to turn to for help. There was no sane voice amid the laughter to talk sense into any of those gathered around to watch before those bodies stopped kicking and gagging at the ends of their ropes.

They were still alive.

The realization hit Nick in his dream with every bit of force that it had hit him with the first time. All those bodies hanging from those rafters were still alive, and their eyes were searching the faces of all the people gathered to watch them die. Those eyes seemed dead at first, but there was still some life in there. It was fading quick, but that life was still in there.

The five men opened their mouths, but only their tongues dropped out in a thick mass of purple muscle.

Some of the men in the house laughed when they saw that. Comments were made and jokes were told as the mob stood around and watched as, one by one, those hanged men squeezed out their last breath.

The air stank of piss and worse. That pungent odor forced Nick's whole body to flinch even though the stench was just a memory. When his leg kicked, he felt a stabbing pain flow through his torso and the dream began to fray around its edges.

But the men were still hanging from those rafters and their eyes were opening wide as they started to take their first look at whatever mystery came after this life.

Suddenly, someone in the mob turned to look at him. Even though he was starting to wake up, the dream was too far along to stop just yet. One person in the mob opened his mouth, letting out words that only those inside his dream could hear. Nick didn't know what that man was saying. He hadn't even known when he'd been standing in that house looking up at those thrashing bodies.

Then, just as it was now, the blood was flowing through his heart and mind with such speed that it made him feel dizzy. The fact that his physical self was laying down didn't matter. The fact that he was dreaming didn't matter. Once that first face in the mob spotted him and spoke up, everyone else in the mob turned toward him as well.

That was all that mattered.

Once that whole mob turned on him, they rushed forward like a rockslide with violent desperation filling their eyes.

That was when Nick twitched again and

the shock of pain from his ribs jolted him awake with his next breath lodged in his throat.

"What's the matter, Nick?" Catherine asked. "What is it?"

It only took a second or two for him to realize where he was and what had happened. The dream was like a familiar torture, yet it still rattled him every time it came.

The little house was still dark. Nick realized that he'd probably only been asleep for an hour or two. "Just a dream," he assured her.

"You want to tell me what it was about?"

"No. Just try and get some sleep."

Nick rubbed his hand over Catherine's arm, comforting her until her breathing became slow and deep. He allowed himself to drift off as well, but also kept his ears open for each and every sound outside the house. Somehow, listening for Skinner to come around again was less taxing than seeing those rafters and hearing those voices.

TWENTY-SIX

"I hope you're happy." Shaking his head and pacing the floor of his office, Sheriff Manes turned from the window looking out onto Fourth Street so he could face the big man sitting in the chair beside a large gun cabinet.

Skinner leaned back with his feet propped up on a desk that used to belong to the sheriff's senior deputy. Scott was dead, however, which made the desk seem emptier even though the deputy's items still littered the top. In fact, the entire office felt empty, which was a big factor behind the sheriff pacing the floor of his office.

"If nothing else," Manes said, "I at least hope you're happy."

Taking a moment to reflect, Skinner nodded and gave the sheriff half a smile. "Actually, I'm feeling pretty good this morning."

Turning to glance out the window, Manes looked toward the eastern sky as if to verify what the other man had said. Sure enough, it was morning. Somehow it just didn't feel like another day should have come so casually on the heels of the previous night. It just didn't seem right. None of it seemed right.

It didn't take much to pick up on the sheriff's rotten mood. That was fortunate because Skinner wasn't the type to invest much into something as trivial as someone else's mood.

"And what's got you all twisted into a bunch?" the gray-haired man asked.

For a moment Manes wasn't even sure how to approach that question. "Are you serious?" he asked incredulously. "Could it be fucking possible that you're serious?"

Skinner let out a low whistle. "Such language. And here I thought you were a fine, upstanding citizen."

"Make one more joke, just one more, and I swear to God I don't give a damn how bad you are with that knife or pistol of yours, I will take you apart." There was no room for jest in Manes's voice. The question of whether he could seriously make good on his threat didn't enter his mind. He was too far gone to be thinking rationally.

His eyes darting about the room, Manes

looked for the familiar faces of his deputies and couldn't find any. There was just the cold visage of Skinner to look back at him.

"The only men I've got left on my payroll are Rich and his cousin, and neither one of them are good for anything."

Skinner snapped his fingers and said, "Oh, that's right. *They're* the fine, upstanding citizens."

Before he could think about what he was doing, Sheriff Manes was flying across the room with his hands open and ready to be wrapped around Skinner's throat. The lawman was stopped in his tracks by a slight flutter of movement that was Skinner's hand and the subtle metallic click that was Skinner's pistol being readied to fire.

"You've been real helpful, Sheriff. Fact is, I don't think I could've gotten this far without you. But as helpful as you've been, I could pretty much do without you by now." After letting a moment of silence pass, Skinner asked in a tone that had darkened into a cold dirge seeping out of his mouth, "You seeing things clear enough now? Or do I have to explain it to you better?"

There was no questioning the fact that any further explanation would have come from the barrel of Skinner's gun, which was aimed and ready to go.

Manes backed away from the other man. It was something he hadn't done since he'd gathered the group of followers who'd once been his deputies. "Jesus," he grumbled as the cold, hard facts presented themselves to him one more time. "Jesus Christ, things are a mess."

Seeing that the sheriff wasn't about to make another play after having his most recent bluff called, Skinner lowered the hammer of his pistol and twirled the weapon idly around his finger. "Aw, they're not so bad."

"Not so bad? How the hell can you say that? How the hell can you sit there and act like it's just another day?"

"These things happen, Sheriff."

"Yeah, but not to me. My men are dead and gone and that . . . that undertaker's helper is still out there alive and well."

Skinner laughed. "That boy hasn't been well for a long time."

"Well he should be a whole lot worse. He's the one that should be dead. Not my deputies."

Manes had wound up facing the window once again. His arms were folded across his chest and he glared out at the locals who passed by his window, knowing better than to look inside. He turned on his heels and jabbed a finger toward Skinner. "You knew about that bastard. Surely, the men that're offering that reward don't much care who brings him in. Why didn't you just do it yourself?"

Skinner didn't answer. Instead, he just watched the lawman sweat and kept spinning the pistol around his trigger finger.

"Who is he to you?" Manes asked. "And who's that other fellow he was asking about last night?"

Furrowing his brow as though the question truly did stump him, Skinner brightened up immediately and said, "Oh him. That's just one of Nick's partners from the old days. Finding him was a real stroke of luck, you know."

"I'll just bet it was. That's when you knew that this Nick person would be coming along real soon."

"Every once in a while you actually talk like there's a brain under your hat, Sheriff. I guess it's not that big of a surprise you could take over a whole town for yourself." Skinner swung his feet down off the desk and stood up the moment the bottom of his boots hit the floor. "You want to get your town back?"

"What are you talking about now?"

"I'm talking about this place. This town

that used to be in the palm of your hand when I first got here. The town that you couldn't hold now if your life depended on it because you don't have any men left to back you and everyone around here knows it."

Although it stung to hear those words, there wasn't much that Manes could say to refute them. "And what are you gonna do about all this? Join me and help me put the fear of God into these people so they'll do what I say? It doesn't quite work like that, Skinner."

"I know more about herding sheep like these than you'll ever hope to. Your main problem is that you've got one man out there who's giving hope to all the others."

"You mean Nick Graves."

"You got it."

Manes laughed at the conversation as well as the entire situation. "Well there's a stroke of genius," he said sarcastically. "I never would've thought of that on my own."

"You can think about it all you want, but you know damn well you can't do anything about it. You need me for that, and I'm willing to lend you a hand with your little grave digger problem."

"For a price, I assume?"

"Naturally. And I won't lie to you. It'll be

a steep price, but one that'll be more than worth it since your town should fall back in line once Nick's gone. At least, you shouldn't have any problems until you get yourself some men. Hell, I might be able to steer some good shooters your way as well."

Staring into Skinner's eyes, Manes felt all his precious control slipping out of his grasp like a set of reins used to steer a mule team along a mountain path. And much like a man who'd let his reins go, the mule kept right on running toward the edge of a cliff, leaving him three options: jump off and take his chances on a fall, ride the wagon right off into oblivion, or fight like hell to get those reins back into his hands.

Skinner watched as the sheriff weighed his options. The gray-haired man knew exactly what the other was thinking and still found it amusing to observe the thought process in action.

"You know I don't have a choice here," Manes said as a simple fact.

Skinner shrugged and replied, "You could always leave here and find some other little town." Smirking, he added, "Or you could run away like a little bitch like you did —"

"Fuck you. At least pay me the courtesy of answering a question."

"Go ahead and ask it."

"When you came here, you had this all planned, didn't you?"

It infuriated Manes no end that Skinner actually had the gall to look confused and insulted.

Putting his back to the window, but refraining from moving toward Skinner, Manes kept his arms crossed in front of him as he spoke. "That other fellow you were after. You could have killed him right off the bat, but you didn't. You gave him enough time to get word to this grave digger and then you buried him. You wanted that damn grave digger here because you knew what would happen. I'll even bet you knew he'd take down my men."

"To be honest, Idid have some men coming after me. This here plan hatched while Iwas in that lovely cell you provided. I knew Nick would be coming for Red, and figured he'd take out some of those strutting deputies if they got in his way. I didn't think he'd go through so many, though. He must've been practicing since the last time we met up." Skinner thought for a second and nodded to himself. "But don't fret about your men. After seeing you fold up last night, I would've just killed the ones Nick missed anyhow."

Despite his better judgment, Manes let

his hand drift down toward his gun. "You son of a bitch. How dare you talk to me like that."

"Like you said yerself, you don't have any choice but to listen. And if you want to test me, just go ahead and move your hand toward that gun one more inch. Even another half inch, and I'll blow the back of your skull right through that window."

When Skinner spoke, there was no threat implied. It was a pure statement of fact.

The door to the office swung open and Rich started to walk inside. He stopped when he saw the two men staring intently at each other.

"Leave," Manes commanded.

Rich hesitated.

Skinner addressed the deputy without taking his eyes from the sheriff. "Get your ass out of here, little man."

Rich waited for a full second before retracing his steps through the door and easing it shut once he was outside.

The mocking laughter rumbled right beneath Skinner's surface, but it shone through perfectly clear in his eyes. "There you go, Sheriff. I guess we can see how much control you really have left in this place. Now what about that generous offer of mine?"

Manes let his arms drop down from where he'd been holding them and leaned over to take a look through the front window. He truly couldn't believe that Rich would take some murderer's orders over his own. But sure enough, Rich took one last look at the sheriff's office, motioned toward his cousin who was waiting nearby, and they both strolled down the street, leaving Manes behind them.

Skinner had already gotten to his feet and was walking to stand directly behind Manes. "You know your choices. It don't matter too much how you got here or what anyone had planned. The only thing you need to think about now is if you want to stay here and lose everything you worked for to some grave digger or let me help you get it all back."

There wasn't much more for the sheriff to consider. Skinner had him by the short hairs and he knew it. That left only one other option besides the one being dangled in front of him by a known killer.

"And what if I decide to go after this grave digger myself?" Manes asked.

"There's nothing stopping you. It's your funeral."

Manes let out an exasperated breath and turned his back to the window. In doing so, he might as well have been turning his back on everything that used to be his former life. "What's your price?"

TWENTY-SEVEN

When Catherine woke up, she stretched her arms out, expecting to feel Nick behind her. But the only thing she felt was a slab of wood. Beneath her there was something that was way too soft to be the same floor upon which she'd fallen asleep. Her eyes snapped open and darted about the room. It took a couple of blinks and some rubbing of her eyes, but she soon realized that she was still in the same house she'd taken Nick to the night before. The only difference was that she was presently on the little bed rather than stretched out on the floor.

"Nick?" she said quietly. "Are you still here?"

The house was only one room, so even with the bits of furniture scattered about, there wasn't much place to hide. Thinking that Nick had left her alone, Catherine started to get out of the bed. Before her feet touched the floor, however, she spotted some movement near the front door.

Nick was still there. He'd just been so quiet and so still that he blended seamlessly into the dusty shadows between the brilliant rays of sunlight that shone through the window. Now that she was up and about, Nick turned to look at her. "It's early," he said. "You can get some more sleep if you like. How you feeling?"

Her hand drifted to the wound on her neck. Although she could feel the crusted blood as well as the sting when she moved her head, it wasn't much more than a minor discomfort. "Better," she replied. "You?"

Nick knew better than to check his wounds. As long as he was conscious, those wounds were making him aware of their presence. Sometime throughout the previous night, the blood had been washed away from his face and strips of material had been tightly wrapped around his torso. Since he wasn't about to head to a doctor's office, that was about all he could want by way of treatment.

"I'm doing pretty good," he lied. "Why don't you go back to sleep?"

"I slept more than enough, thank you. I think I'd feel better fixing you some breakfast."

"I already ate."

"Well, then some coffee maybe."

Nick shook his head. "I was just about to leave." He could see the frown coming even before it turned the edges of Catherine's lips downward. "It should be safe. Nobody even came near this place all night. Ever since the sun came up, it's even quieter."

"Stay here?" she asked in a whisper that barely made it across the room. "Please. That . . . man is still out there. Isn't he still out there?"

"Yes. He is."

"So what are you going to do, then? Go find him and start shooting at each other again? What if he kills you?"

Smiling, Nick walked over to where she was standing and wrapped his arms around her. She melted into his embrace but didn't return it. Instead, she kept her hands tucked up against her chest and rested her head against him.

"I'm not going to get into a fight today," Nick said reassuringly. "At least, not if I can help it. There's too much work to be done."

"What kind of work?"

"The Eddings funeral is being held this evening and the burial is tomorrow. Didn't you get your invitation?"

Catherine pulled away from him and pointed to the floor. An invitation had been slipped beneath the door and was wedged against the furniture that Nick had used to brace it shut. "You really think the funeral's still going to be held?" she asked. "After everything that happened last night, you think folks will want to come out of their houses?"

"You'd be surprised. Most folks would rather go on with their lives after something bad happens. Actually, I'll bet that what happened to us is the talk of the town."

As much as she wanted to say that wouldn't be the case or that the town would be holding its breath when she walked outside again, Catherine knew that wouldn't be right. The people of Jessup may have been gossips, but they were strong. What amazed her was how easily Nick was handling everything. "You're probably right."

"Better that than have them hide like rabbits in their holes. I'll bet they feel a little better not having those three asshole deputies strutting up and down the streets."

"I guess so. But it's not the deputies I was worried about."

"I know," Nick said while holding onto her. "I know exactly what you mean, but I can't hide from him either."

"And what about the rest of us?"

"I'm the one he really wants, Catherine.

That's why I don't plan on being too hard to find. I'll be doing my job for everyone to see while you stay here where we know it's safe. I've dealt with him before, so I can deal with him again."

"How do you deal with a man like that, Nick? Just . . . kill him?"

"Don't worry about it. He's not your problem. Do me a favor, though. Go through these things here and get some idea of what you think your cook friend would like to be buried in. You should also get some idea of what type of service he would like."

"What? I'm not sure I could —"

"Just go through his things, pick out a nice suit of clothes and the rest will fall into place."

Strangely enough, Catherine seemed to look more like her old self now that she had something to keep her occupied. She nodded and said, "All right. It's the least I can do for him since he did try to save my life."

"He did save your life," Nick clarified. "Both of them did. If they hadn't stepped in for you, Skinner would have killed you. I know that for a fact."

Catherine stepped back and walked toward a small dresser that only had two drawers in it. Her hands seemed to work on their own as she began sorting through the dead cook's clothes. "Who is he? Skinner, I mean. How do you know a man like that?"

Nick's first impulse was to tell her the truth. But he knew that telling her about Skinner would have been a mistake.

The truth only would have scared her.

"Skinner is an animal," was all Nick decided to say on the matter. "That at least makes it easy for me to know what he's going to do next."

Looking over at him, Catherine was about to demand that he tell her more on the subject. But before she could say anything, Nick had turned his back on her and was collecting his jacket, which he'd used as a pillow the night before. He slid the jacket on, checked outside through the dirty window, then pushed aside the heavy furniture so he could open the door.

"I'll check on you before too long," he said. "You'll be fine."

Catherine took a deep breath, and before she could let it out, Nick had left. "I know," she said quietly to whatever spirits were listening. "We all will."

TWENTY-EIGHT

Nick had every intention of heading to Dan Callum's place and getting to work. As far as he knew, the Eddings funeral was still on, and the undertaker would have plenty on his plate with what had happened the night before. Once he'd snuck around and put plenty of distance between himself and the house where Catherine was staying by taking back streets and ducking into alleyways, he started to feel more like his normal self.

Emerging at the end of Cavalry Avenue not too far from Mil's, he noticed that he hadn't been too far off the mark in what he'd told Catherine. Although there did seem to be a shadow hanging over the town as a whole, there were still plenty of people out and about. There were even a few smiles to be seen, but Nick had to look intently to find them.

He kept his steps lively but took an indirect route onto Eighth Street. Part of him was hoping to come across Skinner while the day was young so he could get the confrontation over with. But the gray-haired man was nowhere to be found, which wasn't too big a surprise.

As always, the local foot traffic thinned out considerably by the time Nick got within sight of Dan Callum's parlor. The undertaker was just walking around from his own back lot when Nick approached.

"There you are!" Callum said. "I thought you were dead."

"Nice to see you too," Nick responded dryly.

Callum waved off the comment and rushed up to take hold of Nick's hand. He shook it vigorously as he spoke. "I heard about what happened last night, and since you didn't sleep in your room again, I thought something awfully bad happened to you. The sheriff doesn't pull someone out in public like that too often, but when he does, we don't usually see that person again." He paused and scratched his head before adding, "Well, I might see him."

"And today's no different. You see me now, don't you?"

"I sure do, boy. I sure do."

The last time Nick had been called boy

was by people trying to get under his skin, and they had almost gotten their teeth knocked out seconds later for the bad choice of words. Before that it had been Stasys saying it when Nick was young enough to fit the title. This time it sounded more like his father talking than some idiot with a chip on his shoulder, so Nick let it pass.

"Come on back here," Callum said, letting Nick's hand go so he could place that arm over the younger man's shoulder. "We got plenty to do today, and it needs to be done before the Eddings affair tonight. I've had plenty of folks let me know they have every intention of showing up for it."

"That's great news. Nobody seemed scared off by what happened?"

"Scared? Hell no. In fact, most folks are talking like the sheriff's gone for good and all of his asshole deputies went with him." Lowering his voice to a conspiratorial whisper, Callum asked, "Is that the case?"

"Could be."

"I heard there was some devil on the loose with a knife in his hand. He gutted poor Bob Kimnach like a fish and killed the Fontana boy as well. Did you see any of that?"

The shadow that fell over Nick's face was

more than enough to answer Callum's question.

"It looks like you managed to get away," Callum said. "But you look like hell. Did those deputies bust up your nose?"

When Nick tried to smile grudgingly, he felt pain stab through his face and rattle his eyeballs. "And then some. Took some hard shots to my ribs as well."

Callum shook his head. "Could've been worse. Most folks around here think you were killed, but the owner of The Porter House says he saw you taking Catherine Weaver away from there."

"She's safe," Nick said.

"I also heard the sheriff talking about how he ran that bastard killer out of Jessup for what he done to his deputies. That son of a bitch didn't say a word about those other two boys."

"You hear a lot, don't you?"

"Well, there's a lot to be heard since you got here. And I don't mind telling you that fixing those deputies up to be put in the ground is a pleasure. If it was up to me, I wouldn't even have services arranged for them. Hell, nobody but the sheriff is gonna show anyway. But a paying job is a paying job."

"Speaking of which, why don't you show

me what needs doing before it's too late to get any of it done."

Callum turned and led the way around to the back lot of his parlor, where there were five piles of lumber set out at even intervals. "I've just gotten finished getting my ducks in a row. Here's the lumber for the coffins. No need to put your back out on three of them. Those deputies could rot in a hole naked for all I care, but that just wouldn't be proper. Be sure to do a nice job on the other two."

"Don't worry about that," Nick said, knowing that "the other two" referred to the two young men who'd tried to save Catherine. "They'll get the best I can make."

"Good. And once you're done with that, we should be able to get started on the markers. I've got Miss Matthews coming over to help get things set up for the Eddings affair, so that frees us up for one hard day's work."

"I've never turned my nose up at one of those."

"That's good too. Especially since you need to go and collect those bodies before either of us can get started in on any of the rest that needs to be done. Now you see why I'm so glad to see you made it out of that mess alive before that animal with the knife killed you just like he did all them others."

"That's funny, because I was just starting to wish the exact opposite thing."

Although those five bodies had surely been dragged out of sight or covered with a tarp, there apparently hadn't been anyone willing to take them all the way to the parlor. Since he was the low man on the totem pole, Nick didn't complain about getting the dirty work of collecting corpses that had had all night to ferment.

"You don't have to do everything, though," Callum assured him. "I already hitched up the mule to my wagon, so you can just ride down the street and pick those boys up."

"I'll get right to it."

And with that, both men started in on their tasks. Callum headed into his workshop, where he prepared to receive the bodies and get them made up to look handsome for their appointment with the Almighty. Nick took off his jacket, rolled up his sleeves, and walked to the undertaker's wagon.

So far it sounded to him as though the general opinion of the town was that he and Catherine were both lucky to have made it out of a killing spree that centered mostly around Skinner's bloody rampage. Well, if that murderer had ever been good for anything, it was drawing attention.

The only thing left for him to do, he thought, was try to keep people thinking that he was just another a victim. That meant not appearing as though he was anything more than a grave digger, which in turn meant not wearing his gun to collect the bodies. In a way, it seemed odd to be concerned over such things after all that had happened. But then again, something in Nick's mind wanted to go about his life as though he was unaffected by what had happened.

He wouldn't normally wear a gun when running an errand like this one, and doing so now would show that Skinner and the rest had gotten to him. Nick couldn't abide by that. The folks in town had enough to be scared of and didn't need another gunman walking down the streets to add to the mix.

Still, as much as he wanted to go about his duties in a proper manner, there was another duty he needed to consider: defending his life. Grudgingly, Nick strapped on his gun belt and made sure it was mostly concealed beneath his coat. The weight of it there at that moment served only as a reminder that he wasn't a man who could lead a normal life. Perhaps he could never be such a man. For that reason, he hated Skinner and all the others like him even more.

Nick drove the wagon up to The Porter House and saw that the bodies had been moved out of the street.

"Where the hell have you been?" asked the very angry owner of the restaurant. "If I woulda known that nobody was gonna fetch these boys by now, I woulda taken them down to Dan Callum's place myself."

The businessman was about to launch into another tirade when he got a look at Nick's face. "Oh," he said, coming up short all of a sudden. "You were the one pulled out of here by Sheriff Manes."

"Yes sir, I am," Nick said as he climbed down from the wagon. "And I'm sorry for being late."

"Just uh . . . just please get these bodies out of here. They're over in that alley. At least the deputies are. Bob and that Fontana kid are with their families. Both of them were farmers. I can take you to their houses if you'd like."

Nick was already walking toward the alley. He didn't need directions. All he needed was a functioning nose to make his way to those bodies. It was a cold day, but the chill wasn't enough to keep the stink from the air.

The deputies lay on the ground, and a dirty tarp had been thrown over them to keep them out of sight, but that was about it. Shaking his head, Nick realized just how despised those three must truly have been. Most folks would do better for an animal carcass they'd found under their porch. Those three had been left out to rot. The sad part was, it wasn't the first time he'd seen such disrespect for the dead.

"I know it isn't right," the restaurant owner said, joining Nick and the bodies in the alley. "But the only ones sad to see these boys go is the sheriff, and even he didn't come around to help gather them up. You don't look so good yourself. What did they do to you?"

"Gave me quite a beating," Nick answered as he knelt down to gently scoop up the blond deputy's corpse into his arms. The weight of the dead man sent a torrent of pain through Nick's entire body like daggers shooting outward from his cracked ribs. The dressings held, though, and Nick swallowed a good deal of the discomfort. Since he was the one to send them to hell, he figured it was only right that he dig their hole and carry them to it.

The restaurant owner's eyes flashed to Nick's waist, attracted by the glimpse he'd caught of a gun belt. Although he seemed a bit unnerved by the sight, he wasn't surprised by it. "Not that it's my business, but why would they do that to you? Does Sheriff Manes have something against you?"

"Yeah. I wouldn't bow down to the first deputy when I pulled into town. After that, I made the mistake of opening my mouth about trying to call down some real law into this town."

The other man winced as though he was feeling real physical pain. "Oh, that was a mistake. That's the type of thing to get a man killed."

Walking out of the alley, Nick went over to the wagon and set the body down in the cart's narrow bed. "Yeah," he said. "The sheriff saw it the same way." Although the restaurant owner followed him back into the alley and helped move things out of the way, it was obvious he had no intention of touching any of the bodies himself.

Nick picked up Harelip's remains and had to carry them over one shoulder, which made the edges of his vision blur from the pain of his wounds. "If that other man with the knife hadn't come along, I'll bet I'd be one of the bodies here in this alley today."

The other man nodded furiously, completely buying into the account that Nick was feeding him. "He was a mad dog. I was here when he killed my two workers. He was like a man possessed."

There was no need for Nick to stretch or bend the truth in any way when he answered, "Yes, sir. He had the devil in his eyes."

"Well I guess you would know."

Nick stacked Harelip's body on top of Blondie. The corpse landed with a solid thump before Nick turned to look into the face of the other man. For a moment he thought the restaurant owner was hinting at something he knew. But the surprised look in the other man's eyes told another story.

"I didn't mean to be disrespectful," the restaurant owner said quickly. "I just meant you were right there, weren't you? You saw it better than anyone else."

"Yeah. I did." Nick turned and walked back into and through the alley to fetch Scott's body, which was still in the back lot.

Even with two of the three corpses removed, the lot stank of blood and feces. Leftover gunpowder clung to the surfaces of boxes and broken posts like scum on the bottom of a rock. Nick's feet pressed down into the mud, keeping his eyes focused on the one body that remained.

"Did the sheriff ever catch him?" Nick asked.

Temporarily overwhelmed by the grotesque spectacle of the scene, the restaurant owner shook himself out of it and said, "Huh? Oh! Did he catch who?"

"The mad dog killer."

"He says he ran him off. Either that or the crazy bastard got what he came for and moved on. Nobody around here would be a bit surprised if those deputies were killed because of some other rotten business they were in." The man paused and looked down at the body that Nick had picked up and was carrying back to the wagon. "No sir. Not one bit surprised."

By the time Nick had loaded up the wagon and was climbing into the driver's seat, there was a good sized crowd gathered around to watch. It was about the turnout he'd expected after having seen more than his fair share of people curious to see a clean-up like this one.

Nick got the directions to the other two men's homes from the restaurant owner and snapped his reins. The mule strained a bit with the added weight but got the wagon rolling all the same. Compared to this scene, Nick figured that picking up the bodies of the two who'd stepped in on Catherine's behalf would be a much more somber affair. At least, he hoped that would be the case.

As he'd expected, both of the restaurant workers' families were quiet and walked about as if in a daze. With their grief too strong and too fresh to do much of anything else, they simply let Nick take the bodies of their departed loved ones, handed over clothes for them to be buried in, then watched him drive away.

Twenty-Nine

Collecting the bodies took Nick less than an hour to complete, but it seemed a whole lot longer. There wasn't much room left inside the wagon, and the corpses formed a gruesome pile in the cart behind him. Nick did his best to stay away from the main streets on his drive back to Callum's parlor. The undertaker was standing outside the back entrance, waiting for him when he arrived.

Unloading the bodies went a lot faster with both of them on the job. In a matter of minutes Callum and Nick had the corpses placed on tables in the workshop and prepared for the undertaker's professional attention.

After putting the wagon where it belonged and unhitching the mule, Nick headed for the back lot and began hammering together the coffins Callum needed. With no call for quality on the first three, those were finished in just over two hours.

Nick slowed himself down, however, once he started the fourth and fifth. For those two, he sanded down every edge and made sure every corner was straight. He even carved R.I.P. in a practiced, craftsman's script. Those three letters looked plain at first, but a closer inspection revealed the intricate care that had been taken to make the writing more pleasing to the eye. The touches were subtle, but made it seem as though the letters had been written onto the wood with a brush rather than carved by metal tools.

Proud of his work, Nick was stretching his arms and taking a moment to enjoy it when he heard someone walk in the parlor's front door. He stepped through the workshop to get a look at who had arrived and found Callum speaking to a disheveled-looking man wearing a badge.

The sight of that metal star sent a chill through Nick's blood, but this deputy seemed nothing like the rest. In fact, Callum appeared to treat the lawman with genuine respect and friendliness, so Nick just stayed behind and let the two have their conversation without any interruption. There wasn't much more than a few more words exchanged between the two before the deputy handed Callum a large bundle of what appeared to be dark material tied together with twine.

After he left, Callum turned around and spotted Nick standing in the workshop doorway. "That was Rich," he said.

That explained a lot. "I heard Catherine mention him. He sounds like the only lawman worth his badge around here."

"You got that right." Holding up the bundle of material, the undertaker said, "He came by to give me these. They're clothes for the three that were killed. My guess is Rich picked them out himself even though he couldn't stand those three any more'n the rest of us. Rich is a good man. I'm glad he didn't get mixed up in whatever happened last night."

Callum walked past Nick and into the workshop, making sure the door was shut tightly behind him. All three deputies were laid out on the tables closest to him, and the two other men were stretched out on one closer to the back door. After setting the pile of clothes onto the table beside the bodies, the undertaker started going through the pieces of clothing and separating them by size, eyeballing which piece was meant for which man.

"What do you think so far?" Callum asked.

Before Nick could ask for clarification, he saw the undertaker nod toward the bodies. Although they still had to be dressed in clean clothes, each of the corpses had been cleaned up and their gaping wounds roughly sewn together. Nick did his best to ignore the wounds to the face and instead examined each one in a more detached, professional manner.

"You did a good job, sir. It looks like there won't be an open coffin for all of them, though."

Callum walked over to one of the bodies. While each man had his eyes closed as though sleeping, one of them had a third eye that had been carved through his forehead by a quick piece of lead. Over that, Callum draped a white handkerchief in articulate, flowing motions that reminded Nick of a servant draping a napkin over someone's lap.

"There," Callum said after straightening out a few wrinkles. "A wake is for folks to see the face of the departed one last time. Even if they are better off dead, I'd think there's at least one person in town who might want to say their good-byes."

Nick watched as Callum fretted with that handkerchief covering the black hole that had been punched through the deputy's skull. The undertaker kept fretting until it was exactly perfect, tugging until all that was left was the freshly scrubbed face.

"You're a good man, Mr. Callum."

In response, the undertaker merely shrugged. "Just doing my job. Whatever right or wrong they might have done, I'm just supposed to make sure they look good for their first day on the other side. Whatever comes next isn't in my hands."

"But still, most everyone else acts like they couldn't be happier to see those three go. I'm surprised they weren't just dumped in a hole somewhere before I got there."

"How are those coffins coming?"

"They're done. I was just stretching my legs before getting started on the markers."

"We've got to get started on preparing for the Eddings affair. It won't be long before people start showing up. The family will want to see her before anyone else gets here. That reminds me, I need to take her picture."

Of all the rituals that came along with tending to the dead, Nick was only disturbed by one of them, and this was it. He followed the undertaker into the main room where there was a coffin sitting against a side wall. It took both men to move the wooden box onto the table at the head of the room in front of all the pews.

Inside, Mrs. Eddings lay resting. Her skin was cinching in against her face and her eyes were sinking lower into their sockets. Callum had done a good job with the makeup, which gave her cheeks and lips a bit of color. Once the coffin was on display, Nick removed the lid and stepped aside to wait for Callum to come back with a camera.

Something about photographing the body seemed unnatural to Nick. It was respectful to pay attention to details like carving an attractive marker and giving the dead a nice sendoff. But those pictures that were taken of the dead and kept by their families had a way of sticking in Nick's mind no matter how much he tried to sweep them away.

He hadn't even had a lot of pictures taken of himself and his father because they were not only expensive, but taking them was a long, tedious affair. By the time they came out, the subjects' eyes were glassy and far removed from the situation. He knew that was a result of boredom mostly, but he always thought it made the people in those portraits look dead.

While Nick went through his thoughts, Callum had been fretting with the camera and making minor touch-ups to the old lady's appearance.

"All right," he said finally. "Stand back from there."

As soon as Nick was far enough away, Callum took his picture. The flash powder went up in a smoky puff and then it was a matter of having Callum fret with the equipment some more to get it out of the way.

"Take this in the back and set it up next to those deputies, will you Nick?"

"Sure."

"You don't like this part much, do you? I can see it in your eyes."

"No, I guess I don't."

"Strange, but there's always something that gets to a man. Even a man in our line of work has a thing that puts the chill into him. For me, it's always been dressing them. I half expect one of them to start screaming at me or some nonsense like that. Sometimes they'll twitch or kick a bit. Damn unsettling."

Callum followed Nick into the workshop and got to work on the deputies' makeup while Nick set up the camera for the next picture.

"If you don't mind me asking, what is it about the pictures that gets to you?" Callum inquired. "Seems like that's the easiest part of this job."

"I don't like having my picture taken."

"Some of the redskins say it steals your soul. You're not part Injun are you?"

Nick smirked at the joke and shook his head. "Not quite. I can see where they get that idea, though. People's faces look . . . empty in portraits. Like those wartime pictures from the battlefields. My father had a better reason for it, though." Nick reached down the front of his shirt and removed something that hung from a tarnished chain. The jewelry was delicate, but looked even more so in contrast to the rough hands that held it.

"What do you have there? A locket?" Callum asked, unable to hide his surprise.

Nick nodded and opened it with an ease and gentleness that would seem too much to ask for from a man missing so much of his hands. Inside was a picture of a woman in her late twenties. Her hair appeared to be sandy brown and fine as silk. She had the face of a Gypsy and a wide, loving smile that seemed to illuminate the very fabric of the photograph.

"What's the name of that beauty?"

"Her name's Sophie," Nick said. "My mother. Whenever my father would look at this, he would say that people should just stop taking pictures of themselves because there was no way to take a picture better than this one." Looking at the picture for a few moments, Nick started to nod slowly while gently closing the locket. "I think I'll have to agree with him."

Both men got back to work. Callum did his best to make it look as though blood was still flowing beneath the dead men's skin, and Nick hammered together the markers that would be planted at the head of each grave. This time he kept his gun belt off. He did so out of respect for his craft as well as respect for the dead men he worked to honor. Something just didn't feel right about preparing for and attending a funeral while armed. But he was certain trouble was still brewing.

He was also certain he'd find a way to deal with it once it arrived.

For the moment, he went about his duty the way any other man in his position would. He wasn't about to start in on carving the names into the wood, however. First he needed to find out what was to be written and, if need be, come up with a sentiment to go along with the facts.

But even the job of getting those facts together would have to wait. There were arrangements to be made concerning the Eddings wake, which was to take place in a matter of hours. Much like a party with a more somber tone, a wake was a grand affair. In the case of someone like Mrs. Eddings, who was missed by an entire community, it could be a gathering of the entire town, which simply didn't happen very often.

It was a chance for people to not only pay respects, but to catch up on the lives of people who hadn't said much more than the how-do-you-do's of everyday activity. There was food to be served, decorations to prepare, speeches to write, and glasses to fill. As a Mourner, Nick had the added duty to be present for the entire wake and pay especially close attention to the immediate family of the deceased.

All of this kept him so busy that he didn't even notice that Callum was done in his workshop until the flash powder started popping again. After three pops over the course of several minutes, Callum emerged from the workshop while tugging the apron off from where it had been hanging around his neck.

The undertaker fussed with the decorations Nick had set up and greeted the boy who brought the food and drink to the front door. Matthew the printer even stopped by to drop off the slips of paper that were commemorative announcements of the day's ceremonies to be handed out as remembrances. The invitations to the deputies' wake were done as well. As promised, they were rushed and a little smudged, but they were legible, and the undertaker figured that was good enough.

Callum dropped the deputies' invitations in his office and stacked the more elegant ones meant for that night's affair on a small table near the front door. Once that was done, he stepped outside and stretched his arms over his head while grunting with the discomfort of aching muscles.

"Come on out here, Nick," he called over his shoulder. "Take a breather before the guests start arriving."

Nick straightened a picture of a younger Mrs. Eddings that was provided by her husband to be shown next to the coffin. After that, he walked out to stand beside Callum, where they both savored the few moments of peace.

Unfortunately, that peace only lasted for a few seconds before Callum asked the one question Nick had been hoping to avoid.

"Tell me something," the undertaker said. "What does 3-7-77 mean?"

THIRTY

"What are you talking about?" Nick responded, doing a fairly good job of feigning ignorance.

Callum repeated the numbers in a manner that implied he wasn't buying Nick's act one bit. "Three-7-77. It was written in blood in front of The Porter House last night. It was written right by where you were standing, is what I heard. I'm no gambling man, but I'd still wager every dime to my name that you and the one who wrote it are the only ones in Jessup who know what it means."

"I'm still the talk of the town, huh?"

"Not as much as that mad dog killer from last night and the blood he spilled. Actually, most of what I heard is talk about some grudge between that killer and the sheriff that goes back to March seventh of 1877."

"But you don't believe that."

"No, sir," Callum said solemnly. "I most

certainly do not."

"Why?"

"Because I lived here back then and so did Corey Manes. That was a while before he was sheriff, of course, and it sure as hell was a while before this town knew about the likes of that butcher who killed those boys last night."

"You sure about that?"

Callum looked over at Nick and nodded. "I'd stake my life on it. Corey Manes was a deputy, and not a very good one at that. There were rumors floating around about him not being the straightest arrow in the bunch, but a blood feud? No sir. I don't believe that for a second.

"In fact it seems to me that none of the real trouble started until you came to town, Nick, and this other little puzzle seems to fit you right down to the bone. Part of my job — make that our jobs — is to be able to read people and how they react to certain things. We're in the profession of dealing with sensitive matters while trying not to hurt too many folks along the way."

Nick had to smile at that. If only Callum knew just how much that applied to him.

"When I asked you about those numbers," Callum went on to say, "there was a look in your eyes like the one I see when I deliver the bad news to a woman who already knows she's been widowed. You knew what was coming and you didn't want to hear it. That look don't come out of ignorance.

"I may not have known you for long, but I know that you're a good man who means well. I just think that telling someone about this load you're carrying around with you might help. It's like what a grieving family needs to do after they lose someone. They need to let it go before they break under all that weight."

"Jesus Christ, Dan, you don't let up, do you?"

"No, sir. I do not."

Pulling in a deep breath and then letting it out, Nick couldn't believe that someone like Dan Callum had seen so much of what he'd been trying to hide. Despite all of his efforts, the undertaker still saw right though him like he was a first-timer sitting down to a professional poker game.

More than that, he couldn't believe what he was about to say next.

"Three-7-77," Nick explained, "is something that Skinner picked up in Montana."

"Skinner?"

"That mad dog killer. He's got a name. It's Nathan Skinner."

Callum nodded. "Go on."

"His feud isn't with the sheriff. It's with me. We've known each other for over fifteen years, and though we were never really friends, we went through a lot of bad times together and saw a lot of blood spilled. I guess we were kind of like soldiers fighting in the same regiment. We covered each other when the lead started to fly and came to rely on each other.

"But there was no war. We weren't soldiers and we sure as hell never were friends. Well . . . not really anyhow." With an ironic smirk, Nick added, "Brothers in all but blood, maybe, but never friends."

Already Nick could see the change in Callum's face. The undertaker was having a hard time digesting what he was being told. It showed by the paleness in his face and the discomfort in his shifting stance.

"He wasn't always this bad, Dan. I wasn't the same either. When Skinner was younger, he was no mad dog killer. Neither of us were angels, but we were just fighting to get out of our boring lives before we got too old and too roped into anything like a family that needed raising or a business that needed to be run."

Nick shrugged and looked at Callum unapologetically. "Believe it or not, I didn't always want to be a Mourner. . . ."

THIRTY-ONE

Virginia City, Montana
1864

If a man wanted to raise his family in a calm place and run a prosperous business, there were plenty of good places to go. America was full of them. Unfortunately, this place at this time was not one of them.

There were plenty of good men to be found in Virginia City, but there was hardly any law to protect them from the other types who rode through town like they owned every bit of land they stepped on and deserved to take whatever they wanted from those too weak to fight for it. It was a time when the country was already at war with itself. Blood had become such a common part of life that killings didn't seem out of place on or off the battlefield.

Nick Graves was eighteen years old, and this was the farthest he'd traveled since his father had picked up and moved from Missouri into Kansas. Stasys was still in Kansas, which seemed like a whole world away from Nick and his pack of similarly wide-eyed wolves. There were half a dozen of them. That number had been whittled down from the original ten who'd started their ride in Wichita a year before and had been raising hell ever since.

They'd paid their own way across the country using skills learned from sources ranging from fellow outlaw gangs to the Union Army. It was amazing how similar such sources were. In fact, some of the boys riding with Nick still wore their military colors. Others, like Nick himself, had become more accustomed to the brutal guerrilla fighting that didn't get written about in too many newspapers or official reports sent back to the War Department.

There were soldiers riding in the gang as well as outlaws. There were wide-eyed kids out for some excitement and there were men like Nathan Skinner. Actually, there was only one other like him, and that was the one who'd made Skinner into the man he was to become. That man wasn't riding with Nick and his hellion friends. Some doubted he even truly existed outside of a nightmare.

Skinner was the kind of young man who

seemed to have been born wearing a disturbing smile and thinking disturbing things. Although he'd done work for the military, he'd never worn a uniform.

He didn't come from an especially bad family.

He was just a bad man.

The true bad men were a rare breed, and like most rare animals, they made a lasting impression on anyone who crossed their paths.

Nick, Skinner, and the rest of the gang rode into Virginia City with fire in their eyes and ill-gotten gains in their saddlebags. They tied their horses to a post outside the first saloon they could find and then proceeded to hand out the money they'd stolen to the working girls who descended upon them like predators in bustiers.

Once the saloon doors closed behind them, Nick and the rest of his brothers in arms were lost in the sea of debauchery that gave many towns their primary source of income. Inside those walls, the young men felt like kings, and as long as their money kept flowing, there were plenty of people willing to prolong the illusion.

Nick had learned many a swift trick at the card table, thanks to nights like that first one spent in Virginia City. He'd also acquired his taste for brunettes and the sweet scent that naturally flowed from the pores of some women's skin. He'd become a man during that long ride from Wichita, although it was hardly the kind of man that Stasys would have hoped for.

That was something Nick hadn't liked to think about. Not then, and not in the years to come. That was how he'd acquired another taste: namely, the taste for vodka. Lots of it.

Although they'd spent several days in Virginia City, he never recalled there being a sunrise. Mostly, that was because Nick rarely stuck his head outside, and when he did, it was at some ungodly hour of the night. Also, that was because his memories of that place would be forever darkened by what had happened there.

Like soldiers sharing good times and bad, Nick and the surviving members of his gang grew closer the more time they spent in that saloon. Over the course of those days, they joked, drank, gambled, and eventually spent all the money they'd taken prior to reaching the Virginia City limits. But in all that time, Nick had yet to buy a drink for one of the founding members of their tightly knit group.

"Where's Skinner?" Nick asked one of the

members of the gang. While everyone had their uses, this member was kept around for only two reasons: entertainment and wide shoulders.

Ford Fargo knew how to tell a hell of a joke and had been genuinely bright as a young child. As he grew into a young man, that brightness just seemed to get dimmer every year. Even so, he was still good for a laugh. And though he wasn't much with a pistol, his wide shoulders made him a bigger target than most, which made him a definite use in a fight. Most of the others looked after Ford but were more than happy to watch him be the first one to walk into a tense situation and draw a little fire.

Somehow, Ford had managed to stay alive longer than most decoys, which only reinforced one of Skinner's axioms: The Lord looked out for the stupid.

"Hey Ford," Nick said as he sidled up to the big guy with the friendly smile permanently etched onto his face. The other man obviously hadn't heard him the first time, so Nick added a light punch to Ford's shoulder to grab his attention. "Have you seen Skinner?"

Ford shrugged. "Ain't he with a lady?"

"I don't know. I haven't seen him since we got here."

"Got here to this saloon, or here to Montana?"

"Dammit, Ford, just forget it."

Unfortunately, nobody else Nick could find had much more information than Ford. That only made Nick more curious, since Skinner had been disappearing more and more the longer they stayed in town. It seemed doubly curious because neither he nor any of the rest of the gang really left that saloon. Nick walked toward the saloon's front door, refusing the advances of a pretty little brunette who'd shared her bed with him three times since his arrival.

Before he could take hold of the handle, the door burst open as someone came into the place like a charging bull. Nick caught a fleeting glance of one stern face before it was covered. The man who entered pulled a sheet down over his face and took a few more steps inside. From there, he pushed past Nick and stepped sideways to make room for the next group of men who entered the saloon.

All of the men wore sheets over their faces, making them look like ghosts of hanged men since all the sheets were fastened with rope tied around their necks. Burning, intense eyes stared out through holes cut roughly through the fabric of their makeshift hoods, and the vague outlines of their faces could barely be seen behind the material.

Moving as one, the men spread out within the saloon and displayed the weapons they were carrying. Mostly, their hands were filled with shotguns, but there were also a few rifles and pistols in the mix. Because of the crowd inside the saloon, as well as the alcohol flowing through his system, it was hard for Nick to say how many there were. Looking back on it, he guessed there were probably around nine or ten. At the time, however, the group seemed more like a legion sent by the devil himself.

Nick's hand went instinctively to the gun at his side. The Army model Colt was the same one given to him by an officer stationed in Missouri a few years back and was the same one Nick had used to send his first man to hell. Still, even though all his fingers had still been in place back then, the gun felt cumbersome in his hand and he wasn't nearly fast enough to clear leather before one of the masked men turned on him and jammed the barrel of a shotgun into Nick's gut.

"Don't be foolish, boy," came the voice, which sounded like a muffled growl once it made it through the crude hood. "We just came to talk."

One of the other masked men looked over to his partner and Nick. "Is that one of 'em that we heard about?"

The first man nodded beneath his hood, pressing the shotgun a bit harder into Nick until he saw the Colt drop back the rest of the way into its holster. "Yeah, this is one of 'em all right. Where are the rest of you hiding?"

Nick didn't answer. He just stared into what he could see of the other man's face, feeling as though he was staring into a bleached skull with the eyeballs still wedged in their sockets.

The rest of the men fanned out, searching through the crowd with their shotguns held out in front of them.

"We'll find you all sooner or later," the one who must have been their leader shouted. "So you might as well make it easy on us."

Ford was the first one they spotted. He tried to hide from the masked men, but his frame wasn't the type best suited for hiding and he only wound up drawing more attention to himself, as well as to the man he was ushering toward the back door. Ford made it less than two steps before tripping over a board that sat less than a quarter of an inch above the rest of the floor. Under any other circumstances, his graceless stumbling might have been comical.

That night in Virginia City, however, Nick wanted to shoot the dumb lummox himself.

Another of the masked men, this one wearing a burlap sack tied over his head, swept in to take hold of Ford by the scruff of his neck. He stuck the business end of his rifle into the back of another of Nick's companions, bringing both of them toward the rest of the invaders.

After that the locals in the saloon pointed out the rest of the gang just to get the masked men on their way. Forming themselves into a circle around the youthful gang, they tossed Nick in with the rest and marched them out of the saloon.

There had been some rough times once Nick had decided to leave his father behind to ride his own trail. There had even been plenty of times when he'd been in real danger, but his youthful ignorance had made those seem more like days of adventure.

This time was different.

This time Nick was in real fear for his life.

The masked men marched them into a small house. Inside, there was no furniture and the wall separating the two rooms had been knocked down. Over their heads, the ceiling loomed like a black cloud. The rafter spanning the middle of the building caught everyone's eyes. Actually, it was the nooses dangling from the rafter got the most attention.

"Take a look up there, boys," the lead masked man said. "One word from me and each one of you will be swinging from them ropes. If any of you can count, you'll see that we already got enough up there for all of you."

"We didn't do anything," Nick said through his fear. "We didn't even leave the goddamn saloon."

"Yeah. Not yet you didn't. But we heard about you boys, and we don't want your kind around here. You little bastards think you can come through here because we don't have no law. Well, Virginia City does have law and we're it."

All the masked men seemed to stand taller when they heard that. Their eyes shone with deadly righteousness.

Nick looked up at the exposed rafters and the nooses hanging from them. He counted once again just to be sure, then took another look at his companions gathered in the midst of their masked hosts. When he looked back at the familiar faces, he could tell that the rest of his partners and friends were thinking the same thing.

There were five nooses waiting for them.

There were five young men being held at gunpoint.

There had been six members of the gang when they'd ridden into Virginia City.

Nick shifted his gaze toward the masked men and studied each of them in turn. There was no doubt in his mind that he was about to swing from one of those ropes. The way he saw it, that only left him with one other alternative.

"Go to hell," Nick snarled as he reached for his Colt. "Every damn one of you!"

There was a dull thump that rocked through Nick's world, followed by a pain that rushed through his entire skull, starting from the back and working its way to his eyeballs. His vision quickly started to fade and he felt himself dropping to the floor. He didn't feel his body hit the ground and didn't expect to open his eyes ever again.

THIRTY-TWO

His eyes did open. Even so, Nick sure didn't like what he saw.

The first thing he spotted was a pair of eyes staring down at him through a brownish haze. Blinking and shaking his head to push aside some of the throbbing pain, Nick realized that his sight wasn't failing him, but that the rest of the face in front of him was covered by a burlap sack with holes cut out for the eyes.

"Sorry about that," came an eerily familiar voice from behind the burlap sack. "But I had to give you a knock on the head before you did anything stupid."

Before Nick could place the voice on his own, the man peeled back the burlap to reveal his face. "Bet you didn't see this one coming, did you, Nick?" Skinner said with a wide, joyful grin.

Nick sat straight up and felt the world teeter beneath him. Reaching behind to feel the back of his head, his fingers brushed against slick, crusted blood, which sent another wave of pain slicing through him. Saltwater burned the edges of his eyes in much the same way it would after being punched in the nose. Nick swiped them away quickly with the back of his hand and asked, "Where are the rest?"

"The rest?"

"The rest of our gang, Skinner! The rest of our friends!" Looking around, Nick felt sick to his stomach, but not because of the wound to the back of his head. "Where's any of them? Where are we?"

Skinner put a finger to his lips and signaled for Nick to be quiet. "Simmer down, boy. These men," he said, holding up the mask, "are still looking for a reason to hang you. I convinced them that you and I could do more good than harm to this place."

"What are you talking about?" Nick still didn't know where he was. Having gone to the saloon and stayed there, he could have been twenty yards from his horse and never would have known it. "Tell me where we are!"

"You're about two steps away from the grave if you're not careful. And if you don't shut up pretty damn quick, you'll drag me down with you." Skinner waited until he saw that his words had gotten through and Nick was losing his steam. "I knew about these fellas and just managed to track down a few of 'em before they rounded up you and the rest of the boys."

Sitting up and clearing his head a little more, Nick snatched the mask from Skinner's hand. "Who are they?"

"They're the local vigilance committee. They keep their eyes open to take care of any trouble that might ride into their town."

"What about the law?"

Skinner held up the mask. "This is it."

"And you knew about this?"

"I heard about them. That's why I went off looking for them. Unlike the law, these men can be reasoned with so long as you know what to say."

"Which is what, exactly?"

"That I was one of them." Skinner grinned as though he'd just heard one of Ford's jokes. "I told 'em I was a tracker from Cheyenne and that we could scare you boys enough to run you out of town without having to string you up. And don't look at me like the wounded little lamb, Nick. We had our run and it was just a matter of time before we got caught, just like your pa told you. This way, I arranged for us to get out

384

of here without doing it feet first in a pine box."

Skinner had always been a talented liar. The fact that he could talk his way out of nearly any situation didn't come as a surprise to Nick. In fact, it wouldn't have been a surprise if Skinner really did have connections to the law in one or two places and simply had kept them under his hat.

"So where are the others?" Nick asked for what felt like the thousandth time. "Where's Barrett?"

Barrett Cobb was the member of the gang who'd known Nick the longest. They'd ridden together before Skinner had joined them, and he'd taught Nick plenty in his own right. Both of them, however, had learned from Skinner. The strange thing was how two men of roughly the same age could learn such drastically different lessons from the same man. Still, Barrett was a vital member of the gang as well as the closest member of Nick's extended brotherhood.

"They got their scare and left town. Barrett was the first to go. He told me to tell you he'd head up into Leadville and would wait for you there as long as he could. I already met up with the rest and told them to go their separate ways. As for this vigilance committee, I can only pull the

385

wool over their eyes for so long before they get the hankering to string you up again."

Nick had been awake long enough to get a handle on roughly where he was. He could hear the sounds of the saloon, and they weren't coming from too far away. As near as he could tell, he and Skinner were less than a block from where this whole mess had started.

Turning around, Nick nearly jumped out of his skin when he noticed another man walking out of the shadows no more than five feet behind him. It was the one who'd led the masked men into the saloon to round up him and the rest of the gang. Even though the hood was still tied over his head, the sharp eyes beneath it were unmistakable.

"Holy shit," Nick exclaimed as his hand went reflexively for his Colt. But even though his fingers were intact, they did him no good. His gun was gone.

"Relax kid," the leader of the vigilance committee said as he came to a stop next to Skinner. "I've had plenty of time to kill you and didn't do it just yet. You've got your friend here to thank for that."

"So what now, then?" Nick asked. He looked from the masked man over to Skinner, who gave him a subtle nod, which meant he wanted Nick to hear what the masked man had to say.

"Your friends are already gone, kid," the committee leader told him. "I've seen to that myself. They weren't exactly the worst kind we've had through here, but they're not the types we could allow to stay. Then again, plenty of the men that ride with me now started off not too much differently. There's a war going on, and it doesn't just stay on battlefields, rolling along to the beat of a drum.

"Times like these are hard and they breed hard men." Through the mask, the committee leader's eyes darted down toward Nick's empty holster. His hand came up, holding the Colt that had once rested in that same holster. "In rough times, it's easy for a man to go astray."

"My father would agree with you," Nick said brusquely. "Can I leave now?"

"I'm offering you a second chance, kid," the man said through his mask. "Skinner here told us that you boys mostly stole here and there and got into a few scrapes, but were otherwise just out for a ride. Like I told you, your friends are already gone. You can either join them or you can do yourself a favor . . ."

Nick closed his eyes and took a deep

breath. His father had told him this day would come, when he would have to pay for any lawlessness he might have done. Until now, it had just seemed like strict words coming from an old man who didn't want his only son to leave his home in Wichita. Suddenly, Nick wondered if he would ever see Stasys again.

Probably not, he decided. So, resigned to his fate, Nick waited for the committee leader to finish his menacing promise.

". . . and join us."

There would only be a few times in his life when Nick was genuinely surprised. This was one of them.

"What?" he asked.

Still studying Nick closely, the committee leader tossed the Colt back at Nick's feet and took a few steps forward. He waited until he saw that Nick wasn't going to reach for his weapon before untying the rope from around his neck and peeling the mask from his face. His face was clean shaven and the look in his eyes seemed genuine enough.

"You're still alive for a reason," the now unmasked man said. "I'll let you leave here the same way your friends did, or you can stay."

Although at first he was just glad to still be alive, Nick was now so confused that it felt like his head was spinning. This time the dizziness didn't come from the wound he'd been given. "Stay? Here, you mean? Why?"

"Because you keep your wits about you. You're loyal. I hear you're plenty good in a fight, but most of all, you've got stones, kid." The committee leader smirked when he said that last part. "Most scoundrels that come through here are nothing but spoiled kids shooting off their mouths and their guns. You've got to know what I mean."

Nick knew only too well what the other man meant, but he wasn't about to give him the satisfaction of agreeing with him.

"You and Skinner aren't like the rest, though. Men like us are needed in these parts because if there's to be justice around here, it'll take men like us to deal it out."

"At the end of a rope," Nick said. "Isn't that what you mean?"

"If the situation calls for it. But that's nothing new. Sheriffs and judges hang folks too. The only problem right now is that we don't have the benefit of honest, hardworking sheriffs and judges around here. So we can either sit back and let justice be trampled into the dirt or we can enforce it ourselves."

Skinner grinned and chucked Nick on the

shoulder. "I told you coming here would be a good idea."

The funny thing was, when they'd been on the trail, Nick would have sworn that it was the consensus of everyone in the gang to head to Virginia City. Now that he thought about it, however, he could see where Skinner had pushed to come here until he'd gotten everyone to agree.

"Did you have this in mind the whole time?" Nick asked.

Shrugging, Skinner replied, "We were headed for jail or the gallows, Nick. You know that. Hell, we already lost three of our own before we even got through the Dakotas."

"Four. We lost four."

"There you go. Now, we could keep going like we've been goin' and get ourselves picked off one by one, or we could clear out for good like we were talking about. Only thing is, we've burned too many bridges around here to head north, so that leaves south into Mexico. My Spanish ain't too good, so that means I had to find another way. I found this one," Skinner said proudly. "And I think you and Barrett were the only ones worth bringing along. Hell, the others are too stupid to see past the next whore in the next town anyway. Tell me I'm wrong."

Nick's first reaction would have been to say that Skinner was wrong and then storm out of Virginia City forever. But deep down he knew Skinner was talking sense and that the wild look in his friend's eyes had been getting worse the longer they rode together. There were even times he'd wanted to put the trail behind him and start fresh.

Maybe if he started over, he thought, he could make himself into a man his father could be proud of. Maybe then he could sleep at night, content that the soul of his mother wasn't drifting away purely out of shame for what her son had become.

"Let me meet up with the others," Nick said to both Skinner and the committee leader. "I can talk to them and let them know what you're —"

Skinner's hand, which had just been resting on Nick's shoulder, now clenched into a fist and rapped into the side of Nick's face. It wasn't the kind of strike meant to do much harm, but it sent a sting through the younger man's body and sure as hell got his attention.

"You won't tell them a goddamn thing," Skinner said. "Those assholes you call friends will just get you to ride with them one more time until it's your last time. You want to die in a blaze of glory? Go down fighting? Well I've got news for you, Nick. No matter how much you did in Missouri, you're no soldier. I don't see a badge on you, so you're no lawman.

"That just leaves one thing, which is exactly what you know you are. An outlaw." That last comment hung in the air like a fog. Skinner knew damn well exactly the effect it had upon its intended audience. "This country don't put up with outlaws like they used to. Folks are getting tired of men like us, and they're even more tired of the dumb-as-dirt kids you, me, and Barrett have been running with."

So far the committee leader had been silently letting Skinner say his piece. Now he stepped in again and cut in using a voice that was low yet sharper than the blade strapped in the sheath at the small of Skinner's back. "Listen to your friend, kid. You know what's good for you, and staying on the run isn't it. You either buck the tide or swim with it, and my committee isn't the only one around here who don't take kindly to those that buck. There are plenty out there who'd rather help you drown than turn our towns into shooting galleries."

"And what if I say no?" Nick asked. "You hang me and call it justice?"

"No," the committee leader answered

calmly. "I'll see that you get a head start before all of us come looking for you. If you come back, I'll gun you down and be done with it."

"Then you must not trust me."

"I don't. Not yet, anyway. You'd have to earn my trust just like all my men earned it. But once you get it, I can offer you something those dumb-shit friends of yours never could. You can have a home here and start an honest life. You can put the past behind you and start over fresh while putting your skills to use in a way that means something.

"You want a minute or two to think about it? I'll give you that. This committee may work for the law, but we're not bound by it, so we have to cover our tracks. That means this is a onetime offer. Take me up on it, like Skinner, and we can get started with your new life, or you can walk away and never come back." He leaned in closer, staring so hard into Nick's eyes that the two men seemed to be connected by a red hot poker. "And I do mean *never* come back."

In a way that seemed more than a little crazy at first, Nick was taking a lot of what the committee leader was saying to heart. Too much of it struck home for the older man's words to be just so many polished-up promises. Besides that, he'd heard about vigilance committees like this one, and knew they were feared and respected for stepping in to do what the justice system simply could not.

But more than that was what Nick felt inside his own gut. Stasys had always told him to be true to himself, and Nick's self had been worrying for a while that Barrett and the others were riding straight toward the edge of a cliff.

The young were all the same. Animals, men, it didn't matter. They all were driven by instinct above most anything else. At that moment, Nick thought he could trust the committee leader, even though he didn't feel the same toward Skinner. For that reason, he got to his feet, looked the committee leader in the eye, and extended his hand.

"All right. I'll sign on. The name's Nicolai Graves."

Nodding his approval, the committee leader shook the hand Nick offered and said, "You made the right decision, Nick. I'm Red Parks."

Skinner placed his hand on top of the other two, making the truce seem more like an irrevocable pact.

There was another thing common to the young.

They all made mistakes.

Thirty-Three

When Nick stopped talking, Callum felt like he was overwhelmed by the silence that followed. Throughout the story, Callum swore he could see Nick's younger face and hear a younger man's voice describing what had happened that night in Virginia City. Now that it was over, the undertaker saw the years creep in once again and reclaim the storyteller.

Nick looked over to Callum and shrugged. "The man who headed up that vigilance committee was the man I was looking for here. Instead, I find Skinner. That message he left for me was his way of knocking me, just like he'd knocked me to my senses that night when I'd met Red Parks for the first time."

"And 3-7-77?" Callum asked.

"It's a code Skinner picked up from the vigilantes. They'd paint it on a man's door as a warning. Sometimes they'd paint it in blood." Nick straightened up like an old soldier reacting reflexively to a salute. "The numbers add up to twenty-four, and that was how long whoever got the warning had to get out of town."

"And if they didn't?"

"Three feet wide, seven feet deep, and seventy seven inches long. That's how big a hole would be dug for the man who didn't. Red was always a good man who liked to give warnings. But not Skinner. He just liked the blood."

Although the wind was blowing and leaves were getting tossed about, it still felt quiet as a tomb to both men standing in front of the funeral parlor. The cold that was autumn's breath seemed to be made especially for them, chilling Nick and Callum right down to the juice in their bones.

"So Skinner left those numbers for you?" Callum asked.

"Yeah."

"He wants you to leave Jessup?"

Nick shook his head. "He wants me to start digging a hole."

Neither man said too much after that. The simple fact of the matter was that there just wasn't much more to say. Callum and Nick kept themselves busy by seeing to the last preparations for the Eddings wake. The sun was just beginning to dip below the horizon when the first guests started to arrive at the parlor. Callum was there to meet the pair who turned out to be Mrs. Eddings's son and his wife. The undertaker had just put on his best black suit and received the grieving family members with a warm, comforting smile.

A few more of the Eddings family showed up soon after and were ushered straight in to spend some quiet moments with the deceased. Once the guests who weren't members of the Eddings family showed up, Nick stepped out of the spare room in back wearing his own black suit, which was reserved for special occasions such as this.

The long, black coat hung down past his knees, blending in perfectly with his black pants and black vest. A starched white shirt and silver watch chain crossing his stomach were the only things standing in contrast to the dark colors of his clothing. His somber demeanor and downcast eyes even made the very flesh on Nick's bones seem darkened by shadow.

His boots were black and had been polished to a shine for the evening's affair. His black wide-brimmed hat had also been given a special cleaning, and not only matched his suit, but darkened his face even more.

Nick walked through the main room of the parlor without making enough noise to disturb the Eddings family and opened the front door with an equal amount of care. Although he brightened a bit after catching the eye of one of the guests standing outside, he was careful to keep himself from looking inappropriately joyful.

"Thank you for coming," Nick said in a low, formal tone. "If you would be so kind as to wait out here for just a bit longer while the family pays their last respects."

The guests all nodded immediately. Nick's professionalism was impeccable.

Once the family had taken their time alone with the body of their departed member, they let Callum know that they were ready for the remembrance ceremony to begin. When he got the signal from the undertaker, Nick let those gathered outside into the parlor. By then the group standing outside had grown to an impressive size. In fact, Nick wouldn't have been surprised if most of the town had shown up just as Callum had predicted.

As he held the door open, Nick greeted each of the guests with a few words of welcome and a gesture to show where they should be seated. Each of the locals looked at him with a smile that was more than a little surprised. Some of them shook his hand with real gratitude, commenting on how beautiful everything already was.

"This place looks better than I've ever seen it," commented one elderly gentleman who looked older than the town as well as some of the trees planted nearby. "You did a fine job, son. Lord knows Mrs. Eddings deserved it."

Not wanting to hold up the line of guests entering the parlor, Nick accepted the praise with a smile and a nod while gently moving the old-timer along.

The wake was a standard affair. There were several speakers who told stories about the deceased that were both funny and sad. Nick stood at the back of the room and listened to them all. Callum spoke a few words as well before a preacher got up and led everyone in a prayer. Everyone at the gathering bowed their heads as one while speaking the solemn words.

Everyone except for Nick.

He never took part in the religious aspects of any such ceremonies. There were plenty of reasons for this, not the least of which was the fact that he felt he had a long way to go before the Lord above would take time to listen to what he had to say. He simply remained silent until the preacher said, "Amen."

It was dark outside when the line of people started moving past the coffin to take one more look at Mrs. Eddings. The air was heavy with tears and suppressed sobs. There was a constant murmur of people speaking among themselves, sharing tears along with good memories.

Nick had moved up to stand near the coffin, ready to help anyone who needed assistance on their way to or from their seat. Sometimes people would be too weak to make that short walk to the open coffin on their own. Sometimes they were unable to make the walk back. Every so often at an affair such as this one someone would faint dead away, but nothing so dramatic happened here.

Although Nick was needed to assist a few of Mrs. Eddings's close friends and relatives who felt a bit light-headed after seeing the beautifully made-up yet very dead face of the deceased, nobody was so overcome that they needed to be caught. Nick was careful to offer his left hand to those in need while keeping his right hand on their shoulder.

Throughout the ceremony and viewing, he couldn't help but think about the bodies still laying in Callum's workshop. He was sure the town would show up just as they had this evening for the two boys who'd tried to help Catherine. The deputies, on the other hand, would more than likely wind up with a quick send-off and a hole in the ground.

Only Sheriff Manes could force someone to show up for the deputies' wake, and the lawman would be in no position to force anyone into anything once this night was through. Nick knew he would see to that personally.

With the viewing over and speeches done, Nick and Callum pulled aside the pews to make room in the parlor for people to visit and partake of the food that had been provided. All in all, it was a successful affair. The deceased had been sent off properly, and those left behind were comforted in the midst of their common loss. There was only one more thing to be done before Nick's job was complete.

"Excuse me," he said, approaching a tall man with his arm draped over the shoulders of a younger woman. Although much younger, both of them bore striking resemblances to Mrs. Eddings. "You're Mrs. Eddings's children?"

The man nodded because the woman was

trying to get a grip on the sorrow she was feeling. "Yes. We are."

"My name is Nicolai Graves. I wish I knew everyone here a little better, but I would like to offer my sincere condolences."

"I'm Martin Eddings and this is my sister Maribeth. You helped arrange all of this with Dan Callum?"

"I did."

Maribeth pulled in a deep breath and looked up at Nick, but still seemed too weak to say much.

"You did a fine job," Martin said. "Thank you for putting so much work into this. I know you've had some . . . well . . . some troubles of your own since you got here."

Disregarding the mention of anything involving his own activities since arriving in Jessup, Nick merely replied, "It's been a pleasure. I've heard nothing but wonderful things about your mother. I wish I could have met her."

It looked as though Maribeth wanted to cry when she heard that. The wound of her mother's passing was still open and it hurt with every little prod, but the tears didn't come. In fact, there was something in the tone of Nick's voice and the undeniable sincerity in his eyes that acted like a cool, soothing balm on the wounds of her soul.

"Thank you, Mr. Graves," Maribeth said.

Nick reached out to take her hand in both of his, being careful to place his right hand underneath, where it couldn't be seen. "I know what you're going through. Both of you. I lost my mother as well when I was young, and I still miss her very much. Just know that she'll always be in your hearts, and as long as she's there, she'll always be with you."

It was the first time Maribeth had smiled since her mother had departed. She even stood a little taller, as though a weight had been removed from her shoulders. Martin smiled as well, but couldn't find the words to express his gratitude.

"Here," Nick said, removing something from the inner pocket of his coat. "Take this. It will comfort you when nothing else will."

Nick handed over a small, square-shaped book in a black leather cover. It was small enough to fit in the palm of Maribeth's hand, and when she opened it, she saw the pages contained verses of scripture from the Good Book itself.

"It's a Mourner's Bible," Nick said. "It's just a remembrance of this ceremony as well as some selected passages to ease a troubled mind. All of my best to you, Maribeth, and to you as well, Martin."

"Thank you again, Mr. Graves," Martin said. "I wish I could do more to show my appreciation. If you'd like to come by our home sometime for dinner, we'd be more than happy to accommodate you."

"I'll keep that in mind." And with that, Nick turned away from the siblings and walked toward the door leading to Callum's workshop.

The door didn't even have a chance to close after Nick had stepped through it before someone else walked in. Nick was heading for his small room and didn't have to look to see who'd come in after him.

"Something you need to ask me, Dan?" Nick asked, pausing in the entrance to his little borrowed room.

"Just where you thought you were going."

Nick turned to glance at the undertaker over his shoulder. "The wake's done and everyone seems to be doing all right."

"But that don't mean you can just hide in the back here."

"Why not?"

"Because there's people out there who are asking about you." Callum walked past the tables so he could see Nick without having to look past all those sets of dead eyes staring up. "They want to thank you for doing

405

such a fine job here."

"That's good to hear, but my job's not quite finished yet."

Callum winced when he saw Nick reach for his gun belt and buckle it around his waist beneath his black coat. "That butcher wasn't run off, was he?"

"No."

"And what about the sheriff?"

"I expect he's still about as well."

"You can stay here, Nick. People around here know what kind of man you are." In response to the subtle twitch at the corner of Nick's eye, Callum added, "They may not know everything, but they know you stepped in on Catherine's behalf and didn't back down when it came to helping Jed Arvey. Whatever you did in the past can stay buried. You can start fresh here."

"I've heard that before, Dan. It didn't work out too well in Montana, and I don't want to put anyone here at risk. What I thought was buried came around like a bad dream and got some good people killed in the process. Probably more people were hurt than I even know about."

Nick drew his gun from its holster and carefully checked each round in the cylinder. Snapping it shut and dropping it into its place at his side, he stepped into his room and grabbed his patchwork bag, which had already been packed full of his belongings. Sitting on the bed that had yet to be slept in, resting in the imprint left by Nick's luggage, was a small wad of folded bills.

When he saw Nick pick up the money, Callum said, "That's your payment for all the work you did for me. There's a little extra, seeing as how you set me up for my next several jobs and all."

"Thanks."

"You sure you don't want to wait before you go? After all, damn near the whole town's here and will be for a while. I doubt there's anyone at the stables to get your wagon and horses ready."

"I can get my horses on my own. Thanks for the work and for giving me a place to stay, Dan."

"Heh. Like you ever slept here."

"Yeah, well it's the thought that counts. Take care of yourself." Nick carried his bag out of the room, past Callum and out the back door. From there he planned on making one last stop before finishing up his business. Catherine hadn't been at the Eddings wake, so he stopped by the little house where he'd left her to say his good-byes.

There was a message on the door waiting

for him. It was short and to the point: 3-7-77.

THIRTY-FOUR

Nick didn't step through that door.

As much as he wanted to charge inside, he kept himself from giving in to the rage that those red numbers had been intended to provoke. The paint was still wet on the front of the door, and it ran down from the bottom of each hastily written mark like saliva running from the corner of a wild animal's mouth.

He realized that the idea must have been for him to bust into the house with guns blazing and his head filled with the notion that Skinner was inside with Catherine. But Nick wasn't buying it. Whoever had written those red numbers, it sure as hell wasn't Skinner. Nathan Skinner never gave a second warning and he never used paint.

His arm dropped down to his side, pulled back the side of his coat and removed the gun from its holster. The gnarled wood fit perfectly into his gnarled hand, completing him in a way that only such familiar iron could. Pulling in a deep breath, Nick stepped away from the door and walked around to the back of the house.

Catherine saw the shadows move outside the little house's window and prayed to God that it wasn't Nick coming to check on her. Even though she wanted desperately to be found, she didn't want the other men inside the house to get what they'd been waiting for.

"What's the matter?" Sheriff Manes asked from where he was sitting in the middle of the room. "Those ropes too tight for you?"

Catherine could have made a noise through the gag in her mouth or even nodded her head, but she didn't bother. Instead, she just shot Manes a look filled with so much hatred that it nearly stung her own eyes.

"Well it shouldn't be much longer before we get a visitor and this will all be done. Your friend the grave digger should be here any moment, in which case I'll put him down myself. Of course, if Skinner finds him first, this mess is over. At least, it's over for the grave digger. Skinner's working his own angle for now but he's got plans for you, darling, and I doubt I'll be able to stop him once he finds out where I got you stowed." More to himself, he added, "That's why he ain't invited to this little party."

The sheriff stared down at Catherine and winked. "It'll be fun to see what he does once he gets his hands on you. For now, though, he's got another job to do."

Her eyes darted over to the second man inside the house. Rich looked just as trapped as she was, but she couldn't blame the skinny deputy for not helping her. She and Rich had both watched as Manes had emptied out the bullets from Rich's gun and dumped them onto the floor. Apparently, the sheriff was all out of men he could trust.

The movement came again, and this time Catherine was certain she recognized the shape of Nick's wide-brimmed hat moving once again toward the door. Unfortunately, Sheriff Manes recognized the shape as well and crouched down lower in the dim, flickering light of the room's single lantern.

The door's handle twitched and made a shrill squeak as its hinges were dragged against each other slowly. A man stood in the doorway, his frame outlined by the starlight trickling in from outside.

Triumphantly, Manes stood up and raised his gun as his finger tightened around the trigger. His target was already picked out

411

and there was no possible way he could miss.

At the last possible moment, the lawman eased up on his trigger and peered closely at the face beneath that wide-brimmed hat. "Is that you, Bruce?"

Rich's cousin stood in the doorway, cringing at the way the sheriff's gun remained pointed in his direction. "Yes sir, Sheriff. It's me."

"I thought I told you to keep an eye out for anyone headed this way," Manes said as he finally lowered his pistol and let out the breath he'd been holding. "And where the hell did you get that hat?"

Bruce stared into the house as though he didn't know what to do or what to say. He managed to take half a step through the door when it became obvious that he wasn't walking forward on his own, but being pushed from behind.

Of course, by then it was too late.

Falling straight forward, Bruce reached out with both hands to catch himself. More than anything, he just wanted to press himself against that floor and stay there. Since he'd already been relieved of his gun, there wasn't much else for him to do.

Even before the deputy had reached the floor, the man crouching behind him was revealed. Nick reached around Bruce with his right hand and sighted down the barrel at the familiar face of Sheriff Corey Manes.

The lawman might have been shocked at first, but his reflexes were already kicking in. His finger tightened around his trigger and sent a shot through the air that broke the window several feet from Nick. With his other hand, the sheriff reached out to grab hold of Catherine's shoulder so he could pull her in front of him.

Nick stepped back so his left side was covered by the door frame and he took a shot with his modified pistol, clipping a chunk of skin from the side of Manes's face. Before the lawman could squeeze off another round, Nick fired again. That shot would have been a kill if Nick hadn't pulled his hand at the last moment. Catherine was too close to Manes and he wasn't about to risk harming a single hair on her head.

Although she resisted Manes's grip as best she could, Catherine didn't have the balance to pull herself away. Her ankles were tied, severely limiting her options. She looked over to Rich, who was backing away to keep from catching any lead himself. The angry look in the deputy's eyes was enough to convince Catherine that although Manes couldn't trust him, perhaps she could.

Once she saw that Rich was looking at her, Catherine lifted the foot she'd kept pressed to the floor, revealing the discarded bullet she'd been hiding.

Manes had managed to keep his grip the entire time, even while taking another quick shot at Nick. Pulling Catherine up with all his strength, he managed to get her completely in front of him. From there all he had to do was turn his pistol toward her temple and the shooting stopped.

"You want to kill her?" Manes asked. "Then just make one more move that I don't like."

"Some lawman," Nick sneered from his partial cover. Now that Manes had tipped his hand, Nick talked to him like the true coward he knew the sheriff to be. "Hiding behind a woman? Let her go and take care of this yourself. At least that way you might be able to salvage some of your pride."

"Shut your mouth, grave digger. This ends here and now. When you're dead, I think I'll string up your body in front of my office. That'll give this town something to think about the next time they start feeling brave. Toss that gun and step in here."

Nick didn't move.

"I said toss it. Or was Skinner wrong and this here bitch really doesn't matter to you?"

Nick weighed his options in his head and figured he might be able to put a bullet through Manes's head before Catherine got one for herself. If he was wrong, however, she would die anyway. And there was always that last twitch of the muscles that could do her in even if he did get the shot he was after. In the end, he only had one real choice.

Slowly, Nick extended his arm, opened his fingers, and let the modified weapon drop from it.

"That's perfect," Manes said in a gloating tone. "Now come in here and shut that door."

Without picking his feet up from the ground, Nick moved away from the door frame he'd been using as cover. That way, he could use his sense of touch to keep track of where he was and what was next to him rather than taking his eyes off Manes. It was a trick he'd learned from a blind man. Simple, yet effective.

The moment Nick's boot touched a board raised higher than the rest, he stopped. If he stepped forward, his left shoulder would have bumped against the door frame, so he stayed where he was. Manes seemed to be plenty happy with the arrangement.

"All right," Nick said. "Now let her go."

Manes tilted his head and then shook it. He felt comfortable enough to push her a bit to one side so he could move better, but still had most of himself behind Catherine's trembling body. "Get here in front of me so I can see your face better."

What the sheriff really wanted was for his target to come closer so he would be sure not to miss. Nick knew that much for certain and was fine with it. All he needed was for Catherine to get a little farther away from the lawman. Just an inch or two was all he needed. Nick moved slowly, waiting for that little bit of space to be granted.

"Don't do it, Nick," Catherine said. "He'll kill y—"

"Shut up, bitch!" Manes roared. As soon as those words came from his mouth, he saw Catherine preparing to snap forward with her hand. Not only was she intending to scratch him across the face, but she moved her head forward also, as if to bite him on the cheek or any other piece of him she could tear off.

The woman's strikes were sloppy and desperate. Manes avoided them by straightening his arm and leaning back so he was out of her reach. But in that awkward position, he couldn't dodge her nails while still keeping his pistol aimed at her head.

Seeing that, Nick smiled.

Only then did Nick step all the way from the door, exposing the hand he'd been hiding as well as the gun he'd taken from the deputy who still lay on the floor. Bruce's pistol was a clunky Smith & Wesson, but that didn't mean Nick couldn't use it. His left hand might have been damaged, but his body recalled enough of his previous experience to know what to do. Besides, at that close range, Nick knew he would have been hard-pressed to miss Manes's snarling face.

Nick brought up the deputy's weapon just as Manes looked his way. Shock and fear flashed across the lawman's face in the fraction of a second before Nick squeezed the trigger. That look of shock only grew more intense when the hammer of Nick's weapon dropped to make a hollow, metallic *click*.

One thing Nick hadn't considered was the possibility that Sheriff Manes would send out a patrol carrying an empty revolver.

"See, Rich," Manes said after letting out the breath that he thought was going to be his last. "This is why I don't trust you or your asshole cousin with a loaded gun. I figured if you did have bullets, you'd only try to shoot me in the back or you'd get your gun taken by someone without shit for their brains." Savoring his moment of victory, he lifted his gun so he could take careful aim and added, "Looks like I was right."

At that moment, from behind Sheriff Manes, came another sound of metal on metal. This time, however, it was the snap of a cylinder being shut and a hammer drawn back.

"Yes, Sheriff," Rich said after loading the single round that Catherine had kicked over to him. "It does look like you were right."

That single round went off like a cannon inside the little house and tore a messy hole through the lawman's rib cage. Manes had just been turning around to make sure he was hearing correctly, only to get his suspicions confirmed by the white-hot flash of pain as lead pierced flesh and bone to tear straight through the tender organs inside him.

Nick may have been holding an empty gun, but that didn't mean he was helpless. Already launching himself into motion, he was nowhere near the door frame when the sheriff's finger clenched around his trigger and blasted a hole into a nearby wall. Instead, Nick had rushed into the room to come around on Manes's other side. From there, he knocked the gun from the lawman's hand and pulled him away from Catherine.

Even though Nick managed to scoop his gun up from the floor, he didn't need to use it. Manes staggered and bumped against a wall, sliding down to land in an awkward heap with blood pouring generously through the wound in his side. His body twitched a few times, but they were only reflexes. The weak light inside the house played across the lawman's face as he stared up at whatever dead men saw. His mouth hung open and the rest of his body caved in a bit once it surrendered the spirit that had kept it moving.

Catherine rushed forward but stopped just short of embracing Nick. "Is he . . . ?"

"Yeah," Nick said. "He's gone."

Turning toward the sound of footsteps, Nick raised his pistol to cover the remaining deputies.

"Hold up, now," Rich said. "This doesn't have to go any further."

Nick sized up both lawmen in the space of two seconds, then stepped forward and holstered his modified Schofield. "Both of you had your chance to prove yourselves a minute ago." He extended his hand. "Thanks."

Bruce shook Nick's hand. When it came to Rich, Nick tightened his grip around the deputy's hand and looked him straight in the eyes.

"But that doesn't mean you're through yet," he said. "There's still one more favor I'd like to ask."

"Go ahead and ask it."

"Later." Turning to Catherine, Nick took her in his arms and hugged her so powerfully that he lifted her off her feet. She squeezed him back with everything she had and kissed him with enough passion to make him forget about where he was and what had just happened.

All he could think about as he tasted her lips and felt her breath pass into his mouth was taking her away somewhere and shutting out the rest of the world. Unfortunately, he knew that couldn't be. As much as it pained him, he set her back down, ended the kiss and forced himself to pull away.

"You won't have to stay in this place again after tonight," he said simply.

Catherine didn't like the sound of that. The expression on her face said that much. "So . . . with Sheriff Manes gone, you figure that other man will leave?"

Nick's pause lasted only a second or two, but it felt like a world of silence passed between them. "Yeah. Something like that. So will I. It's the only way you can stay safe."

"Why would you think something like that?"

"Because they'll keep coming for me." And that was it. Nick let his hands linger on her as long as he could before walking toward the door. "Do me a favor," he said to Rich as he was about to step outside. "Tell Jed Arvey and his family when it's safe for them to come back to their home." Nick told the deputy where the farmer had gone and started once again to leave the house.

"When should I talk to them?" Rich asked.

Nick lifted his nose to a cold breeze and pulled in a full lungful of the autumnal air. It smelled like distant rain and burning leaves. "You'll know when."

THIRTY-FIVE

The first place Nick went was the stables. There was a note tacked to the front door that read, CLOSED FOR THE NIGHT. TRY AGAIN TOMORROW. He didn't pay attention to that, and got to work opening the door on his own. It was latched from the inside, but it wasn't anything that a little bit of know-how and a piece of bent steel couldn't cure.

Nick pressed his shoulder against the doors and pushed as hard as he could until there was enough space between them to slide the metal hook in and pop the latch. He'd learned that from a horse thief back when he was a kid, and had never forgotten the simple techniques. Truth be told, most folks didn't expect anyone to steal from them, which always worked to a thief's advantage.

But Nick wasn't interested in stealing horses. He wasn't even interested in getting his own animals and wagon. Once the door came open, he stood in the doorway like a statue clad in black until his eyes adjusted to the thick, shifting shadows. Before too long he could distinguish the shapes that were stalls, the ones that were horses, and the one that was the man he'd been looking for in the first place.

"I knew I'd find you here, Skinner," Nick said in the darkness as he made a subtle adjustment to the holster he wore.

Skinner had been leaning against the stall where Rasa and Kazys shifted nervously. "Really? I guess you were listening to me during all those years we rode together after all, huh?"

Nick nodded, but in the darkness, the motion looked like it could have been an illusion. "Don't waste time tracking a man down when you can just sit back and wait somewhere you know he'll need to go. That's how we got Steve Wright outside of Omaha when nobody else could."

"Heh. I remember that. Ol' Steve cashed in for a pretty penny. Of course, you an' me have got bigger prices on our heads nowadays."

"Yeah. I guess that's what you'd call progress."

Stepping into the wide row that ran down

the middle of the stables, Skinner studied Nick carefully. Even in the darkness it was plain to see the disgust that slid over his features. "Fuck you, kid. Nobody that digs holes and builds boxes for a living can look down their nose at me. Red always thought he was better than me too."

"Is that why you killed him?"

"Yes," Skinner replied after taking a moment to think it over. "It is. And you should be thanking me for it too. After the way things turned out in Montana, I'll just bet you were out to kill him yourself. Well, I figured he was in town hiding from somebody, and I tried to hold off on killing him until they got here. He held out for almost five days. You should've been there when he kicked off. It was a hell of a sight."

Nick didn't say anything to Skinner, but the intensity in his eyes practically made them burn in the dark.

But Nick's silence didn't matter. Skinner was in his element and could feel the effect he was having on him. "He started to cry toward the end," Skinner said in a quiet, almost childlike tone. "He said he was sorry and that he was in just as much hot water as everyone else. You know what, Nick? He even said he was sorry for what we done to you."

"Shut up," Nick hissed. The words came out of him like steam before a volcano erupted.

"He cried like a little woman. Kind of like that sweet number of yours here in town cried when I gutted her friends."

"Shut . . . up."

"He cried like your pa did when me and Barrett went to pay him a visit while you were in that jailhouse in the badlands. Remember that? Remember how it took a while for us to break you out? Remember when you asked what took us so long?"

Skinner was trying to get under his skin. Nick knew that. Before a fight, he always played on his opponent's emotions as a way to amuse himself as well as to gain an edge. As much as he tried to keep that in mind, Nick was having a hard time shutting his ears to it. Mainly, that was because Skinner rarely lied about such things as hurting people. There were so many demons following him around that Skinner didn't have to create any more.

As if reading Nick's thoughts, Skinner grinned and settled the question once and for all. "I remember it well enough, Nick. He cried, 'I so sorry, Sophie. I make our son into man like this.' " Skinner shifted his voice into a sobbing mockery of Stasys, complete with overexaggerated accent. When he was done, he smiled and looked through the shadows at Nick. The other man hadn't moved from his spot. The blackness of the shadows mingled seamlessly with the blackness of Nick's clothes, leaving only a sliver of white from his shirt and the cold glint of his eyes to break the inky shape.

"You finished?" Nick asked.

The anger that had crept into his voice before was gone.

The tension was gone.

There was so little humanity at all in Nick's tone that his voice sounded more like a trick of the wind than anything that could have come from flesh and blood.

Skinner straightened up and took a few steps back until he stood at one end of the stables and Nick was at the other. "No," he replied, dropping the games and turning almost as cold as Nick. "I've only gotten started. In fact, I like it here so much that I think I'll keep this town for myself. There's plenty of folks like you and me in these parts. They run to Mexico or Canada or wherever they can go to be safe. Well, if Manes had one good thought in his life, it was to make some extra coin by charging runners like you and me for sanctuary here. I could get rich from providing a service like that. What do you think?"

Nick didn't answer. He'd become so still that his form began to blur around the edges and blend into the shadows.

But Skinner didn't need a response. "Eh, to hell with it. I could get plenty rich just bringing in the heads of my old friends like you and Red. It's tricky cashing in the reward, but it's worth it. And you, Nicky boy, will be the mother lode that'll set me up for life."

"There's just one problem with that plan," Nick said, his words drifting from him like whispers from a lingering dream. "You've got to bring me down before you can cash me in."

Skinner's smile had seemed cruel and taunting at first. Now, however, he appeared to be genuinely amused. "Is that all you got? You're bluffing the wrong man, kid. You're lucky you can hold a shovel after what was done to you. Besides that, Manes told me about that sorry excuse for steel you've been carrying."

The shadow standing opposite Skinner moved slightly as Nick allowed the front of his coat to open. His gun belt was still around his waist, but this time the holster was sitting diagonally over his belly instead of hanging straight down at his hip.

Shaking his head, Skinner dropped his hand down to his Colt, which put the one Nick had carried in his youth to shame. "You can practice all you want, Nick. You can even get a gun that you won't drop in that half a hand of yours, but there's no way in hell you can think you're quicker than me."

The only response Nick gave was to shift his left foot back so his shoulders were lined up toward Skinner. It was a classic duelist's stance, which presented a thinner target to an opponent. It was also a blatant challenge.

"You want to die?" Skinner asked. "Is that it? You'd rather get shot than go through what Red had to go through, huh? On second thought . . . I can't say as I blame you. All right, then," he said, shifting into his own sideways stance. "For old times' sake."

What fell over the stables once Skinner's words had faded away was something beyond silence. The sound of horses' hooves rustling against the straw-covered floor could still be heard but seemed to come from miles away. Even the shadows seemed like thick soup drenching the innards of the stables.

Outside, the world went about its business and everyone else went about their lives. But inside that drafty building, with only the horses and mice to bear witness, two men stood waiting to make a move that would determine which of them would walk out alive.

Skinner took everything in, figuring in his head the possible threat that Nick could pose. He'd seen the younger man fight in his prime. He knew he could have beaten Nick then and he could beat him even easier now. That only left the possibility that Nick wanted to go out fighting. He had to admire that.

Nick had seen Skinner gun down dozens of men throughout the years. He'd gotten so good at it that he took to using a knife to alleviate the boredom. Nick had learned a lot from Skinner, and not one lesson was something to be proud of. The older man knew how to kill, and though he preferred to draw blood slowly, he could do it fast as well. Very, very fast.

The seconds ticked by, wearing away at both men like a file grating against their skin. Nick was not only concentrating on his odds of surviving, but trying not to give Skinner any subtle thing to use against him. Like poker, a standoff was as much a mind game as it was physical.

Nick's brain was starting to itch after all

his figuring.

His fingers were starting to tense.

The noise of the horses was starting to get to him.

Reflexively, he flexed his right hand and winced at the old pains which coursed from the gnarled remains of his fingers and ran up through his arm.

Even in the darkness, Skinner picked up on that wince the way a shark picks up on the scent of blood in the water. The tension lifted from him and the decision was made. Nick may have been a bad man at one time, but now he was the gunfighter's equivalent to a cripple.

Easy pickings.

Skinner's hand flashed to the grip of his pistol and his finger snaked over the trigger.

At the first sign of motion, Nick reached for his gun as well. The twisted, specially carved wood conformed perfectly to his hand, and the gun lifted from the holster with just his two whole fingers beneath it.

Already anticipating the smoke and envisioning the blood, Skinner cleared leather and turned the gun upward to take aim. The cocking of his hammer was like the backswing of Death's scythe.

Nick kept his eyes focused and his breath steady, his confidence in his customized weapon unwavering. The handle wasn't the only part that had been modified specially for him. To compensate for his lack of fingers and the speed he would lose on the draw, the barrel had been carved with deep grooves nearly as wide as the pinky that Nick was missing on his left hand.

Those grooves, complete with slightly raised edges, caught on the inside of his holster to twist the gun as it came up so the handle pulled in tight against Nick's hand. That way, all he needed to do was hook the trigger guard, lift, and tighten his grip as the gun was slapped into his palm.

A shot blasted through the stables. It whipped through the air and drilled through Skinner's forehead, sending his brains spraying in a fine mist across the stable's back wall.

Skinner blinked once and tried to speak. He tried to pull his trigger, but didn't have the strength. He didn't even have the strength to remain on his feet. He could see Nick walking toward him, drawing closer in his undertaker's clothes as if to bury him right then and there.

Nick kept the gun trained on Skinner, stood over him and watched him die. His hand wasn't hurting. It never had been. The twitch and wince was a carefully thought-out bluff that Nick knew Skinner wouldn't be able to resist. Skinner seemed to realize this only as he stared up at the dark figure looming over him and emptied his lungs in one final gasp.

"So tell me," Nick said as he knelt down and looked into Skinner's glassy eyes. "How's the view from down there?"

EPILOGUE

Omaha, Nebraska
Four Days Later

Normally, any man walking out of a building carrying a sack full of money had a right to be nervous. Even though that man wore a sheriff's badge pinned to his shirt, there was the chance that he could run into someone willing to test his mettle to get his hands on enough money to set him up for several very comfortable years.

What worked in this man's favor was the fact that word had already spread on whose body he'd brought in to earn that money. It didn't matter how lanky he was or how awkward he appeared to every passerby, the fact that he'd gunned down Nathan Skinner was enough to buy Rich plenty of space from even the baddest of Omaha's bad men.

Rich did his best to keep the nervousness from showing as he quickened his steps toward the corral at the end of the street.

Once there, he hopped up onto the seat of the wagon that was waiting for him and dropped the payment at the driver's feet.

"It's all there," Rich said.

Nick looked down at the sack, which was actually one-half of a saddlebag with a piece of the middle connecting strap still attached. "I believe you. Looks to me like they threw in an anvil or two as a bonus."

"Between the reward offered by the local and federal law, there wasn't enough cash to cover it." Rich glanced around nervously and lowered his voice. "Some miner came through here not too long ago. There's some gold in there as well."

Nick used the toe of his boot to open the flap and take a look inside for himself. He ignored the wink of precious metal, but nodded in satisfaction when he caught the sight of all the folded bills beneath the rocks. "Tell you what, Rich. You keep that gold for yourself."

"What? Really?"

"Sure. It's probably just iron sulfide anyway." Nick returned the deputy's stare and broke out into laughter. "Why don't you keep it and pawn it off on the next idiot who don't know any better when cashing in a bounty."

"That's just great. I come with you all the

way to Omaha, drag that disgusting carcass through this whole damn city for you, and this is the thanks I get?"

"Well I couldn't exactly bring him in myself."

"And why not?"

Instead of answering the question, Nick snapped the reins and got Rasa and Kazys moving. But before he pulled out of the corral, he yanked back on the reins and set the brake again. "Tell you what, Rich. You take that gold back to wherever you got it and ask for a horse instead."

"But if these rocks are worthless —"

"Then just remind them that you don't take any guff from anyone, including the departed Nathan Skinner. My guess is they'll even toss in a nice saddle."

"So you're not driving me back to Jessup?"

Nick shook his head.

"You did a lot for me, Nick. You did a lot for my town."

"And this evens things up. When you get back, give my best to Catherine. Take care of yourself, Rich." He paused and cleared his throat. "I mean . . . take care of yourself, Sheriff."

"My cousin and I could help you," Rich offered. "Hell, it's the least we can do."

"Appreciate it, but no. There's some people I need to find, and when I do, I'd prefer not to have the law anywhere close to me."

Rich climbed down with his fool's gold in hand, leaving the money under Nick's boot. The nuggets looked impressive enough, but the more he thought about the look on the face of the man who'd handed them over as part of the reward, the more Rich was inclined to believe what Nick had told him.

There was a crack of snapping reins followed by the rumble of wagon wheels and Nick was gone.

He had appointments to keep with some very unlucky people.

The employees of Thorndike Press hope you have enjoyed this Large Print book. All our Thorndike, Wheeler, and Kennebec Large Print titles are designed for easy reading, and all our books are made to last. Other Thorndike Press Large Print books are available at your library, through selected bookstores, or directly from us.

For information about titles, please call:
(800) 223-1244

or visit our Web site at:
http://gale.cengage.com/thorndike

To share your comments, please write:
Publisher
Thorndike Press
10 Water St., Suite 310
Waterville, ME 04901